The Anvil's Mark

The Queen's Blade Book 3

D.K. Holmberg

Copyright © 2024 by D.K. Holmberg

Cover by Damonza.com

All rights reserved.

No part of this book may be reproduced in any form or by any electronic or mechanical means, including information storage and retrieval systems, without written permission from the author, except for the use of brief quotations in a book review.

Want a **free book** and to be notified when D.K. Holmberg's next novel is released, along with other news and freebies? **Sign up for his mailing list by going here**. Your email address will never be shared and you can unsubscribe at any time.

www.dkholmberg.com

The Anvil's Mark

Chapter One

My blade vibrated in my hand, suggesting a powerful magical source.

I hadn't felt anything quite like this since dealing with the aelith powder, and I had not come across any since I had returned to Busal City. I clutched the blade tightly, focusing on the part of myself that allowed me to use some magical energy as well, so that I might pick up on the power here, and possibly even identify the source.

The road along the shoreline was busy, as it often was. Some of the activity was tied to the row of docks, which opened into the rest of the city, and the transportation hub of the city itself. Some of it also came from merchants that traveled along this road, winding around the city rather than through it, for ease of transport and a more scenic route.

I was out here because I had picked up on power.

As the Queen's Blade, I had no choice but to chase this power, especially because there had been several attempts to bring power into the city ever since I had come here, and I was still trying to understand all that was involved in my responsibilities.

This time, however, I was not alone.

"You look like you've found something," Jos said.

Jos was an Investigator, someone who had a little talent with my own ability but was not nearly as potent. Many Investigators served Busal City, all of them looking into the dangerous magical items that entered the city, trying to discern what was a threat and what was not. I had taken it upon myself to be much friendlier with them than my predecessor had been, partly because I had come to understand that they added value to my investigations. Not only that, but technically I supervised them, so I needed to ensure that we maintained an effective working relationship.

"Unfortunately, I think I have," I said, looking down at the shorter man. Shorter, but broader in some ways. "Don't know what it is."

He looked at the blade I was holding. "Is that doing anything?"

This was Jos's way of asking more about how I could pick up on things that the Investigators could not. They had various fabrications that were useful in identifying magic, and I had little doubt that he had taken out one from his pocket and was probably concealing it in his hand, but he wouldn't be able to pick up on the power quite as well as I could. The Investigators simply did not have the same technique, and fabrications did not share the kind of power that I naturally possessed.

"Something like that," I said. "I'm not so sure that you need to be a part of this."

"I thought the deal was that you were going to incorporate us into your investigations a little more," Jos said, sounding irritated.

Then again, the Investigators were often irritated with me. Thankfully, they had grudgingly started to accept me as more than just a replacement Blade for Waleith.

"That was the deal," I said. "And I have been making a concerted effort to keep you a part of the investigations."

More than that, even. My predecessor, my mentor, by the name of Waleith, had known the Investigators were useful, but he had also known that they could not be effective in more dangerous situations. I was still not entirely sure how much Waleith knew about the threats that had begun presenting themselves in Busal City. When I had been brought here, I had been told that I could serve in many ways, but I had not known that I would need to dig into so many forms of dangerous power. Waleith had implied that danger was rare, and I had uncovered that it was anything but rare.

I had started to wonder if the ongoing threats that we had uncovered were tied to a greater conspiracy, and that was the reason that Waleith continually disappeared from the city.

"Come along," I muttered, waving to Jos to follow me. I didn't slow, though I didn't need to.

When we passed people on the road, I tried to move

to the side, not wanting my bulk to intimidate them too much, as I was a large man, and I was well aware of how that could be perceived. Some made a point of veering out of the way, as if to avoid me altogether. Others looked at me, then at Jos—who had quite an intimidating presence as well—before scurrying out of the way. Still others just stopped, as if frozen.

I didn't know if they recognized that the pin on my lapel marked me as a member of the Queen's household —or at least, a person who served the Queen's household —as it was entirely possible that there were those around the city who did recognize such things.

We reached the end of the harbor street and then paused. From here, the road narrowed, working its way out toward the open water, but it was much less hospitable, and far more difficult to traverse for wagons and anybody that was not traveling on foot. The road also worked its way around the north side of the city and then eventually met up with the main thoroughfares that led into the city itself.

This wasn't what I wanted to be doing, but ever since the councilor I'd detained had hanged herself in her cell before I'd had a chance to question her about who else was involved in her treason, I had not known how else to find answers, other than to chase every possible lead I had.

"Which way?" Jos asked.

"What do you detect?"

He shot me a look. "I thought this was about what you were able to pick up on."

"I think that we can test each other, right?" I offered him a hint of a smile, though I didn't expect him to return it. "We use similar techniques."

Jos grunted. He pulled out a small circular item that was wrapped around his middle finger. "Similar? Do you rely on this kind of fabrication to do your job?"

"Mine is somewhat different," I admitted. "Did Waleith ever talk to you about what he was able to do, the reason that he had been selected as a Blade?"

"Just that it was something that your kind was born into. He said that I really couldn't understand so I shouldn't argue with a Blade, simply because I should know my place." He sized me up. "And I'm not going to argue with a Blade."

I chuckled and veered to the left, staying on the road. Whatever I had picked up on was coming from this direction. It was powerful. Powerful could mean something massive, a large quantity of magical items—either fabrications or something that was naturally occurring—making their way into the city, but it didn't necessarily have to be. I had some experience with the potency found in smaller items, and trying to negate the power found within them.

"Your fabrications give you a general sense of magic being used, right?" I asked the question as I was hurrying along the road, scanning the city and then farther along the road itself. I even peered north, into the pastures that surrounded the city, but I didn't expect to feel or find anything there. "Not that I have a lot of experience with your kind of fabrications, but I presume that you are using some device that permits you to identify power."

Jos shrugged. "You know that it does. It sort of vibrates."

I nodded. "Well, my blade does something similar. Maybe not quite the same, but I can feel it when magic is used. And it doesn't take all that much."

I could pick up on the fabrication that he was carrying, even though it didn't seem to have all that much power in it. And given the training that Waleith had put me through, I could now identify many types of power, and threat levels, as I focused on magical items. Most of them were easy, and they were becoming so familiar to me that I could identify what others were carrying around me. Not always, though. There were times when the magic I picked up on remained unfamiliar, such as now.

"But you can tell if something is dangerous or not, yeah?"

"I can tell if something is powerful or not, but the danger..." I shrugged. "It's not always obvious to me if something is dangerous until I get closer to it and have a chance to inspect it."

And he knew that. It was part of the reason that the Investigators were required to consult me on any haul of items they collected. At first they had hesitated to do so, because they had wanted to prove their own worth and had not thought that they needed to consult with me. Increasingly, however, they felt open to drawing me in, because I had made it clear that they would get the recognition for everything they had done. I didn't want any additional recognition.

"So why isn't my fabrication indicating anything up here?" Jos asked.

I wanted to tell him that his fabrication was not powered by him, whereas my fabrication was powered by me. I wanted to tell him that had he not been with me when I had first picked up on this power, I would not have included an Investigator in this search. Not on a search like this that could lead to nothing.

However, I had come to the conclusion that saying anything like that, which might be considered offensive to the Investigators, was counterproductive in my desire to build a workable relationship with them.

"Your fabrications are not quite as potent."

"But you're the Queen's Blade. Can't you get me a better fabrication?"

He looked at me expectantly, as if it were my decision, as if it had nothing to do with the different type of fabrication that Investigators had.

"I doubt the Queen cares that much about what fabrication I get you, but your job does not require anything more complex than what you already have."

He frowned, and I waited for a moment, thinking that he would argue with me, but he didn't.

Then the power that I had been feeling began to intensify.

Something was happening—somebody was using it.

I started running.

"Where are you going?"

I ignored Jos as I darted forward, away from the city. I had no idea as to why I felt it so potently.

At this point in the city, just beyond the border, the landscape consisted of rolling hills dotted with small shrubs, a few twisted trees, and the occasional meadow flower. It didn't offer much to obscure anything, which left me wondering why I had picked up on something so potently that I could not see. I had expected to practically run into whatever it was that had caused this burst of power. There was no sign of it, however.

Until I walked through what felt like a cold rain shower. The moment I passed through it, I felt my blade trembling, a familiar resistance working against it, as the magic trembled... and then shattered.

Then the scene in front of me shifted.

There were three people near a stone pillar with a small spherical item resting on it.

They didn't notice me at first. Perhaps they weren't aware that I had somehow carved through the power that was shielding them, but they were all looking down at the item on the pillar, and one of them was whispering something, which I couldn't quite hear.

"What was that about?" Jos asked.

Then, and only then, did the others look up.

One was a muscular man, sword strapped at his side, and something about him struck me as familiar. He had a long scar along his neck that worked up toward his ear before disappearing into his hairline. His deeply tanned face turned into a scowl as he saw me. The scars seemed to change, looking more like they were hiding tattoos.

"Deal with this," the man said.

One of the others turned toward me.

And then a fourth person—a slender woman—appeared, different from the others, approaching with a quiet confidence and no real expression of concern in her eyes.

The woman had on a long dark cloak, and she had a slender rod in one hand, which she flicked, causing it to extend into a staff that was perhaps two feet taller than her. She wasn't tall, so the staff itself was not even as tall as me, but she began to spin it, causing it to whistle through the air. The whistling struck me as dangerous, but not only that, it also felt powerful.

"Get behind me," I said, pushing Jos back.

"And let you fight? What are you talking about?"

"What does your fabrication tell you?"

I didn't wait for him to answer.

The two on either side of the tattooed man had weapons as well, but they weren't ready as I darted toward them, putting myself in between them and the woman. *Split them up and make them easier to attack.*

The spinning staff continued to whistle through the air.

I turned toward the woman. She was the first threat I had to deal with.

I had brawled quite a bit in my days in the army. It wasn't something that I was proud of, but it was something that I had gotten fairly good at. Fighting required a certain fearlessness and discipline, but brawling did not. It just required one to be willing to face someone else.

It required one to be willing to get hurt.

When I had served as protection in the tavern in

Lavrun, I had been willing to fight, partly because I had felt I had no other choice and no other chance to do anything of value, but also partly because I hadn't really known any better. My time in the army had made me feel that brawn was all I had. Since leaving that town, and since becoming a Blade, I had started to feel I had a little more value.

I had still not managed to become much more of a fighter than a brawler.

So when the woman swung her staff at me, I simply lunged at her and swung outward with my blade, trying to catch her hand, her wrist, or anything to keep her from spinning the weapon and using whatever magic was infused in it.

The staff caught my fabrication blade, twisting it, and I nearly dropped it.

She swung it down, the change in direction so fast that it caught me off guard. It slammed into my shin with a painful crack. For a moment, I worried that she had shattered my leg, but the pain swept through me.

Some magic was definitely infused in the staff. I pushed against it, recognizing how I needed to resist it, and did all that I could to try to overpower her attack. I didn't know if anything more would happen, but I wasn't going to simply wait and see what else might occur.

That staff had left pain surging through my leg, but it was pain that I could tolerate. The magic, however, threatened to freeze me in place.

Jos cried out.

I flicked my gaze around, trying to figure out what he

had been doing, before wishing that I hadn't. The woman smacked me in the shoulder, then the back, sending me stumbling. I crashed toward the other three, who were still surrounding the pillar. I brought my blade up, already pushing through the magic, and slammed it down on the center of the pillar.

This was the source of power here, and if I could stop it, I could stop whatever they were doing.

The blade hovered in the air for a moment. It met a resistance, and I couldn't identify the source of it, though I could tell that it was magical. I pushed again, forcing my blade down as much as I could, until the resistance, and the power, crackled, causing it to explode outward.

My blade slammed into the pillar, which cracked before starting to crumble.

I scooped the spherical item off it and stuffed it into my pocket.

Then I spun.

I made a quick survey of everything around me.

When I had blasted through the magical protection, the rippling wave that had been building swept out, catching the others. I expected them to be lying motionless on the ground, but only one was.

The scarred man was already starting to get up, and I noticed a strange chain hanging loose around his neck. Probably some sort of fabrication, or some other magical item, from the way that it felt to me. I stumbled toward him, pain throbbing in my arm and my back where I had been struck, and kicked him until he fell unconscious.

Then I turned.

Where was the woman?

Jos lay in a heap near where one of the others had been. He had managed to knock one of the attackers out, and he lay not far from him. A small fabrication rested on the man's chest.

Not on it. *In* it. Jos must have stabbed him with it.

Jos had probably used the fabrication to drain magical energy from the attacker. Such a technique was impressive, but I didn't know if Jos even understood what he had done.

The other attacker had scurried away, and only the woman with the staff lingered.

She regarded me, this time with a renewed focus and a look in her eyes that told me she wanted to ask a question. I understood the question, and I wasn't about to give her an answer. She wanted to know how I had managed to destroy the pillar.

"Anything else you want to try?" I asked.

The woman's staff continued to spin, though she did not make any attempt to move toward me again. I didn't know if she waited because she wondered what else I might do, or if she waited because they had something planned.

Was that the only item here?

There was a very real possibility that they had other magic in reserve, and I just hadn't picked up on it. The strange buildup of pressure had faded the moment I had crushed that pillar, but I still had the spherical item that had been on it in my pocket. Did that mean that the item was somehow responsible?

Or had they been using the pillar to power it?

Questions I didn't have answers to, and I wouldn't get answers unless I had a chance to interrogate these people.

"We don't tolerate magic in Busal City," I said.

I waited a moment but had already started to plan what I was going to do. I was going to need to get to the woman, knock her down, and then get to the others.

I had started to plan my approach when she raised her staff, brought it down in a sharp crack, and a wave of power rippled out, throwing me backward. I came to land next to one of the men, and when I looked up, she was gone.

Chapter Two

I hurriedly searched the man that Jos had stabbed, finding him not breathing and a heavy bloodstain covering his chest where the fabrication had pierced it. I took the fabrication out, wiped it on the man's jacket, and then slipped it in my pocket. He didn't have any coins, or anything else that would identify where he was from, as I suspected he wasn't local. The only thing he had was strange tattoos on one arm.

When I was done, Jos started to sit up, rubbing at his chest and groaning.

"What happened?"

"Don't really know," I said, looking around. "I am not entirely sure what they were doing, and I don't know if they will return." I looked over at the other fallen man, who was still unconscious but, as far as I could tell, still alive. That was good, because we needed to talk to someone about what had happened here. "I did, however, manage to destroy that altar."

"You think this was some sort of religious ritual?" Jos got to his feet, and he started to look around. "I haven't seen anything quite like that before."

"I don't think it was, but honestly, I can't say with any real certainty. It was something, however."

He looked down at the other man. "What do you want to do with him?"

"Question him."

"What do you think he's going to tell us?"

I shrugged. "I don't know. But we can't keep him here." I let out a heavy sigh. "Which means bringing him back into the city, and to the constables."

"You think the constables will help?"

When I nodded, Jos shook his head slowly. "You really are quite a bit different than Waleith, aren't you, Joha?"

"What's that supposed to mean?"

"It just means that Waleith would never have asked the constables for help."

"Well, he probably wouldn't have brought you out here, either. I'm going to trust that you and the others will gather the pieces of the pillar and bring them to the city, where we will need to test them."

"What if more of their people come out here?"

"I doubt it," I said. Something told me that they would avoid it, for several reasons.

For one, they would probably not know what I was capable of. The woman had certainly seemed suspicious in a way that left me thinking that she would hesitate until she had a better assessment of what sort of danger I posed. And for another, I suspected that I had stopped whatever they had been trying to do. Not that I had a good idea about what that was. The pillar was gone. And though the small sphere remained intact, I didn't know what to make of it. Which was one more reason to get back promptly, so that I could take the time necessary to analyze it.

"Can I entrust this task to you?" I asked Jos.

He regarded me with a little irritation. "You can trust me. Is that your way of testing whether you can?"

"No. You were hurt. It's not an insult, nor is it a comment about your abilities."

At least, it wasn't entirely a comment about his abilities, but then, I wasn't sure if he was going to see it that way or not.

"I'm going to be fine. What do you think we will find?"

"Honestly, I don't know. Maybe nothing. But it had power."

"The pillar? Or was it what they had on it?"

It was a good question, and it was not one that I had a good answer to, as I didn't know whether the pillar or the sphere had been the primary focus.

"Just bring the pillar back, and let me know what you uncover."

"I can go back with you," Jos said.

"I want you to gather as much information about this site as you can, and I'll send people to you."

He looked like he wanted to argue, but he nodded.

I grabbed the fallen man, who groaned softly as I did, and then slung him over my shoulder.

I made my way back to the city. I followed the same road that we had taken out, pausing at the Investigator station. I looked inside to see one of the newest Investigators, a boy by the name of Ryal, sitting at a desk and making a note in a journal.

"Oh, hey, Zaren," he said, looking up at me. "What do you have there?"

"Trouble," I said, smiling inwardly at how he called me by my first name. He sat up straighter. "Jos is just outside the city to the north. Follow the road. Grab two or three Investigators if you can, along with the wagon. There's an item out there that I want you to bring back into the city so that you can run some tests on it."

"You want *us* to do this?"

"We've already dealt with the bigger threat, so you don't have to worry about anything happening," I said.

He mouthed the word "threat."

"But we do need to look into what it was intended to be used for. Jos can fill you in. Can you do this?"

Ryal nodded. "Glad to. Thanks for letting me be a part of it. I really appreciate—"

"Just work quickly," I said, cutting him off.

If I let him talk too long, he was going to go into how he was so appreciative that we had given him the opportunity to serve as an Investigator. Ryal actually had some natural talent. I hadn't had an opportunity to talk to Waleith about whether there were others like me, who could be identified and trained as Blades, but I suspected there were. Ryal was somebody the Investigators had suggested, as they claimed that they had used fabrications to discover him. I wasn't sure if that was possible, or if they had some other way of identifying talent, but either way, it was good to bring more people in.

And I was starting to think that we needed more Blades, though rebuilding a contingent of Blades could prove challenging. Considering what had happened, and how the trainees had been killed, the Queen might not even want to restore that program. At least, not in the same way.

I carried the man along the street, getting a few strange looks, until I reached the constable station.

It was busy. Then again, it was often busy when I came here, and I no longer got strange looks when I headed into the constable station, as I had when I had first come here. I was a known entity now, and most put up with me, though I knew that was because I was friendly with the Captain. There were some who still didn't care for that friendliness, who looked at me askance, such as Reg, who I'd met when I had first come to Busal City. He looked up from his desk as I passed, still carrying the man on my shoulder. He opened his mouth as if he was going to object, before clamping it shut again.

"Bring us a new friend?" Lijanna asked.

She came out of the back, wiping her hands on her pants, then paused to squeeze the hilt of the sword she had sheathed at her side. She was tall, and though I hadn't seen her fight, I suspected that she would be skilled. Someone like her didn't get her rank within the constables without having a measure of skill.

"Somebody who decided to make things a little difficult today," I said.

She arched a brow. "Oh? Anything we need to know about?"

"Not sure," I said. "Possibly. Ran into a little trouble on the north side of the city. I have some of my Investigators out there, so if you come across them, give them a little space?"

She nodded.

I fully expected that Lijanna and the other constables would investigate, especially given recent events.

"Anything going to cause trouble for us?"

"I hope not," I said. "Say, can you put him in a cell for me? I'm going to need to question him, but I have to wait until he comes around."

Lijanna snorted. "Always having us do your dirty work, aren't you?"

"I don't know if I'm having you do dirty work. But I would appreciate it."

"For you?" She grinned. "You know I'm happy to." She tapped on a nearby table. "Say, Darish, can you give me a hand?"

Darish got up. He was a wide man with broad shoulders and a bit of a gut, but he had the look of the kind of man that I had served with in the army, somebody who would welcome a bit of a scuffle. A brawler, like me. Not a fighter, not as I suspected Lijanna was. He grabbed the man easily, pulled them off my shoulder, and then slung him over his own. "Which cell?"

"Back one. And give him a little food and water when he wakes up so that we can get some information from him." Lijanna looked back at me. "Because we are going to need some information."

I nodded.

With him off my shoulder, I stretched and then made my way back to the Captain's office.

Jaqarl Harent was a man that I had served with years ago, though he had been in the navy, while I had been in the army. Since coming to the city, however, he had been an ally, and somebody that I made a point of ensuring I maintained a rapport with, which had ended up being quite useful, especially given everything that we had encountered recently.

I knocked at his door, which was slightly cracked, before poking my head inside.

For a former military man, he was not the neatest or most organized person. His office was filled with books, stacks of papers, maps, and even items that had likely been confiscated all throughout the city. Piles of debris littered the floor, and he sat behind a desk that was overflowing with even more paper and books.

"What is—oh. You. Do I even want to know what you have going on now?"

I chuckled as I took a seat across from him and leaned back, crossing my arms. "That's the greeting I get?"

"You and I both know what greeting you deserve. What kind of work did you bring me this time? I'm still looking into what happened with Sivara, and I haven't come up with anything." The look he gave me suggested that he hoped I might have something for him, so I shook my head. "Damn shame she offed herself before we could get answers."

"Or convenient," I muttered.

"Or that," he agreed. "So, what do you have?"

"What makes you think I brought you any work?"

"You're here in my office," Harent said, holding up one finger. "And you have that smug look on your face." He held up a second finger. "And you have a little tension to you that suggests that you want something from me." He propped up a third finger, then began to wiggle them.

"Well, you're not wrong. I don't know if you have to be involved in this, but I do want you to be aware of what I just encountered, because who knows? Maybe it's something significant."

I filled him in on what Jos and I had encountered.

"Don't really know what it was about." I reached into my pocket and drew out the small item that I had pulled off the pillar. "And this..." I shrugged. "It doesn't even have any significant power within it."

"Maybe that doesn't have the power. Maybe it's the pillar."

"I don't know," I said. "It just felt a little strange."

"Well, the kind of things that you get involved in generally tend to be strange, don't they?" Harent leaned forward, holding his hand out. I gave him the item. He held it up to the light, turning it in place, before he handed it back to me. "So do you want to tell me if that is a fabrication or something else?"

"No marks on it," I said. "And all fabrications have some markings on them. I don't really know what this is, honestly. And I can feel something within it, but I'm not entirely sure what."

"So is it dangerous or isn't it?"

"Well, if it is dangerous, it's not the kind of danger that I'm going to ask you or your people to deal with."

"Thank you."

"This is my responsibility."

"No," Harent said. "I'm just thanking you for letting me know that you are dealing with something. That way, if you're running around the city, getting into trouble, I know if we need to help you."

I snorted. "*You* need to help *me*?"

"I seem to remember us having a pretty big part in ensuring your safety during some of these recent events."

"Maybe a little bit," I said.

"What else?"

"Is it that obvious?"

"It's obvious that you want something. And seeing as you just told me about this," he went on, pointing to the spherical item that I was still holding, "I am curious."

"You have a new prisoner."

"What else is new?"

"You're not concerned about the prisoner?"

"Should I be?"

"Depends upon what he is in here for."

"And depends upon what we uncover."

"Probably," I said. "And honestly, I don't know how much he will tell us. I had Lijanna drop him into a cell, and hopefully, we can find out something from him, but..." I shrugged. "Otherwise, the Investigators are securing the pieces of the pillar."

"Sounds like you have it all taken care of."

"Mostly." I shifted forward before sticking the sphere in my pocket. "There is something else that I wanted to ask you, but I'm not sure how to go about it."

"You were in the army. Make your request. If it's not something that I can help you with, then I'll tell you."

"I need to learn how to fight," I said.

This fact had been weighing on me for a while, but dealing with a woman who was clearly skilled had made it even more apparent.

"You need to *what?*" Harent laughed. "You do realize how ridiculous that sounds coming from *you*, don't you?"

"I realize that," I said. "Which is why I'm asking *you*. It's something I've been thinking about for a while, but this situation sort of drove the need home."

"Because it's ridiculous or because you figure that I'm the right person to help?"

"A bit of both. When I was facing the woman with the staff—"

"You didn't tell me that it was a woman," he said.

I snorted. "Fine. There was a smallish woman who had a staff and dealt with me somewhat handily."

A smile began to spread on Harent's face.

"Partly because I think she knew how to fight. I have

gotten into a lot of fights, have been a brawler, but I'm not much of a fighter."

"So you want to learn to fight better? Do you need to do that for your job?"

"Probably not generally," I said. "But considering everything I've been through so far since I came to Busal City, I can't help but feel it would be useful. I can't just keep getting away with throwing my size around. And I need to know how to plan and strategize when it comes to the different people that I deal with."

"Not a bad idea," he said. "But it's not going to be easy. You had training in the army, Joha, but the kind of training that you had is not the kind of training that is usually all that helpful. It's too regimented. You need to learn useful skills. How to incapacitate somebody quickly. How to keep them alive." He regarded me carefully. "And you probably aren't wrong. You need to know how to handle different styles, because I can tell you that there are fighting styles that are more or less useful in certain situations."

"So you are willing to do this?"

"Oh, not me," he said, shaking his head. "I don't think that I would be of much use to you. I was never much of a fighter. Us navy men don't engage in a lot of hand-to-hand combat, you know."

"Thanks," I said.

Harent snorted. "I'm not saying that I'm not willing to do it. I'm just saying that you will need to learn from somebody who can actually teach you the things that you are looking to learn. And that's not going to be me. I will make some arrangements, though. You might not like the process."

"Why not?" I could immediately think of several of his constables that I would not be all that thrilled to be paired up with to fight and train, including Reg. He didn't strike me as all that skilled a fighter, but I knew not to judge a man without having a chance to see him in action. And if he was the one Harent thought I could learn from, I could easily imagine him having far too much excitement about the prospect.

"Why don't we just start with Lijanna?" Harent said, looking down at his notebook before looking back up at me. "She can teach you some basic hand-to-hand fighting. And if you get into anything more advanced than basic, she can help you there as well."

"Lijanna?"

"You don't think you can learn from her?"

I snorted. "Actually, I'm glad it's her. She always struck me as somebody pretty capable."

Harent smiled slightly. "*Pretty* capable?"

"What?"

"Oh, I'm not going to spoil this one. I'll let you find out for yourself."

"Why do I get the feeling that I'm not going to like this very much?"

"You will," he said. "Anyway, this little issue that you had outside of the city. Is it going to be a problem for us, or for the city, the same way that it was before?"

"I don't know," I answered. "Waleith told me that all sorts of magical items move into the city at any given time. Some are benign, the kind that I need to have the right amount of discretion to overlook." I had found several things like that and had learned to ignore anything that did not have the potential to cause much trouble. "Others are not so benign and can be quite dangerous. He told me that it wasn't all that common to have repeated threats coming into the city, but now I'm starting to think that he might have been misleading me."

"Where is he, anyway?"

"I don't know," I said. "After we dealt with Sivara, I thought he might stay, especially since we had been dealing with a councilor."

"Still surprised that he let you handle that on your own."

"Thanks," I said.

"It's not to disparage you. It's more about the fact that you hadn't been in the city, dealing with these things, for all that long. It just surprises me that he didn't want to have a bigger part in that investigation."

"He probably thinks he is giving me a little autonomy," I said.

"Maybe," Harent said. "At least, I hope that's all it is."

"What else would it be?"

"Don't know. Waleith has always been a strange one, though."

"I think he has to be," I said. "Especially with all that he has done to help the Queen."

"I've got stories about that, if you'd like to hear them," he said.

"You know I'd love to hear them."

"I don't know how true any of them are, but why don't we get a drink some evening? And I can share with you all that I know about Waleith. Including the fun rumors, and the not-so-fun rumors."

"I think that the not-so-fun rumors are probably the ones I need to hear first."

"No," he said. "You need to come up with your own opinion."

"It's like that?"

"It's just like it is," Harent said. "You don't have to like everybody you work with. You just have to work together." He set his hands on the desk. "So now we're working with you."

"Is that your way of saying you don't like working with me?"

He laughed. "If I didn't like working with you, I would suggest a few others that you could train with."

"And you still might," I said.

He laughed. "I still might."

Chapter Three

After chatting with Harent a little longer, and establishing a training schedule, I made my way over to the cell block. I hadn't spent much time here in the cells, but then again, I hadn't really needed to, as I wasn't usually the one responsible for holding anybody here.

The scarred man was curled up and facing away from me, though he was breathing regularly. I stood outside his cell for a little while, watching him. The water jug was untouched, and there was a plate of bread and cheese resting in the corner, both of which were also untouched.

There was some power here.

I couldn't tell the source of it, although I suspected that it came from the man himself. Within the constable station, however, there was always a bit of power, because the constable station had some innate natural—or perhaps not so natural—protections on it. The building was one of the older buildings in the city, and many of the older structures had etchings on their stones that I suspected were tied to an ancient kind of power.

The man continued his steady breathing.

But his shoulders seemed a little more tense than they had been before.

"I can see that you're awake," I said. I stayed within reach of the bars of the cell and grabbed for my blade, feeling the familiar, and surprisingly comforting, weight of it in my hand.

The man's demeanor didn't change. The only thing that I could tell had changed was his breathing had quickened just a little.

And so I focused on the power that I could feel, and began to use the blade, pushing some of my innate magical resistance through it. I didn't know if the man was going to react in any way, but I suspected that he would be aware of what I was doing.

His breathing started to quicken further.

There was a faint heaviness in the air, and it took me a moment to realize that it came from what he was doing. Did he have something on him that I had not noticed? I'd stripped the chain from his neck and shattered the links in it, disrupting whatever magic might be found within the chain itself, but I uncovered very little to be concerned about. I didn't know what to make of him, or the change within him.

The resistance intensified.

"Hey," I said.

One of the constables poked her head into the hallway, looking down toward me.

"I need to get into the cell," I said.

"Does the Captain know?"

"The Captain doesn't know that I'm going into the cell, but he knows I brought this prisoner here, and I need to make sure that he isn't going to escape."

The constable's eyes widened slightly. He was a younger boy, and clearly new to the constabulary.

"If you have any questions, get Lijanna, or the Captain, and let them know that the Queen's Blade wants to get into the cell. Does that work for you?"

His eyes widened again.

"Will you do this for me?"

He hurried forward. "I heard that you come around here. I'm Nerak Los."

"Nice to meet you. Unlock the cell, but don't go too far."

"Why?"

"Because I'm going to ask you to lock me in with him."

"You're going to have me do *what*?"

I just waited, and then he unlocked the cell, which allowed me to step inside. Once inside, I hesitated, then pulled the door closed.

"Lock it," I said.

Nerak did so. And then I crouched down in front of the man.

"So," I said, holding my blade, "you want to make it seem like you aren't awake, but I can tell that you are. Do you want to talk to me about what you were doing outside of the city?"

He still didn't move.

"I'm perfectly happy to drive this blade into your back, and considering what I was able to do to your little friend with the staff, you may not want to take that option. How about we talk?"

The pressure was building, and given that I had removed all the items on his person, it left me thinking that he himself had some power. I had dealt with a few people with magic of their own. Not well, and I didn't know if I could do anything to disarm him very easily, short of simply using my blade.

"Sorry about this," I muttered, and then I jabbed him in the right shoulder with my blade. *Might as well give him another scar.*

"What are you doing?" Nerak cried.

"I'm talking to him."

"The Captain wants us to keep our prisoners alive."

"And I'm trying to keep the constables safe," I said, not turning.

The man still had not stirred, so while I suspected he was awake and alert, he was trying to make it seem he was not.

"I'm going to get the Captain," Nerak said.

"Please," I said.

When he scurried off, he left me alone with the man.

"Now," I said, "you might as well stop pulling upon whatever power you are trying to use. I can feel it, and I don't like it."

That elicited the most reaction. He started to struggle.

I had crouched next to him, and it took very little effort to drop a knee onto his back, which kept him from squirming anymore.

"Not like that," I said. "If you do that, then my blade is going to dig into your shoulder more, and I don't want you to bleed all over the cell."

"You don't know what you're doing," the man said.

He had a strangely accented voice, a little thready, though I didn't know if that was because my knee was on his back and I was keeping him from speaking clearly, or if that was his normal speaking tone.

"Maybe not," I said. "Why don't you start with what your little group was doing outside of the city?"

"You don't know what you are doing," he said again.

Once again I began to feel the strange resistance building. It suggested to me that he possessed some sort of magic. And now I understood why he and the other man—assuming that he had some sort of magic of his own—had joined the woman in her attack. If he had some innate power, the same way that Talina had innate power, I could easily imagine him using that before I had an opportunity to deflect it.

"Fine," I said. "What was that pillar?"

I took the chance that the pillar was the key, because the sphere didn't seem to have much power in it. Either they had drained it, or it had not been significant.

"What is this, Joha?" Harent asked from outside the cell.

"He was getting ready to attack," I said.

"I told you, Captain, he stabbed the man."

I looked back to see Nerak standing behind Harent. He looked nervous. His face was ashen, and he was twisting the fabric of his jacket in both hands. He was really far too new to be put in charge of the cells.

"I'm sure he had a good reason. Tell me you had a good reason, Joha."

"He's using magic," I said. "And unfortunately, you may not be able to hold him here."

"Probably not," he said. "Normally, anybody who has that kind of ability is taken elsewhere."

He didn't say it, as he didn't need to, but "elsewhere" meant the palace itself, where there were natural protections that could hold those with magical ability. I didn't know how I felt about taking somebody to the palace and having to explain to the Queen—or worse, Prince Dorian—why I had done so. I had enough issues with what we had dealt with in the city during my tenure already.

"Just let me see what else he can tell me. That is, if you don't mind."

Harent shook his head. "I don't mind, but just keep him from bleeding all over the place, if *you* don't mind."

I turned back and kept my knee on the man's back. "Now that we have that settled," I said, "why don't you tell me what you were doing? You can start with the pillar, and then you can go to—"

The man jerked back.

The suddenness of it surprised me.

He slammed his shoulder all the way up to the hilt of

the blade, and warm blood spurted around my hand, making the blade slick so that I almost dropped it.

I pushed my knee onto the man's back, yanked the blade out of him, and then rolled him over. I jammed my free hand up against his throat, holding him down. His eyes widened as he regarded me.

"I don't know what you thought you were going to achieve there, but it's not going to work."

"You don't know..."

"I don't think you want to stay in there much longer, Joha."

I looked over at Harent briefly. "What?"

"You might have negated something here, but there is power. The obvious kind. I can feel *heat*. You don't feel it?"

It *was* getting a little bit warm, but I didn't know why.

I had used my blade, and that should have negated any power the scarred man had. It had worked against Talina, so why wouldn't it work here?

Then I noticed something. He had markings on his skin. Tattoos, similar to the ones that I had seen on one of the other men at the pillar. These had been faint, so faint that I hadn't even seen them before, but now a darker hue started to work along them, until the pressure again began to build.

It was the markings. That was what gave him power.

It wasn't him. Or maybe it was, through these tattoos, but somehow he had power flowing through him.

I used the blade, carving through one of the markings.

There was resistance to it, and it felt like I was trying to cut through metal, so I forced the blade down, cutting across his left cheek and the marking that was getting darker and darker with every passing moment. Behind me, and behind Harent, Nerak gasped.

"Get him out of here," I grunted.

Some of the resistance began to fade, but not all of it.

It was as if the markings were taking on some of the blood...

Blood. That was what it was. The tattoos were drawing in this man's blood, as if the blood itself was somehow powering them.

How is that even possible?

Now I could pick up on the changing heat much more readily. It was obvious now. He was powerful. It was building. It was uncomfortable.

I grunted, and as I focused on the heat, and the power within it, I started to work my blade across the man's other cheek and then moved on to the arms, and finally I just froze. The building resistance was too much. It was as if with every passing moment, he was drawing more blood into his tattoos, using that to empower himself in a way that I wasn't going to be able to stop. I had never heard of anything quite like this.

"Any suggestions?" I asked Harent. "Short of killing him."

"Why?"

"Well, I don't know what he's going to do here, but he's building to something."

"In my station?"

"Pretty much," I said.

"You can't let him destroy the station," Harent said.

I grunted. "I'm not going to disagree with you, but I'm looking for any suggestions. Have you ever used anything that might negate power? Or have you ever heard of anything quite like this?"

Harent was quiet for a moment. "No. So do what you need to do."

"We need answers," I said. And increasingly I couldn't help but feel this answer was much more crucial than I had realized. I hadn't really understood what had been going on outside the city. And now I started to wonder if perhaps it had been even more dangerous than I had realized, and if perhaps the Investigators were in danger.

Which meant that I needed to deal with this quickly and get to them.

Even though I had cut through several of his tattoos, it didn't seem to have done anything. And I couldn't wait any longer. *So much for answers.* I muttered a curse under my breath, raised the blade, and then jammed it down into his chest.

There was a surge of wind, and I was pushed up, but only briefly. The surge of wind didn't push against my weight so much as it pushed against my innate antimagic ability. That ability was potent as well. I remembered how Waleith had been surprised by it, by what I could do, and it was part of the reason that he had chosen me in the first place.

The look of surprise on the man's face told me that he

hadn't anticipated that I could deliver a fatal blow. He had been convinced that stabbing himself deeper, and using his tattoos, would be enough to save him.

And if I hadn't used my own innate ability on him, it might have been enough. He sagged, almost deflated, and the tattoos began to fade.

I stood, pulled the blade back, and wiped it on him before slipping it into the sheath at my side.

"Sorry about the blood on the floor," I said.

"Would you care to tell me what this is about?" Harent asked.

"I would love to know," I said.

"Those tattoos. They came and then went. What is that?"

I shook my head. "I don't know. When we were dealing with these people outside of the city, they had somebody who had the same sort of markings, but I don't remember them coming and going. They were just there."

"And you've not seen anything like this before?"

I backed toward the door, which Harent pulled open, letting me out of the cell. A part of me was a little concerned that the now-dead man might somehow come back to life. He'd obviously had some connection to power, and it had been enough that he could withstand even a knife to his back and still fight. Maybe he could come back from the dead as well.

"I don't have all that much experience with different magic. Mine is more of a learn-on-the-job kind of situation. Waleith was trying to give me more information, but..."

"So when do you think Waleith is going to return?"

I stared through the bars of the cell, my mind churning. "I don't know. Probably not soon enough."

In my time in the city, there had been many occasions when I had felt my inexperience. However, Waleith had tried to train me, and I had been making progress. I had been able to defend myself, and others, as I had progressed. Not only that, but I had been instrumental in keeping Talina from reaching the Queen and had even stopped Sivara's plot against the Crown.

Why did it seem like everything kept getting more and more complex?

"You're going to need to get some answers, Joha."

"I realize that." I let out a sigh. "Can I help clean this up?"

"No. I've got some people who can do that. But why don't you stay here, just in case?" He locked eyes with me, as if waiting to see if I was going to tease him about the idea that I needed to wait just in case a dead man came back to life, but I did not. I'd had the same thought. "And then we can talk about what else we need to do. If anything."

I nodded. He wasn't wrong.

I was growing increasingly concerned about just what it was that I had gotten myself into. Again.

Chapter Four

"He did *what?*" Jos asked.

I had gone to see him after helping Harent clean up the mess in his cell. I had not wanted to leave that for him, as it was entirely my fault that it was there, even though I knew he didn't blame me for what had happened.

"Stabbed himself," I said. "I don't suppose you saw anything when you were cleaning up the remains from the pillar?"

Jos motioned for me to follow him, and we went through a door in the front of the office and into the warehouse behind it. I hadn't spent that much time here, but enough to recognize where he was taking me. The sense of pressure built the moment I passed through the door. It wasn't unexpected, as this was the place where the Investigators stored most of the items they found.

Jos paused in front of a small shelf near the front of the warehouse. The warehouse itself was relatively empty, as they had started bringing items to me at my home and to the palace grounds so that Matherin could help deal with them. As the Queen's chief fabricator, Matherin was more than happy to deal with some of the magical items.

"It's right here. I've been trying to piece it together to see if we can discern anything from the structure, but it's not really all that intriguing."

I leaned forward and took a moment to study the artifact. Jos wasn't wrong in that he had been trying to put it back together. It was something like a puzzle, though it had been cracked, leaving pieces that had shattered and sheared free. I ran my hand along the surface of one piece, testing for any residual energy, but did not detect anything. That was unfortunate.

"Did you pick up on anything?"

"No. None of us have, actually. We tried with a few different fabrications." He said the last with hesitation, as if he was a little concerned about what I might say to it. I wasn't. It was exactly what I had hoped they would do. "Haven't picked up on anything, though. There are still some tests we can run."

"Good. Keep running through them, and let me know if you come up with anything."

Relief swept across his face, and I felt a little guilty about it, as it was likely because he had feared that I was going to take the investigation away from them. The Investigators, including Jos, were proud and wanted to feel that the work that they did was important. I had to be careful that I didn't take that from them, even though there were certain aspects of what they did that I could do better—and faster. In this case, the investigation was something that they could do relatively well and effectively, primarily because they had some useful fabrications. And since we didn't detect anything magical about the pillar, I wouldn't find anything, anyway.

"What do you think they were doing out there?" Jos asked.

"I don't know. There was another person out there with tattoos, but they weren't like the ones on the man we brought in."

"Not bleeding?" He started to laugh but stopped when I didn't join him.

"Not bleeding, and honestly, it just doesn't make that much sense. Why outside of the city? Why, when someone might have detected what they were doing?"

"Maybe they didn't expect you out there."

I frowned. It was not unreasonable to assume that was the case. And if only the Investigators had been in Busal City, it probably would have been safe. But the magic had drawn me, a Blade.

However, I still didn't know what *kind* of magic it had been.

"We have to keep the others alerted," I said. "I don't know what they might be after, but this is nothing like what I've encountered before."

"What about Waleith?"

I shrugged. "He might have some experience with things like this." There were certain things that I simply didn't know because I hadn't had the opportunity to train like a true Blade.

But that wasn't to say that I couldn't learn.

I knew another Blade in the city. I hadn't visited with Asi in a while, but she knew things, and it would be a simple matter for me to go and ask her if she could help. Assuming she would be interested in helping.

"Anything else interesting I need to know about?"

"Not lately. We've dealt with some of the strange fabrications around here, but not much more to be concerned about. Since we took down that councilor, things have been quiet." Jos said this with pride, which was a good thing.

I pressed my lips together, frowning as I swept my gaze around the warehouse. It was unfortunate that this threat was present, and it was unfortunate that it was now going to occupy my thoughts.

"Let me know if you hear anything."

"You got it," Jos said.

I headed back out and paused in the street. I focused as Waleith had taught me, letting the sense of magic sweep around me. There was nothing obvious here, just a lingering undercurrent of energy, one that washed over me and radiated everywhere around. It was comforting in a way. There had been a time when I had feared magic, when I had believed that all forms of magic were dangerous. I no longer did, though I still felt that magic, in general, had more faults than benefits.

Maybe in that way, I was more like a true Blade.

The strangeness of the attack and the magic the man

had used in the constable station suggested a power that was worrisome. And considering everything that had happened in the city since I had been made a Blade, I couldn't help but question whether it was all connected. And that connection left me with a curiosity.

A curiosity that I didn't have a good answer for.

I found myself walking over the bridge leading across the harbor without really meaning to. I paused about halfway across to move out of the way of a wagon drawn by a pair of horses, and I nodded to the well-dressed man seated atop it. I instinctively tested for any magical energy within the vehicle and found nothing, though I hadn't really expected to. It would be too dangerous to move things so openly here. The bridge itself had its own magic, which I had found a little surprising at first. I hadn't always been attuned to it, but right now it radiated power and connected to me.

When I neared the far side of the bridge, I saw a short, compact figure waiting.

Asi was the only other Blade that I knew besides Waleith. It was a good thing that I had her as a resource in Busal City, especially considering how infrequently Waleith was in the city. She had trained at the training compound, and had been a bit irritable with my presence in the city at first, but I had thought that due to the fact that I had been named the Queen's Blade. In fact, I had come to see that she was just stubborn, and a bit isolated.

She had her fabricated blade held in hand, and it was long—nearly as long as her forearm. It looked like a sword for her.

"Didn't expect to see you over here, Zaren."

I glanced at the blade she was holding. "You're obviously expecting some sort of trouble. So what is it?"

Asi looked at the blade for a moment and then slipped it into her sheath. "Nothing."

I arched a brow, regarding her for a long moment. "No?"

"It's nothing that I can't deal with, so I don't need you to get worried about it. Unless you think you're now my superior."

I shook my head. "I don't think that's how it works. Honestly, I don't really know. Waleith didn't leave me any instructions."

She snorted. "Not surprising, and no. You won't be my superior, and even if you were, I don't think... Well, I guess I don't even know what I think. What's going on?"

"Do you have time to talk?"

"Talk? That's all this is about?"

"It's about an investigation."

"Oh?"

"A new one. At least, I think that it's a new one. I don't know if it's tied to the other ones yet. Considering how everything seems connected, it might well be."

Asi glanced down at the water's edge, resting her hand on the bridge, tracing the stones with her fingers. Her brow wrinkled, her gaze going distant, which left me wondering if she detected something.

"I don't see anything," she said. "Don't feel anything, either."

"Right," I said. "Talk?"

"You really can be a pain, can't you, Zaren?"

"I'm not trying to be."

Asi motioned for me to follow, and we headed along the harbor road until she stopped at a tavern. The city on this side of the harbor was a bit dirtier, dingier, and more run-down than on my side of the harbor. In a way, this side of the city suited me better, though I didn't have the opportunity to spend much time here. I couldn't imagine what it would be like to have the freedom that Asi had, nor to have less concern about the Queen and serving her. Then again, I wasn't terribly concerned about what the Queen asked of me, because I wasn't forced to report to her regularly, though I had to be better at it than I had been so far.

"You coming?"

"I'm coming," I muttered.

The tavern reminded me of the very first time that I had met with Asi. Of course, there had been a Guild member there at that point, and this tavern didn't have a minstrel who left me worried that they were a part of the Guild. I still had to resolve that episode, but I wasn't sure what that was going to entail, or if I would even have an opportunity to do so. The members of the Guild were secretive enough that finding them was going to be difficult without leaving the city. Even if I could, it would take me from my responsibilities here. That was reason enough for me to let it be—at least until the Guild decided to come after me.

Asi took a seat at a table, motioning to one of the

servers, a younger man with a broad face, a scruff of a beard, and a dirty apron, and he scurried to the back.

"Somebody you know?"

She shrugged. "We can't all have fancy places like you do, Zaren. I have to make do with what I have."

The tavern was quiet, and most of the tables were empty, save for one table near the back, where three people sat hunched forward, playing a game of cards. There was a steady conversation among them, and every so often, one of them would slap the cards down on the table, and another one would get angry or push coins off the side. It reminded me of the tavern in Lavrun where I had served as a bouncer.

"Have you detected anything recently?"

Asi shrugged. "Over here? Just some minor things. I don't have Investigators helping the way that you do on your side of the harbor."

"Do you want some?"

The question seemed to catch her off guard, and she regarded me strangely for a moment. "Is that a sincere offer, or are you just playing with me?"

"Well, it was a sincere offer, unless it's offensive, and then I guess I would take it back." I shrugged again. "The Investigators have been useful. Not all of them, and I still think that I have some work to do to make them feel they can trust me, but increasingly, they have been useful. I think that we could probably get them to serve over here as well. Only if you want help."

When the server came back, he set the mugs of ale on

the table. Asi flipped a coin to him, and he caught it out of the air.

"Thanks, Ms. Blade," he said.

He hurried away, and I started to laugh.

"What?" she asked.

"Ms. Blade?"

"It's sort of what he calls me."

"You don't feel the need to try to mask who and what you are?"

"No real point in it. Most people on this side of the city have a pretty good idea about what I do. I don't wear a marker quite as openly as you do," she said, motioning to the pin that I wore on my lapel, "but I have to carry a blade, and the constables aren't really all that secretive about such things, if you know what I mean."

"I don't, not really, but I suppose that it makes sense. And having others know that you are a Blade is probably useful as well."

"Useful, and not."

"Sounds confusing," I said.

"Confusion is the enemy of peace."

"What was that?" I asked.

Asi waved a hand. "Something one of my mentors used to say."

She fell quiet for a moment, and I suspected she was thinking about what had happened at the training compound, and how many people she had known had been lost.

"I'm sorry."

She shook her head. "Arin was killed before, by...

Doesn't matter. Not anymore. Anyway, what were you going on about?" She took a long drink of her ale before setting the mug down on the table.

I hurriedly filled her in on what had just taken place. When I was done, she stared at me for a long moment.

"You sure about that?"

"About which part? Destroying the pillar, getting attacked, the strange orb, or—"

"The markings," she said.

"I'm sure about that," I said.

She let out a frustrated sigh. "Damn. Just when I thought things were settling down for little while. Now you go and bring in the Anvil?"

"The what?"

"You don't know?"

"Obviously not," I said. "Otherwise, I..." I shook my head. "Can you tell me what's going on?"

"The Anvil. It is an organization that I only know about through three things. One is the tattoos. Two is the fact that they are powerful because of number one. And three is that they tend to try to get involved in aspects of the world, and politics, that they shouldn't."

I stared for a moment. "Politics?"

"They've been known to try to influence events. Always for financial gain, of course, but dangerously so. So if they are here, the situation will be difficult. Dangerous, even."

"And everything that we've been dealing with already is possibly tied to that."

"Oh, don't say that," she said.

"Why?"

"Because it makes sense, Zaren. We don't need anything like that to make sense. If the Anvil is involved, it's going to be beyond our ability to deal with."

"Beyond the Blades?" I frowned. "Isn't this what we do?"

Asi leaned forward, taking another drink, and when she set it down, she did so with a light thud and regarded me with a darkened glare. "This is what we do, but not like this, if you know what I mean. This is dangerous for many reasons. For one, the Anvil is more powerful than most of the entities that you have dealt with. I suspect that your time is spent primarily dealing with fabrications and the like."

I nodded.

"And that's sort of all I deal with. The powder that you came across was a little unique, but again, not too difficult. The Anvil is something else altogether. Powerful. Widespread. And they aren't afraid of breaking a few eggs in order to get what they want. Not if the profit is high enough." She shook her head. "So if you have been looking into why—and how—one of the council members got involved, here is your answer."

I sat back. I had thought that it was tied to money and banking, but there had seemed to be another element behind it. Otherwise, why would somebody want to take on the Queen? But now...

"So let's just say that this is the Anvil," I said, "and that they have been behind this all along."

"You just said that they are here, so they *are* behind it," Asi said.

"Fine," I said. "How do we deal with them?"

"We?"

"Right," I said. "How do we deal with them?"

"Let me tell you what I learned at the training compound. When it comes to the Anvil, always send word. Never deal with them on your own. Do you know why?"

"I'm gathering that you're going to tell me."

"Because they are too dangerous. Too much for one person to take on."

"So you just ignored them?"

"No. We didn't just ignore them. There were people who were trained to deal with them."

"Highly trained Blades," I said.

She nodded. "Exactly. People who could counter the Anvil, who were trained in finding them, sniffing them out, and dealing with them. I imagine that it was difficult for you to handle the one?"

"A little," I said. "I think we surprised them when we came upon them, or at least upset what they were planning. But the man was a little challenging. He didn't want to die."

Asi snorted. "Of course he didn't want to die. He had to finish his job."

"So we get ahold of the ones who can handle the Anvil?"

"We don't. When the training compound was destroyed, they were all killed."

I clenched my jaw. And then I reached for the ale and took a long drink before setting it down. "So," I said, "is that why they went after the training compound?"

"I don't know. But I am starting to think that maybe this is far more interconnected than we know."

"I've been feeling that for a long time," I said.

"Well, now you have some more proof. What are you going to do about it?"

"The only thing I can. I have to be the Queen's Blade."

Chapter Five

After ensuring that Asi was going to help me keep an eye out for the Anvil, something that she assured me she would do because she was equally concerned about their presence in the city, I returned to my side of Busal City. I wandered around the entire city, looking for answers, but was not able to pick up on anything. It reminded me of when I had first trained with Waleith in the city, attempting to pick up on different strains of power around me and make sense of the sources. So far, I had been able to identify very little.

Certainly nothing like the tremoring presence of the Anvil. If there was something here, I should have picked up on it by now, so I didn't think that I had overlooked anything.

Occasionally I came across some Investigators, and I checked in with them to see if they had come up with anything, but over the next few days, all was quiet. I knew that I needed to fill in the Investigators about the

Anvil, but considering the danger that Asi had implied they posed, I hesitated to do so. And that hesitation left me a little troubled that perhaps I was no better than Waleith in keeping the Investigators from knowing what was happening in the city around them, and in fact, I was probably acting entirely like him. And if that was the case, then what was that going to mean for me, and what did that make me?

I didn't know.

I only knew that danger was brewing, and increasingly, I couldn't help but feel that everything I had dealt with was too dangerous even for me.

At one point as I wandered through the city, I ended up near Dara's shop. I had probably ended up here intentionally, though I hadn't done so purposely. I hesitated, feeling for the vague sense of the fabricated energy that came from inside, and though I could pick up on the strains of fabricated power in her shop, I did not know if she was using anything dangerous. I didn't *think* so. And considering the fact that Waleith must have known about this fabrication shop and had done nothing, I had so far left it alone. But then, I wondered whether I had left it alone because I had simply not been concerned about the kind of magic that was found within the shop or because of Dara.

I hadn't seen her much since my return from the Isle of Erantor. Which was hard, and harder than I had expected. She was really the only person that I knew in the city and cared about here. I had gotten to know Waleith and people within the palace, and there was certainly Harent, somebody I had worked with before, but there was something different to be said about spending time with Dara, and the connection that I believed the two of us shared.

"Go on in, you big idiot," I muttered to myself.

A man near me looked over.

I forced a smile, and he scurried on.

I pushed open the door. I had to get this over with. Not only because I had to stop putting off visiting Dara but because it was entirely possible that she knew some useful information. Or at least, her employer might. She had certainly been helpful with dealing with the fabrications that had been moving around the city before.

The feeling of power struck me the moment I pushed open the door, and I stepped inside. I let it wash over me and did not attempt to fight it. Still, the energy began to dissipate quickly, which left me wondering if Dara knew that I was there, or if she simply stopped because somebody was there. If it was because it was me, well, then I had to be a little more careful, and I had to wonder what else she might have picked up on.

I moved toward the counter. Dara was where she always was when I came to the shop, working behind the counter, and she had a lump of partially shaped metal in front of her. This looked like a small building, though I doubted that was what it was intended to be. Most of the time, Dara made sculptures of animals or other figures, which were shaped with her unique form of magic. I didn't think that she was fabricating anything, but I did think her sculptures were used as fabrications.

The smile that curled her lips was not nearly as broad as it had been when I had first come here. "I was wondering when you might come back around," she said.

"It's nice to see you," I said.

"Is it?"

"It is. How have you been?" I cursed myself for the stupidity of the question. I needed to have a real conversation with her, not a faltering conversation. This was somebody that I wanted to spend time with, so why should I act like such an imbecile?

"About as well as could be expected," she said. "I've been busy. But then, you would know that, wouldn't you?"

"How would I know that?"

"Because you've had your boys running around here a lot more lately."

"My boys?"

"You know. The Investigators. They've stopped in a few times. More than usual."

I hadn't realized that. But then, I had empowered the Investigators to investigate as they were supposed to. Why should I intervene?

"I'm sorry. I didn't know."

"It's fine. We aren't doing anything that's illegal," Dara said, choosing her words carefully, and she regarded me for a long moment, as if daring me to challenge that assertion. "And it's told me how you feel about things."

"I don't have anything to do with that, actually," I said. "But I can. Talk to them, that is."

"Would you?"

"I..."

If Dara was involved in anything dangerous, or if her employer was, there was no reason for me to keep the Investigators from investigating. In fact, I didn't want to be seen as having some sort of bias. So I had to be careful here.

"As long as nothing untoward is happening, I suppose I could."

"Untoward? And how would you decide that?"

"Come on, Dara."

"What can I do for you, Zaren?" She straightened, resting her hand on the table, and there was a tension in her posture that hadn't been there before.

"I came by to say hello, and that's it."

"Well, you have done that. I'm a little busy now. Unless you would intervene."

I breathed out heavily. This was how it was going to be now? Could our relationship have changed so much? But then, by nature of my position, how could it be anything else?

"I'm sorry I interrupted. I'm just looking into something. A group that gathers power, from what I understand of it. So if you hear anything about people who call themselves the Anvil, can you send word?"

Dara stiffened. "What was that?"

The sudden change in her demeanor suggested that she had heard of the Anvil. Which surprised me, especially as I had not heard anything of the Anvil. Maybe it was better known here than it was in other places.

"You know of them?"

"If you have gotten involved with them, Zaren, you need to get out. I don't know what you are doing—"

"I'm not doing anything. I suspect that they have been active near the city," I went on, deciding to stick with that aspect, as it was the truth, "and I'm trying to ensure that they aren't active in the city. So if you hear anything, please send word."

Dara held my gaze for a moment, and it looked as if some debate raged behind her eyes. "You don't know what you're doing, do you?"

"With them? I'm trying to protect the city."

"No," she said. "You don't even know what they are, do you?"

I thought about what Asi had told me, and figured that was enough. "I have a pretty good idea. Why?"

"And I imagine everything you know is that they use power to pursue wealth."

I shrugged. "Something along those lines."

"It's not just money. It's power."

"So money and power. Great."

"And if they are here..." Dara shifted nervously, her gaze flicking toward the door before turning back to me. "If they are here, Zaren, you need to get help. This is going to be more than you can handle."

"I'm usually all right in such matters," I said.

"I get it," she said. "The big soldier who thinks he can handle all sorts of problems, and... Well, this is something different. This is not the kind of thing that I would expect you to be able to handle on your own. And they have plenty of experience with big men, strong men, like yourself. And they don't fear them."

I considered the man that we had encountered and realized that maybe she was right. "So they won't fear me. Well, I guess I don't have much to say about that."

"You aren't concerned?"

"Why should I be concerned?"

I was, and I started to worry that without Waleith, or any others who really knew how to handle the Anvil, this was truly going to be outside my comfort zone. What I wouldn't give to have some way of reaching Garridan, but I didn't know if he would even help if I were to do so. Would the Guild even care?

For all I knew, the Anvil and the Guild were working together.

"You should be concerned because people get caught up in their machinations."

"How did you get caught up in them?"

Dara shook her head. "It doesn't matter."

"Seems like it does."

She closed her eyes for a moment, squeezing her hands, and while her eyes were shut, the metal sculpture that she was working on began to deform, taking on a rippling shape. I felt the effect of her magic losing control and noticed the power rolled out of her and impacted the sculpture itself. The process was a little unusual, but it didn't feel painful, and it didn't feel dangerous. It just felt strange. Strange that she would lose control. In all the time I had known Dara, which admittedly was not all that long, she had never lost control over her ability around me.

"My brother got involved with them," she said. "I don't know what happened to him, but that's sort of how it goes."

"He was killed by them?"

"He joined them," she said.

I didn't know what to say. "I'm sorry."

"So just be careful. I don't want anything to happen to you."

"You don't?"

"Not like that."

"Well, I can take care of myself."

"This isn't about defending yourself. This is about them forcing you to serve."

I frowned at that. "*Forcing* me to serve?"

Dara nodded. "That's how they get you, you know. They find your weakness, and they force you to serve. Somebody like you, somebody who obviously has some strength, and your own innate talents," she went on, eyeing me for a moment, "would be appealing to them."

I started to smile. "So you're saying that they would try to force me to join them?"

"Force you, and once you are one of them, there's not a lot you can do. They have ways of compelling people to stay with them. Don't ask me how I know."

I watched her, and I wondered what else she had been through with the Anvil, and just how bad it was. What had her brother ended up needing to do that had hurt her, that caused her to have this kind of reaction?

"I don't think their techniques would work on me, anyway," I said.

"Because you're a Blade? I don't think it makes much of a difference. They have experience with these things, Zaren. Whatever you think you can do, whatever you think you are, they can work around it."

They sounded horrible, not that I was going to say that out loud.

"I'll be careful."

"Just figure out what they want, and it might be best if you give it to them."

I stared at her. "You want me just to give away whatever it is they want from the city?" I shook my head. "I'm afraid I won't be able to do that. I'm the Queen's Blade, and I have obligations. Not only to the Queen but to the city."

"Well, I just hope you don't draw their attention."

I said nothing. It was already too late for me to avoid drawing their attention.

What would they do?

There was the look that they had given me when I had fought them off. A look of curiosity? Maybe that was what it had been. But maybe it had been something else as well.

Maybe they had been appraising me. And here I had thought that I had scared them away, but perhaps that wasn't it at all. I had intervened in whatever they had been doing, but maybe that disruption would only be temporary. And if so, would they keep coming after me?

I wasn't going to be forced to serve.

Or could I be?

They find your weakness. That was what Dara had said.

What was my weakness?

I didn't know. Maybe it was her.

"Thanks for sharing your concerns with me," I said. "I won't bother you anymore."

"It wasn't a bother," she said. "And..."

"I know."

She looked down at the sculpture. "Sacred Souls. I'm really sorry. You must think that I am just jumping at shadows."

"I think that you're scared about this, and I am sorry."

"Don't be sorry. Well, not for that. And I'm glad that you warned me. Otherwise, I might've been surprised by their presence in the city."

"Do you think your brother might be here?"

Dara was quiet for a moment. "No."

"How can you be so sure?"

"Because I'm sure."

I didn't push. There was no reason to. But I wanted to know more. "Anyway, if you find anything useful about what they have been doing, what interests them in Busal City, can you let me know?"

"I'll let you know. I imagine that I should send word to the palace."

"That would be the best way," I said.

She shook her head with a laugh. "I can imagine the looks I would get if I headed up to the palace. Would I even be permitted access to you?"

"Well, I don't actually live at the palace," I said. "Though I think they would let me, it's not really what I want."

Dara nodded. "So your boys, then."

"I imagine they wouldn't be so pleased with you referring to them as 'my boys,' but yes. Any of the Investigators can get word to me."

What would Jos and some of the others say if she came trying to get word to me? Then again, now that we had a better working relationship, it was quite possible that they would actually deliver a message to me.

"It really was nice to see you, Dara."

"And you," she said.

She turned her attention back to her sculpture, and the distant look in her eyes left me troubled. Not for myself, despite what she had claimed that the Anvil might try to do. Rather, it was for her, and for what had happened to her.

What had she been through with her brother?

And would there be a way for me to learn more, short of pushing the issue with her? Would I even dare? No. I wouldn't. There was no point, and if her brother was gone, it was unlikely to make much of a difference, anyway.

I left her, saying nothing more, and headed back out into the street, determined to continue my patrol, and my investigation. But now I was worried about what I might find, and afraid that it might force me onto a path that I might not want to take.

Chapter Six

The knock at my door jolted me awake. How long had I been asleep?

I hurriedly jumped to my feet, grabbed my blade, along with an overcoat, and hurried to the door, pulling it open.

It was Harent.

"They have you running errands now, do they?" I asked.

"Got something you need to see," he said, without any sort of preamble.

"What time is it?"

"Late."

I looked past him. There were streetlights along my street, but that was not surprising, especially because I was close to the palace, and the extra light was beneficial to avoid anybody sneaking up to the Queen's residence. But beyond that, I could still see that darkness hovered over the city. Fog had rolled in from the harbor, and it lay over the street like a blanket, shrouding it in a thin and wispy mist. It was a little unnerving, but only because Harent was at my door.

"Do I need anything?"

"Just you. And that blade of yours." He looked at the blade I clutched in my hand. "Don't know if it's going to be necessary, but I figure that it can't hurt."

"Let me get my boots."

After finishing getting dressed, I met Harent in the street. He nodded to a pair of constables at the far end of the street, heading away from the harbor—and toward the palace.

"You have an escort?" I asked.

"Let's just say that I am a little on edge."

"You wanted my blade, so you're obviously concerned about something magical."

"Just come with me."

I followed him. We headed up a slow hillside, past the palace, and we continued off to the west. The cityscape shifted as we moved past massive manors and into a quieter section of the city. There were some shops here, though it was late enough that they were all closed, and there was no sign of anybody out in the street. There were no lanterns lit inside the homes, either. It was empty. Dark.

"Care to at least fill me in?"

"You've been seen marching around the city," Harent said.

"I have."

"Figure it's something tied to what you brought to my station."

"I don't know," I said.

He grunted. "Don't need you lying to me, Joha. I'd rather have us work together."

I breathed out heavily. "I'm not sure what I know. I talked to the Blade on the other side of the harbor—"

"You know the other Blade?"

"Why does that surprise everybody I tell?"

"It's just..."

"Let me guess. That's not something that Waleith would have done."

Harent shrugged slightly. "Well, it isn't."

"Anyway, I was talking to her, and she recognized the tattoos."

"She did?"

"She said that they are used by an organization called the Anvil." I checked for any sign of recognition in Harent, but he didn't react whatsoever. "And from your lack of response, you haven't heard of them."

"Some sort of criminal enterprise?"

"Apparently, a dangerous criminal enterprise," I said. "And the only two people that I have spoken to who know anything about them fear them."

He was quiet for a bit. "And now they're active here?"

"I don't know if it was a one-off or if they're interested in something. I like to think I scared them away, but the other Blade seems to believe that wasn't likely."

Harent grunted again. "Well, it's probably a little

disappointing to you that you can't just go and scare people like you usually do."

I glowered at him. "Usually?"

"You know. You loom over them, looking all intimidating and the like."

"I thought I actually *had* intimidated the Anvil."

"Any sign of them?"

"I have the Investigators checking, and they probably have all sorts of fabrications set around the city to help ensure that if any magic like that is used, we will pick up on it."

He nodded carefully. "All right. So you're using your resources. And now you have me and the constables looking into things."

"I'd say that you need to be careful with this one," I said. "If there's even a hint of anything magical, you need to involve me. At the least, involve the Investigators."

"Which is why I have you here, Joha."

We stopped in an unlit street, and the darkness was difficult to pierce. There were no streetlights here. But a strange odor hung in the air. A pair of blackened figures stood just up ahead, and as we approached, Harent nodded to them. They moved off to the side. Constables, both of them, I realized.

I looked at Harent. "What's this about?"

"Down the alley," he said. "Once we get down there, I can show you what we came across. So get moving."

"You know, I'm not one of your constables to command."

"You're going to want to see this. Trust me."

The fact that he had woken me up suggested that it was significant. Actually, the fact that he had been awoken and was here along with me suggested that it was significant.

I reached the alley, and a constable handed me something. It was a small arcane lantern. They were expensive, and incredibly valuable. He twisted the knob, letting out some of the pale light, which cast a bluish hue over the alleyway. The color wouldn't be bright enough to waken anybody. I moved into the alley but paused when I saw this wasn't really an alley but some sort of old and weathered courtyard. With the walls closing around me, it *felt* like an alley.

And there was something familiar here.

Another pillar.

It looked just like the one that I had shattered outside the city. This one didn't have any sense of magic coming from it, however. I approached and pressed my blade up against it, rotating around it.

"This what you described to me?" Harent asked.

"Pretty much," I said.

"Figured so."

"Why all of this?" I asked, looking at him. "Why get you up in the middle of the night?"

"Because of those," he said, pointing past the pillar.

I frowned, angling the light. Harent took it from me, adjusted a dial, and the light shifted from blue to a pale yellow. It brightened everything, and I saw three bodies lying in a heap at the back of the courtyard. I moved toward them, doing so carefully, slowly, and then I crouched down beside them. One was an older man with sallow cheeks, a pale complexion, and what looked to be a slit beneath each ear that ran lengthwise down toward his chest. There was no sign of blood, though.

"How can they cut him like that and not bleed him out?" I asked, though I didn't really expect Harent to answer.

"That's the question my men had," he said. "Honestly, it's surprising they found this. I think it was the smell."

I wrinkled my nose. "What do you think the smell is from?"

"Can't say. Don't know. Not them, or at least, not obviously them."

It didn't seem to me the smell was coming from them, either. I moved on to the next body. This one was a woman. She was a little younger than the first, but still older. Probably in her forties, with some flecks of gray in her hair, and the same slits beneath her ears, running down toward her chest. This one had a few droplets of blood on her, but not much. Not nearly as much as I would have expected from this kind of wound. I moved to the third, finding a dark-haired man.

"Anything on any of them?" I asked.

"Not that we've been able to find. We checked them over, but..." Harent shrugged. "We couldn't find anything. We weren't really expecting to, either."

"Why not?"

"This was obviously something intentional. Don't know what it is, but it looks to be some sort of weird ceremony. That's why I wanted you to see it, and tell me if you were able to pick up on anything."

I turned back. "No," I said. "Not clearly. So I think you can bring your men back down here. I'm going to have the Investigators take the pillar and bring it to their warehouse, where we can run tests on it." Unfortunately, I doubted we would uncover anything, as whatever had happened here was already done, and whatever magic had been here was already spent. It wasn't tied to the pillar.

Unless the pillar was the key.

I crouched, looking at the pillar, looking at the dead bodies, and had my mind churning.

"When I was talking with Asi—she's the other Blade—she mentioned knowing something about the tattoos. That's a pretty defining characteristic for the Anvil. I wonder if these pillars are tied to those tattoos." I frowned. "But why bleed out these others?"

"Perhaps the blood somehow powers the pillar," Harent said.

I stood, looking over at him. "Do you really think something like that could be the case?"

He shrugged. "I'm not a Blade. How am I supposed to know these things?"

I snorted. "You say that like you might know something."

"I say it like somebody who is just tossing around ideas. Not because I know anything. Sacred Souls, Joha. I've seen some strange things in my time in the city, but this is up there."

"I need to find out if anybody in the palace knows what happened to Waleith."

"Normally, I would tell you that we'd rather not have him around, but I'm starting to think that it might be necessary."

"Same."

Not that I was afraid of drawing Waleith in, but the idea that there might be something strange going on, something greater than what I could know and find on my own, was troubling.

"Thanks for getting me up."

Harent laughed. "Oh? Figured you'd want to play with this."

"I'm not so sure that I wanted this, but I'm also not so sure that I have much choice in the matter. Maybe keep the bodies someplace more secure."

"What do you think they're going to do?"

"You saw what happened with that other guy," I said.

The comment made Harent pause. "I will see what I can do."

I turned to the pillar. It was intact, so I wasn't sure if I wanted to leave it that way, because there might be some power still within it. The idea that there could be something magical still powering this pillar was troubling to me, and it was the kind of thing that left me thinking that the best course of action was probably the safest one.

I held my blade up above the center of it. There were no marks, no writing, nothing to suggest that this was anything magical. It was just made of stone. I hesitated a moment, then tried to lift it. It was incredibly heavy. I could barely get it a hand's height above the ground before I nearly dropped it. I settled it back to the ground and looked over at Harent. "How did they move it here?"

"Don't know. We don't have any word about what they were doing or who brought it here. I just brought you here."

I thought about the pillar that the Investigators had brought to the city. How had that been so portable in one piece? Or maybe it hadn't been.

"Stand back," I said.

"You're going to do that now?"

"You want me to wait?"

"I don't think I want to be around you when you're doing your Blade thing," Harent said, backing down the alley.

"It's not like it's going to infect you, or affect you. It's just going to deal with the power here."

He stared at me and then shook his head. "Sacred Souls, Joha."

I grinned. Then I pushed the blade down.

Right before the blade pierced the top of the pillar, I began to feel some resistance. I had to push through it. There was more, and it was stronger than I had anticipated. I had felt some resistance when I had done this outside the city. This, however, was surprising, because I had felt nothing from it before.

How was that even possible?

It shouldn't have been. I should have been able to pick up on this kind of power within the pillar. Had the blade not been in my hand, I... Well, I didn't even know what I would have found.

I pushed.

Then I started to feel the power pushing against me, resisting me, until I noticed a steady, slow cracking that began to work its way through the pillar. And then I forced the blade down with a grunt. The blade slammed into the top of the pillar, where a spiderweb of cracks began to spread outward.

And something else happened. It was odd, and a little unpleasant, to see some sort of liquid starting to spew out from those cracks.

"Is that—"

I cut off Harent. "Blood," I said, looking over at the dead bodies. "The pillar is filled with blood."

But why?

The cracks started to spread.

Harent yelped, and then he shot me a look before scurrying back down the alley. I stood there for just a moment and then decided that I didn't want to be there when the pillar exploded, and I hurried away. At the end of the alley, I stood, holding the arcane lantern up, and watched as the pillar cracked, and the blood pooled along the ground. Then the pillar fell into a pile of debris.

What was going on here?

Chapter Seven

The palace was quiet.

There were days when the palace was a maze of activity, from servants to visitors, but today was not such a day. I wondered if the Queen was in meetings, or perhaps she wasn't even in the city. I didn't visit with her often enough to know her comings and goings, and I doubted that she would even give a thought to me or want me to know what was happening.

I was tired. I hadn't slept much after the strange night. Once the pillar had shattered, the constables had run off to gather some Investigators, and then they had collected the remains of the pillar, piling them into a wagon, which they then transported back to the warehouse. It was one more thing that I was going to have to look into and see if I could figure out the power within it. Seeing as I hadn't felt anything, however, I doubted that I would pick up on much from it.

Harent had set some of his men to patrol, looking for

anything similar, and he was planning to scour the city. If there was power in the city that I couldn't detect, then it wasn't going to be easy to uncover whatever the Anvil was after.

Which was why I was here now.

I needed help. I needed somebody who had an understanding of power, and the Anvil, that I did not. And it was time that I started looking into such things in a way that would provide me with more answers, though I wasn't sure if there were going to be answers. Without Waleith, I didn't know what I could find.

I wasn't slowed passing through the gate and into the palace itself, and once inside the palace, I paused and didn't have to wait very long before Hobell came toward me, as if he had known that I was coming. He probably had long before I had arrived.

"The Blade," he said, his words tight, clipped, as he flicked his eyes around. He was always looking around him, always searching, as if checking for threats that only he could see.

"Good to see you as well. Is the Queen available?"

He pursed his lips in a frown. Previously, he had always refused my requests to visit with the Queen, and I half expected him to do the same again. But he surprised me. "She is incapacitated at this moment. I am sorry."

"Incapacitated?" I frowned at that. It seemed a strange turn of phrase.

He paused, as if debating what to tell me. "She is unwell."

"Anything concerning?"

"Not that I'm going to share with you, but she does have her physicker with her, so no need for you to be alarmed."

I wasn't completely alarmed, but the idea that the Queen wasn't well while the Anvil was active in the city had me a little concerned.

I had no idea of the purpose behind the pillars, the purpose behind the sacrifices—and that was what I suspected they were. All I knew was that something beyond my comprehension was taking place here.

"I'm not alarmed. Is Prince Dorian available, then?"

He watched me for a moment. "I suppose that I could send word to him. You will have to wait, as he is quite busy."

I snorted. It had been my experience that Prince Dorian was always quite busy. And when it came to me in particular, he tended to be *especially* busy. I wasn't sure if it was just because of how I had been chosen, and that he didn't really care for the fact that I had been selected as a Blade, or if it was that he didn't like Blades in general. Whatever it was, he had never cared much for me. The feeling was relatively mutual, and honestly, I couldn't help but feel Waleith didn't care much for him, either. Which was probably part of the reason that Dorian didn't care for me.

I was guided into a small sitting room, where I waited. I hadn't expected him to give me much in the way of accommodation, as in the past, when I had been waiting on the Queen or others, Hobell had never really treated me with much more than a cursory amount of respect. I didn't know if that was because he didn't see me as a part of the Queen's household or if it was because he felt that I interrupted the flow. The room was well appointed, with portraits on the walls. I recognized the Queen and her deceased husband, but the others I didn't recognize. Probably the Queen's parents, but I didn't know much about Crown politics, nor did I know much about the line of succession, other than the fact that the Queen's father had ruled for a decade prior to dying from a fall down the stairs in the palace itself. Supposedly mysterious, though I wondered how much of that was just rumor.

I worked my way around the room, looking at each portrait, studying them. They were quite well done, though I didn't know much about art. They looked lifelike. At least, lifelike enough that I could imagine some of these people in life.

The door came open, and Prince Dorian strode in, sweeping his gaze around the room before settling it on me. He had a haughty air to him, his hands clasped behind his back, as he regarded me for a long moment. "What is it?"

"If you don't want to visit with me, I can certainly wait for the Queen."

"No," he said. "You cannot. She is—"

"Sick?"

He frowned. "Hobell should not have spoken about that."

I tapped on my lapel pin. "I am a part of the household. I am her Blade."

"Yes," Dorian said. "I suppose you are. What can I help you with today?"

"I need to know if there have been any reports of Waleith."

He arched a brow. "You came to the palace, interrupted my meetings, simply to ask me about Waleith?"

"Something's happening in the city."

"Oh?"

If there was one thing that I had not been that good at ever since coming to the city, it was reporting issues that came up. And even though the Queen might be incapacitated, that didn't mean that I couldn't—or shouldn't—report to her adviser.

"I don't know all that much about what I'm going to tell you, so—"

"So you have come here prematurely?"

"I came here hoping that I could see if you, or the Queen, knew anything about when Waleith would return. What is happening is the kind of thing that he is better equipped to investigate."

"Go on."

"Have you heard of the Anvil?"

His expression barely changed, but just enough that I suspected that the term was familiar to him.

"Good. That's going to make this easier."

I filled him in on what I had interrupted and then about what had happened the night before.

"Honestly, I have no idea what these pillars are, and after talking to Asi, it seems to me that the Blades once had a way of dealing with this kind of power, and that most Blades were not supposed to intervene."

"It would be a mistake," he agreed.

"You know something about them?"

"Stories," he said. "Have you heard about the civil war in Tur?"

"Rumors," I said. "Stories from there don't really reach us here. And it was a decade ago." Back before I had been in the army, but there had still been stories about it.

"Apparently, the Anvil were behind it." He turned and shrugged slightly. "They disagreed with the flow of salt coming out of Tur, and they thought to push through a different ruling class. It didn't work out quite as well as they had hoped, but ultimately they managed to acquire the salt flow that they wanted."

"So they were behind it, but what else should I worry about?"

"If you really dig deep enough, you will find that kind of story. Especially about the Anvil. It is not uncommon for there to be a plethora of rumors about them."

"So that's all that you think this is? A rumor?"

"I think that a rumor like that would serve their purposes, yes."

I wondered about that. Maybe it was a valid point, but considering what we had encountered in the city, I was still concerned about even a rumor.

"Why would that be the case?"

"If I told you that there was a terrifying Blade of incredible power, strength, and ferocity that terrorized the criminals who thought to bring dangerous magical items into the city, what would you think?"

I laughed. "I'm not sure I am terrifying."

"And who said that I was referring to you?"

I hesitated for a moment. "Let's say there was a terrifying individual like that."

"Let's. And if rumors began to spread along the shoreline, to people who intended to bring in items of destruction, what do you think would happen?"

"It might cause them to pause."

"Exactly. Pause. Take a moment to consider if a course of action was still viable or if they needed to make additional preparations and plans. And if that were the case, then you can see why rumors like that would be valuable, especially for somebody who wants to convince another to take a different path."

"So you don't think this is anything particularly dangerous or magical."

"You are a Blade. What is your experience with fabrications?"

It was a strange conversation to be having with the prince, but stranger still was that it was the first time that I'd had a conversation with him where I felt he was actually engaged in the conversation, and not simply irritated by the fact that I had come to talk to him or the Queen. And I felt more like an equal, at least in some respects. Not a true equal. There was an obvious power differential between the two of us, and I doubted that I would be able to overlook that, or that Prince Dorian would ever overlook it, but that didn't change the fact that he almost certainly was treating me a little differently. Could it be because of what had happened in the city recently, and how I had dealt with the aelith powder, and revealed the plot against the Queen?

I hadn't spent a lot of time talking to the prince, but this did strike me as a possibility.

"I have seen quite a few fabrications, especially since I came here."

"Exactly. Since you came here. And in that time, what has your experience with those fabrications been? Are they safe, or are they dangerous?"

"I would argue that quite a few of them are dangerous," I said.

Dorian nodded. "Quite a few. But not all?"

What did he know?

"You mean like my blade."

"Your blade," he said, glancing down at where the blade was sheathed at my side, "or perhaps even the house sigil that you wear. A device that is designed to protect you and others who bear it."

I glanced down at the pin. I supposed I hadn't given much thought to that.

"And so there are fabrications that are useful, even beneficial, but there are also fabrications that are dangerous. But one thing is consistent with them. They can be used for a variety of purposes, can't they?"

"And these are just fabrications?"

"It is possible that they are, but it is equally possible that there is truly some other power involved. You are the Blade. Find out." He offered a tight smile.

I nodded to him. "Thank you. And if you hear anything about Waleith, I would appreciate it."

"I'm sure that whatever he is doing is considered crucial to the Crown, so I don't know if there is much I will be able to offer you."

Prince Dorian had started to go when I spoke up again.

"I don't suppose there is anyone that you know who has other stories about the Anvil? Anything that you might have heard would be helpful. Mostly because I would like to know more about some of those rumors."

He glanced back at me, and there was a look in his eyes that suggested that he was a little annoyed. "Rumors are not going to be of much use."

"Probably not," I said, "but if I hear enough rumors, maybe I can see if there are trends within them. And maybe I can start to puzzle out some of the details that are real, and others that are obviously fantastical."

And what I really wanted to know was whether there were rumors about sacrifices, the draining of blood, and strange pillars of power. Because if there were not, it would suggest that this was an aspect of the Anvil that they wanted to keep quiet. And if that was the case, then they would not want those stories spread, even by me.

Right now, the only stories that I had of the Anvil were from the prince—and I suspected that he didn't fear them, or at the very least, he thought they were not much of a threat—and from Dara, who very much feared them. I needed a measure of balance, but there didn't seem to be one. And until I had a balance, I doubted I would be able to find anything useful that would make much of a difference to me.

"I'm sure that if you talk to Waleith, or your other Blade companion, you will get one set of stories. And you are known to frequent the docks." Dorian regarded me, sweeping his gaze up and down. "So if you talk to any of the sailors, you'll hear one story or another." He chuckled. "Though I don't know how much faith to put in such stories."

"I thought the point here was that I couldn't put any faith in any of the stories, and that what I really needed was to try to understand if there were similarities."

"Yes. I suppose that would be true enough. Anyway, please keep me informed, or the Queen, of course, if you come up with anything more that we need to hear about. In the meantime, I trust that you will do your job. You will serve as the Queen's Blade. And you will ensure that this danger is dealt with." He regarded me with an intensity in his gaze before stepping through the door and leaving me there once more.

Chapter Eight

I didn't wait for very long after Dorian left. As I was heading out, Hobell swept toward me to intercept me, as if to keep me from leaving. That was odd, but then again, I'd had quite a few experiences that suggested he was an odd man, and somebody who was quite particular about the activity within the palace—a place that he very much considered his domain.

"How was he today?"

I shrugged. "A little better than my usual experience with him."

Hobell frowned. "You have difficulty with him?"

"Let's just say that I get the sense that he isn't particularly enamored of my role here in the city." I shrugged again. "I don't blame him. I had something of a nontraditional approach to my training."

"Yes," Hobell said, wrinkling his nose. "'Nontraditional' would be one way of putting it. I think that had it been anybody other than Waleith who had recommended you, you would've had a very different welcome in Busal City."

I smiled tightly. "As in a worse welcome?"

"Just different. It is unusual for a newly promoted Blade to serve as the Queen's Blade."

"There aren't very many Blades around."

"Not very many doesn't mean that there are none, now, does it? And given the way that things have turned out since your assignment in the city, perhaps..."

Was that Hobell's way of saying that he thought that someone like Asi or another Blade should have taken this job?

I didn't necessarily disagree. It wasn't as if I felt deserving of this role, just that I felt I could serve. I had helped the Queen, after all, and in a way, I had proven myself, though I wondered if others would be able to fulfill this role better than me. Then again, I did not know how many Blades remained other than me, Waleith, and Asi. Maybe that was all there were.

"I appreciate your concern, and the fact that you obviously don't view me as worthy of my post, but I am doing my best and certainly want to honor what the Queen has asked of me."

The Queen herself had asked me to serve. I couldn't deny that, and neither could Hobell, something that we both understood.

"Well, be that as it may, you must continue to serve as she has commanded, now, mustn't you?"

I nodded. "And I will. Send her my regards, and let her know that I will stop in when she is well."

"I am not your errand boy," he said.

"I didn't say that you were. I just asked if you would give the Queen my regards."

Hobell harrumphed and then strode away from me, heading down the hall, and pursued one of the other servants. I heard him shouting an order about cleanliness before I headed back out of the palace itself. Only then did I pause.

There might be something else that I could do, another place that I could visit, to try to get some answers. It was a place that I had avoided going to, inasmuch as there really weren't all that many answers that I thought Talina would offer, though I did feel she enjoyed taunting me. Thankfully, there wasn't a whole lot that she could do to me, either. But if anybody might know of rumors of the Anvil, it would be somebody who had a connection to real power, something that was beyond simple fabrications.

I was veering around the palace grounds when I heard a steady hammering coming from Matherin's shop. I paused and poked my head in the door to see him standing over his table, pounding out a flat section of metal. His face was tight with concentration, and sweat dripped down his brow, but he shook his head every so often, as if to fling the sweat free.

"Close the door, or leave me alone. Either is fine."

"I just heard the hammering, and I thought—"

"I don't care much what you thought, but I do not need the distraction."

"You look like you need a fan," I said.

"It is delicate work."

Matherin pounded the metal with a large hammer, and the labor struck me as a little amusing. *Delicate?*

"It seems more physical than delicate."

"And you do not know the first thing about what I do, much like I barely know what it is that you do. Now, is there anything that I can help you with, Blade, or have you merely come by to interrupt my labor?"

"I suppose I just came by to ask you about fabrications," I said, shifting where I stood. I had pulled the door closed, as I didn't want to upset him any further than I already had. "And in particular, about different types of fabrications."

He glanced over. "Are you looking to have some sort of fabrication education?"

"I hadn't really intended to, but I wonder if you might help me understand certain aspects of fabrications. I am naturally attuned to different types of magic."

"You are a Blade, so you would be."

He said this simply, as if there was no question about it, which still surprised me. Matherin obviously understood quite a bit about what I could do, and the intricacies of it, but then again, considering the fact that he was the one who had made my blade, and the others that were used around the city, I suspected that he very much did know what I could do.

"Well, are there types of magic and power that I wouldn't be able to detect?"

He paused midstroke and frowned at me. "What are you concerned about, exactly?"

"A kind of power that I cannot detect. At least, not easily. But power, nonetheless."

"That would be rare," he said. He brought his hammer down again, then paused. "Not to say that it is impossible, though. There are plenty of people who understand the concepts of what you can do, and use the knowledge in order to avoid the consequences."

"Consequences?"

"Your ability to detect power is unique. And you have proven yourself capable. Quite capable, I think."

"It is not just detecting it, though, is it?"

"No. It has just as much to do with interrupting."

"Exactly. And yet in order to interrupt power, you need to have an understanding of power. And unfortunately, your lessons are incomplete. I think that if you'd had time and an opportunity to have more formal training, this would not be the case, but you have needed to learn on the job." He hammered again. "That is not to say that your education is lacking. Or at least, that it is by necessity lacking. In fact, I would argue that given everything that you have uncovered about your ability, you can very much use it in ways that others who have had formal training wouldn't be able to." Another hammer blow. "Why are you asking?"

"I came across something recently. A kind of power. It seemed to be tied to tattoos, from what I have seen, though I'm not sure if I understand how. And there was one woman with a staff who handled me and my magic better than I'm used to—"

Matherin's hammer faltered, and it clattered to the ground behind him.

"What did she look like?"

I shrugged, surprised by this response. "Slender. And she seemed completely unconcerned in what I was doing."

"Did you see anything unique about her?"

"Like what? What are you concerned about, Matherin?"

"It is probably nothing," he said, turning his attention back to his work.

"And if it's not?"

"Then it may be dangerous. A Daughter of Inkasa."

"A what?" I asked. "Would she have been with three others doing something strange outside of the city? Some sort of ritual? I interrupted something they were doing with a pillar, and a device on it—"

"You must be careful. You especially. If they managed to draw your talent..." He shook his head. "No. Quite dangerous."

"So you fear the Anvil as well?"

"What. This Anvil?"

I snorted. "Well, not *your* anvil. I was told that it was some nefarious underground organization that is either incredibly powerful or searching for power and influence, and—"

"No. That is not what I'm talking about. I am talking about the Daughter of Inkasa. Dangerous power."

"What's involved?"

It had been simple chance I'd come here to talk to

him, but if he knew something, then it was useful, valuable, so that I could continue to learn more about what the Anvil was doing.

"Just difficult," Matherin said. "And dangerous, and the kind of thing that you might not be able to detect. It is tied to the kind of power they possess. It has the potential to be masked, though perhaps if you have enough focus and concentration and talent, it might not be masked from you." He looked me up and down. "Yes. Perhaps not from you. I will have to think on this."

"Does it have anything to do with blood?"

He frowned. "Blood?"

I described what we had encountered, and he shook his head.

"I don't know the techniques involved. I don't think that I could know the techniques involved. It is considered a dark use of power, and one that would be incredibly difficult to master. And you say that you saw more than one of these pillars?"

I hadn't actually said that, but I suspected he had inferred the truth.

"At least more than one," I said. "Possibly several."

"And what makes you think that this was the Anvil?"

"Because of what another Blade said."

He sighed. "Interesting. And dangerous, I suppose. I will have to think on this."

"If you hear anything, would you let me know?"

"I will. But think on this yourself, Blade. There is the possibility that you will have to deal with more than one threat."

I hesitated with my hand on the door. "More than one?"

"I have not heard of any Daughters of Inkasa working with others. They are mysterious, sticking to the shadows, working in secrecy. But if they have decided to align themselves with another, that might be dangerous. And as I said, unusual."

"So you don't know if this is what I have started to be concerned about."

"I do not. But continue your investigation, and be careful."

I nodded. Then I slipped out, stepping out into the grounds, and hesitated a moment. And here I had thought that I was starting to get some answers, but perhaps the answers that I happened to be getting were more dangerous than I realized. What if there was more than one dangerous activity taking place? What if there was something more afoot, something far more nefarious?

I had to be careful.

And I was going to need to work quickly as well.

Chapter Nine

The prison was dark, and it smelled a little musty, though it didn't feel all that different from the last time I'd been here. I nodded to the guard, who acknowledged me briefly before letting me pass. The pin on my lapel ensured I was rarely stopped in places like this, and if I was, I simply had to show the guard who tried to delay me my blade. Everybody on the palace grounds understood the purpose of the Queen's Blade, and so I had very little difficulty with access.

"Have you had any issues with the prisoner?"

"Not with that one, sir," the guard said. He was a short man with broad shoulders, sandy blond hair, and a stern expression. He was young, and I couldn't imagine just how unpleasant this task was. Boring as well. It was unlikely much took place in the prison cells, but it was a necessary type of work.

"And the others?"

"There's only the one, sir."

"And how is he?"

I had rarely visited with Jasar, but mostly that was because I didn't have much interest in dealing with my past, and he had tried to taunt me with my past and how little I understood. Of course, at the time, he had been right. I had not known all that much.

"Quiet. Most of the time. Sometimes he gets a little wild. We've had to have the Queen's physicker here to administer a sedative from time to time."

"Jamie comes down here?" I asked, surprised by that.

"Jamie, sir?"

"The Queen's physicker. I didn't realize that he came here."

"He attends to any needs on the palace grounds," the guard said.

"Of course he does," I said. "I know the man, and so perhaps I will have some words with him as well."

Maybe Jasar had said something to Jamie. Or maybe not. Either way, I figured that it wouldn't hurt to talk to Jamie about his experience in the prison, and with Jasar and what he was doing here.

As I made my way along the row of cells, I glanced into them. Most were empty, as these were only for high-profile prisoners, those who had somehow caused great harm to the Crown. There was another reason that this prison was here, buried beneath the palace itself, but it was something that many people wouldn't recognize. The very first time I had come down here, I had detected a hint of magical energy, but I had not been able to do much with it, and had not dared to even try. There was power here. That power suggested to me that it was designed to hold people of power. And yet Jasar, at least, didn't hold much power. Talina, on the other hand, was something else entirely.

Jasar's cell was the first one that I came to.

He was curled up on the floor, with little more than straw for his bed, and a bowl of water rested near him. He had a chamber pot, which left me wondering how often it was emptied, as I could easily imagine that he would use it as a weapon against the guards. I cleared my throat until he looked up. His hair was haggard and long, gone greasy, and he was unshaven, his beard having grown in the time that he had been imprisoned here. A wildness had entered his eyes.

"Oh, look. The great Blade has come to pay me a visit."

"Not you," I said. "And not great."

He laughed, a bit of that wildness in his eyes now entering his voice. "Isn't that the truth! Not great, not at all. Not barely."

I frowned at him. "Not barely what?"

"Not barely anything, of course." He started to cackle again. "Have you found the truth? Or have you not even bothered looking?"

I just shook my head. "I don't know what truth you think I need to find, but I can assure you that I know more than you."

"If you knew more than me, you would be dead." He laughed again. "But maybe your time is soon."

"Oh? Or maybe yours is."

"If I'm still here, then yes."

"Are you not afraid?"

"Of you? No. But I am afraid of those who chase power." He cackled. "As you should be. As you should be, Blade." He said the last with a sneer, and then he curled back up, lowering his head so that no part of his face was visible anymore.

I let out a sigh. It had probably been a mistake for me to even get caught up in talking to him.

"He's a strange one, isn't he?" the guard called after me. "We've tried to keep him quiet, but every so often he gets to chattering. Claims that someone is coming for him. Thinks that it's not safe here."

"Well, if he tells you anything useful, send word to me."

"Of course. He'll probably get wild again right around dark. That's when he tends to get really riled up." He shook his head. "We have a few things that we can try, but most involve us going into the cell, and we don't like doing that. He scratches, you see."

"Just make sure you have your leathers on," I said.

"And he bites."

"I can understand why you would leave him alone."

"Best to just let him scream. You learn to tune it out after a while."

I said nothing and headed farther down the hall until I reached the door at the end. This cell was special. I assumed that it had been here from when the palace had been built, and probably from a time when magic was far more common in the city—and when there were fewer people who feared magic. It had been unoccupied until Talina had come here. I didn't know if she needed to be in this cell any longer, as Talina would likely not be able to do anything, as I believed that I had drained most, if not all, of her magic by piercing her with my blade. But I didn't know if she would recover. And I had not been interested in finding out, so this was simply a safety precaution, and it was one that everyone, including the Queen, had agreed was probably for the best.

I tapped on the door, looking through the bars to see Talina near the back of the cell. She was chained and couldn't reach the door, but I wanted to get her attention so that I could ensure that her chains remained intact. They did. When I tapped my blade on the lock, it came open. The locks in the palace were one of the few things that had their own sort of power, and I was able to use my blade as a key. I stepped inside and then closed the door behind me.

The smell here was even worse than it had been in the main hall.

It smelled something of rot, but there was another undercurrent to it that I couldn't quite place.

Talina looked weak and frail, though I suspected that was an illusion, especially considering what I had come to know about her. She was probably putting on something of a show. And it was possible that she controlled how she appeared. I held on to my blade. I didn't want to need to use it to carve through any magic, but if it were necessary, I wanted to be ready.

"You came back to play," Talina said, her words and her voice still strong compared to how she looked. "Better you than Waleith. You don't take your pleasure in pain."

That was a strange comment. How often was Waleith here?

"I came to ask you questions," I said.

She inhaled deeply. "About Erantor?"

That caught me off guard. What did she know about me?

Learning that my father had come from Erantor had been surprising, but it hadn't really changed anything for me. He was still the man I'd known. A farmer and a soldier, like me. But it did mean there were things about my distant family I didn't know—and maybe couldn't.

"If you think to surprise me, you won't."

Talina smiled. "Oh, I can still surprise you. Have you gotten very far in your investigation?" She took a step toward me, dragging the chains. They were heavy, and as far as I had been able to tell, fabrication marks had been etched into them by Matherin or someone like him, to ensure that whoever was imprisoned here would not be able to use any magical ability against whoever came in. Not only that, but they were designed to make it impossible—or nearly so—to escape. "I seem to remember the last time you came to talk with me. It's been a while, though. And I imagine that your little investigation has been slow. Troublesome, in fact."

"The last time I was here, you mentioned that the treachery ran deep."

She laughed. Unlike Jasar, there was no wildness to

her laugh. It was merely amusement. Despite her frailty, her time in the prison had not broken her.

"Treachery? Oh, yes. Treachery always runs deep."

"And it's more than just the council?"

I hadn't come back to her ever since dealing with that episode, and I was curious about how she was going to react. I had done my own investigations, searching for anyone else who might have been tied to what Sivara had been involved in, but had not found anything more. Those who served under her, and were employed by her, had seemingly been removed from her goals. They had served her, but only her.

"Council, is it?" Talina laughed again. "Oh, that is quite lovely."

"Why?"

"You think your council can cause problems?"

"I honestly don't know. The council works directly with the Queen and provides some guidance, so I would've assumed it possible."

"It would make them exposed, yes. It would make them a tool, even. But do you think the council has the key?" She shook the chains. And despite the fact that she was chained and I was not, I still tensed. I made a point of avoiding taking a step away from her, but it was difficult. "A tool, Zaren."

Talina said my name somehow possessively, as if she and I were old friends rather than adversaries. She had attempted to assassinate the Queen, and I had been the one to stop her.

"So there is somebody wielding the tool."

"Oh, yes. And I suppose that is why you are here, isn't it?" She tilted her head to the side, regarding me for a long moment. "Yes. I can see that it is the reason that you are here. You have questions. Let's see if I have any answers for you. Perhaps you will release me for good behavior." Her smile shifted again.

"Your release is not up to me."

"No. It is up to your Queen. And perhaps whoever follows her."

"So you still think that somebody intends to replace the Queen."

"Think?" Talina straightened, and when she did, she looked strong and confident and not at all like a prisoner. "I don't *think*. I know."

"Who is responsible, then?"

"That, unfortunately, I do not know. If I did, then perhaps I would be more use to you. And to your Queen. And if I did, I would not still be here, now, would I?"

I didn't know, but she was probably right. If she knew something, she would have been able to barter with that information for her freedom.

"Do you know anything about the Anvil?"

"Fools is all."

"You don't think the stories about them are useful?"

"And what stories are those? Of little boys who think to topple realms? Of those who think they can incite war and gain power? Of men who claim to grasp the power that they cannot comprehend? Are those the kinds of stories that I should be concerned about?"

"So you don't believe they are true."

"I think you're asking because you don't know."

"And you would be right," I said.

"And I think the fact that you don't know means that you should not confront them."

"Why?"

"If the stories are true, then they are dangerous. If they are not, then someone wants you to believe that they are. Either way, it would be dangerous for you, wouldn't it?"

"And what about the Daughters of Inkasa?"

Talina was quiet. "Where did you hear that name?"

"It doesn't matter. I thought you didn't fear anything."

"Where did you hear that name?" She took another step toward me, yanking on the chains.

"It doesn't matter."

"Oh? And you think that you can handle something like that? You really are a fool. Young, naive, and soon to be dead. Perhaps the treachery is even deeper than I realized."

"What is that supposed to mean?"

"It means what it means. And it means... Well, let's just say that by the time you understand the truth, the truth will hurt. Perhaps maim. Perhaps destroy." She backed away. "I'm tired of this conversation. Leave me."

"You know something. And if you do know something, it might help you."

She turned away from me. "I doubt there's anything that you can do to help me. In fact, I'm quite certain of it."

"What of Waleith?"

"What of him?"

"Could he help you?"

Talina looked over her shoulder at me. "Why would he help me? He cannot even help you."

Chapter Ten

I twisted in place, trying to position myself so that I could defend myself against the next attack. Lijanna came at me, moving fluidly and quickly in such a way that I could barely even react. She was faster than I had anticipated, but I should have known that she was quick. Skilled, even.

"You have to keep your defense up," she said. "Not every attack is going to be one that you can simply bludgeon. Some will bludgeon you."

I glanced down at myself before looking up at her. "Me?"

"You are a Blade, Zaren. Don't you think that there are other kinds of powers in the world that might be able to fight back? Some that are even more potent than you?"

I didn't know what she understood about what I could do, though I had to suspect that she at least had a passing understanding. That had to be part of the reason that Harent had suggested that she be the one to work with me.

"You're probably right. And I guess I'm a little distracted."

"With what the Captain said you dealt with the other night?"

It had been two days since the second pillar had been found. Two days since I had gone to talk to the Queen and found her incapacitated, and had spoken to Prince Dorian instead. Two days since Matherin, and then Talina, had made me even more concerned about what we were dealing with in Busal City. I still didn't know anything about those pillars, but if Talina in particular was concerned about what was happening, I knew that I should be equally concerned. And yet there had been no sign of anything similar happening since. I had spent my time searching, as had the constables, but we had come up with nothing. Neither had the Investigators.

So perhaps we had disrupted whatever the Anvil had planned, but I was starting to think that we had not. Not truly.

"It's a significant danger," I said. "I don't honestly know much about it, other than what I have seen and what I am starting to hear about."

"Did they really bottle the blood?" Lijanna crossed her arms but still looked like a coiled spring ready to strike at any moment.

"I don't know if 'bottled up' is the right phrase, but it was inside this pillar. And that pillar was a fabrication, or maybe something else. Whatever it was, it had a purpose."

"It's so strange," she muttered, shaking her head. "You know, we didn't have that many magical threats in the city until you arrived."

I arched a brow at her. Hobell had insinuated the same thing. "Are you suggesting that I'm somehow involved?"

"Are you?"

"No. I'm serving the Queen. I happened to come to the city after there had been an attack on the other Blades, which had necessitated my recruitment."

"Yes," she said. "I'm aware of the timing and the circumstances. It's just…"

"We are here to train."

I didn't like the implication. It troubled me. It wasn't the first time that someone had suggested that the nature of the attacks had changed since my arrival in the city. Before I had come here, the Investigators had managed to handle almost every threat within the city. Waleith had had a role, but he had needed very little help. And in this case, I was in need of quite a bit of help. Too much, in fact. To the point where I had started to question my competence.

Lijanna darted toward me, launching herself quickly.

This was the first formal training session that we had arranged, and we were conducting it in the small courtyard outside the constable station, where others would often come to spar. At one point, a few constables had come out to watch, thinking that it would be quite entertaining to see the massive Blade battling with Lijanna, but they had quickly dispersed when they had realized that I had nowhere near her level of skill. When Harent had claimed that she was competent as a fighter, I had expected her to be skilled, but this was something else.

Lijanna moved with a series of quick strikes before her leg caught me in the belly, doubling me over.

She darted back.

"Again, that was the same technique, and you again failed to defend it."

"I'm trying to keep track of what you're doing. Larger men don't move very quickly."

"And that will be your downfall. I realize that you have... well, whatever it is that you can do that makes you so special, but when it comes to defending yourself and blocking dangerous attacks, it seems nothing you do is all that successful. Now, do you think that you can follow it if I go a little slower?"

"I can follow." However, as I said this, I still had quite a bit of doubt.

Lijanna moved again, and as she had said, it was the same series of strikes, with the same outcome. She moved quickly, and I could barely keep up with her. With each strike that she landed, I felt ridiculous. She wasn't as strong as me, but she didn't have to be. It was all in the momentum. When her kick struck me in the belly, or the thigh when I managed to turn aside, or once on my backside, which she seemed amused by, it still stung. None of them would likely bruise me very badly, but I had the very distinct notion that she was pulling her punches—or kicks, as the case may be.

"You aren't following," she said. "I don't get why Harent thought *I* should work with you. You still don't even know the basics."

"Why don't we step back and work through them again?"

"I have shown you a dozen basic techniques. These are the foundation to this fighting style."

"And I am still trying to keep them in mind."

Lijanna paused, crossing her arms again. "If you'd like, we could revert to how you would fight in a bar."

"I don't want to do that."

She smirked. "Why? Don't think that you could reach me?"

"My concern is that I might hit you," I said.

She shrugged. "Go on. Give it a try."

I considered it for a moment before heading over to my jacket and taking the pin off my lapel. I held it out for her. "Only if you wear this."

"What is this? I'm not a part of the household, and if somebody saw me wearing it, it would only end up with me getting into trouble. Maybe that's what you want." She frowned. "Is that what you want, Zaren? You know, if you're not careful, people are going to start talking about you."

"Apparently, people are already talking about me."

"Not like they will."

"Anyway," I said, "it is a fabrication. It's supposed to defend you, or at least deflect some attack. I haven't given it a lot of opportunity to test it." If I was going to go at Lijanna in full fury, I wanted to at least know that she wasn't going to be knocked unconscious. Assuming that I could even hit her. But I was curious. If I could strike a blow, maybe we could change the dynamic of how she was instructing me.

"Fine," she said, taking the pin. She fixed it to her shirt. She was barely breathing hard, and this despite how many flurries of attacks she had struck me with.

"Now, are we going to go at this again?"

"You said that I should pretend that I was handling you in a tavern, right?"

"Right. What is that like?"

"Well, when I was in a tavern, I had no difficulty in the occasional hit that might get through my defenses. I knew that if I got to a person, I could wrap them up and either crush them long enough to keep them from fighting me or get to them and knock them unconscious."

"So," she said with a faint smile, "get to me."

"Come at me."

"That's not how we are doing this."

"You said if it was like a tavern brawl, right?"

"I did."

"Well, a tavern brawl is not me chasing somebody. Because if I did, they would generally run. In this case, it's somebody who's had too much to drink and thinks that they can challenge me."

"Does that happen?"

"Not just in taverns," I said.

"I'm sorry. I guess I didn't think about that. But I should have."

"It's not your fault. You didn't make me like this."

"Anyway, if you want, I'll even use the same technique I've been using."

"And I will ignore what you've taught me."

"Maybe don't ignore *all* of it."

Lijanna came at me.

The first time she did, she came in with three punches and a quick strike, then darted away before I was able to react. But because I wasn't thinking about how to handle her, I was better prepared for the strike, and I could brace myself. It still stung, but because she was still pulling her punches, it didn't hurt quite as much as it might have. The second time she came at me, I stepped to the side, and I swatted at her, using a backhand strike that caught her on the shoulder and spun her to the side. Lijanna corrected herself quickly, dropping low, and then she knifed toward me and kicked the back of my leg. I dropped forward but also brought my hand back again, catching her in the shoulder.

She danced away.

"Sorry about that," she said. "I told you that I was only going to stick to the same attack, and in that case, I didn't. I added to it. That wasn't fair of me."

"Someone dies in a fair fight," I said.

"What?"

I shrugged. "If I try to fight fair, then I'm more likely to die. If you try to fight fair, you're more likely to die."

"So you don't think there is honor in fighting?"

"The only honor in a fight is ending it."

"All right. I like that idea. I think I can work with it. So let's try this again. I'm going to start with the initial attack that I have shown you, but I'm going to mix it up. If you hit me, I will reset."

"Don't reset," I said. "I can handle a few bruises."

"You're going to have more than a few," she said with a smile.

"Am I? Let's see."

Lijanna darted at me again. She moved more fluidly and quickly than she had so far, and she seemed freer. Maybe she had been restrained by trying to stick to the same technique as much as I had been. But this time, because I had been anticipating how she was moving, I turned and simply braced for the first of the strikes. When it hit, I pushed her away, giving her a hard shove. She went tumbling back before catching her balance and then spun around to kick. I braced, bringing my hands up to block and keep myself from getting kicked in the face, but I also brought my knee up, which then caught her in the leg where she was trying to kick me. The force of it sent her tumbling back.

She cried out and then landed in a pile.

"Lijanna," I said, hurrying over to her.

She was laughing. "Well, isn't that a thing," she said. She got up, running her hands down her legs, and then looked up at me. "This fabrication. That is incredible. Why don't we all have them?"

"I don't know. I think the Queen likes to control the

types of fabrications that are used in the city. And this is just for me."

"Just you? Not anybody else in the household?"

"I think others in the household have some, and yet maybe not all. I don't even know if all the pins serve the same purpose."

She laughed. "At least that solves one problem."

"Which problem is that?"

"About whether or not you could even get to me. And you can. So I think I am going to change how I have been instructing you. You might be right. You can't fight quickly. But you can use your strength. I think that if I help you take advantage of the fact that you can take a few blows and keep fighting, you might be able to end the fight more quickly."

"I think Harent wanted me not to take so many blows. And honestly, when I asked him about learning to fight a little better, that was sort of the intention."

"We have to take advantage of your strengths. I can teach you technique. I can teach you to understand different forms, different fighting styles, and I can teach you to recognize them, so that if somebody comes at you, you have a general idea about what they might do, which will help you anticipate. But you are still going to need to rely upon your size. You're massive. Use that."

"You're right. I just never really wanted to take advantage of it."

"Are you afraid of it?"

"I think it is more that I am afraid of trying to hurt somebody."

"It's not always about hurting. It's more about ending, isn't it?"

That was what I figured as well.

"Thank you," I said.

"For fighting with you? Honestly, I really wasn't terribly worried about you. You are big, and big is slow. Most of the time." Lijanna shrugged again. "People tend to misjudge me. Much like I suspect you get misjudged. So..." She shook her head. "That clever bastard."

"Who?"

"Oh, Harent. You know, I'm sure he set us up so that we would challenge each other, but also so that I inevitably learned something. He's always trying to prove that there are ways that I can handle myself differently."

"But you are high-ranking within the constables."

"That doesn't mean I can't still learn."

"Let's keep working."

"Let's."

Chapter Eleven

There was a note waiting for me in my home when I returned. I sat on the chair at the small table, dwarfing it as I looked down at the note. It had been resting on the table itself, the wax seal bearing two lutes crossed over each other, waiting for me. Somebody had gotten into my home, left the note, and then gotten out.

And they had been completely unconcerned about the idea of breaking into a Blade's home.

And mine, at that.

The Guild.

I slipped open the note, doing so cautiously, wary that there might be some sort of poison inside. Learning that the Guild were assassins had left me thinking that they might have some desire to deal with me, though I was thankful that I had seemingly not made a true enemy of them. That wasn't to say that I was pleased with them. Considering what had happened the last time I had interacted with the Guild, I was a little concerned about the prospect of them operating in Busal City.

But I had known that I was going to need to work with them. I had known that this issue would come around again. I had known that there was some reason that they had been active in the city, so I had to be prepared for what that might mean, not only for me but for Busal City itself.

It was a request to meet.

That was worrying.

However, with what was going on in the city, there was a real possibility that they knew something. I didn't know who of the Guild was here, but somebody obviously understood the role I played in Busal City. I doubted it was Garridan.

I contemplated what to do. It was a simple request, with little more than the name of a tavern on it.

I assumed that they wanted me to come alone, which was probably fine, as I doubted that the Guild was going to take any action against me in a tavern, especially since they could easily assault me in my home. But I wasn't sure what else they might try.

I was still tired for my training with Lijanna, and a little bruised. My training had gone better when I had stopped focusing on what she was trying to teach me and used the forms that she had shown me, and simply reacted. She had seemed a little irritated, but I wasn't sure if that was because she hadn't been able to get away from me as easily as she had wanted—as I had managed to strike her a few times—or because I wasn't learning any faster than I had been. At the end of the session, she had reluctantly taken the fabrication off her lapel and handed it back to me.

"I can see about getting you one," I'd said.

"I'm not sure that it should just be me," she'd said. "All of us would benefit from that. Or at least, from something similar to it."

"Let me talk to the Queen."

"You have to go to the Queen in order to do something like that?"

"At least let me go to her fabricator."

"If you think so."

I wasn't about to just start handing out such fabrications, even though it was entirely possible that fabrications like mine had already spread throughout the city from minor fabricators, like the ones that Dara worked with.

I got up, made sure that I had my blade, and then headed out of my home. It was starting to get late, and the sun was setting, with a cool breeze coming in from the harbor. It was pleasant, and I was surprised that I would feel that way. Then again, I had started to feel a bit more at home, at peace, in Busal City over the last few weeks, even though some of the threats here could easily overpower me. Perhaps it was the stability. Or perhaps it was the fact that I had a sense of purpose, and I felt I was actually doing some good. Maybe that was all I really needed.

If that was the case, then what did that say about me?

It didn't take long to find the tavern. I had to ask

around near the docks and checked a few places, as I suspected that the Guild would want to meet near the docks. But surprisingly, the tavern was removed from the shoreline and in a nicer section of the city. The shops here were a little higher-end, and the signs better painted. The clientele that wandered the streets looked as if they had more money.

So when I reached the tavern, a small place called the Roaring Cassera, I found myself hesitating just outside it. I didn't feel any magic inside. I had started doing that more often of late, testing whether there was any magical danger around me. I didn't really expect anything along those lines, but it was the fact that I had come to rely upon that ability that was a little startling, especially considering how short a time I'd had access to this innate ability.

But in this case, I knew better than to just ignore the possibility of a magical force out there waiting on me, courtesy of the Guild.

I felt nothing.

Not nothing at all, as around the city there was always an undercurrent of power. But I didn't feel anything acute, any dangerous pressure, and so I entered the tavern, sweeping my gaze around it. It was a nicer place than some of the taverns that I visited, and certainly nicer than the one that I had gone to with Asi, as it had floorboards instead of just compacted dirt. The walls were paneled, and it was well lit, with lanterns hanging from hooks on posts in the middle of the tavern. A long counter ran the length of one wall, with three stools, occupied by well-dressed men who were drinking, leaning close to each other, and chatting quietly. A few tables were occupied, most by young couples, though there was one where a pair of men were huddled close, their voices hushed. Some business transaction, if I didn't know better. There was no sign of a minstrel.

"Sit anywhere you want," a voice said from behind me.

I turned to see a blonde woman carrying a tray sweeping out of a side room. She flashed me a smile and then waved her free hand to the various empty seats around the tavern.

I was thankful that I now had employment where I didn't have to worry about money. My house was provided to me as a benefit, and I received a regular stipend from the Crown, so I was never really in danger of going broke. I was earning more than I ever had before. Certainly more than I had in the army, and the work was generally easier and more interesting. But not always. I knew that my compensation was tied to the danger involved in the job itself, but that didn't mean that I couldn't enjoy the perks.

I took a seat at a table, and the woman eventually made her way back over to me.

"You're new here."

"Is it obvious?"

She shrugged. "We get our regulars."

"Oh?"

"And we get some who want to be regulars and others

who are just passing through." She smiled. "Which are you going to be?"

"Just meeting someone here."

"I see. Well, while you're waiting, I can offer food and drink." She pointed to a chalkboard where a menu was written.

I scanned it. "I will take the potato soup, the bread and cheese, and the dessert." It didn't specify what the dessert was. "Along with a mug of ale."

Her smile continued to widen. "An appetite. You know, the cook likes that."

"I hope the food is good."

"Some of the best." She ventured away, and once she disappeared, there was a slight commotion near the back of the tavern.

I looked up.

And my heart sank for just a moment.

It was Garridan.

There was nothing outwardly remarkable about the man. He was of average build, if a bit slight—though that didn't surprise me for a minstrel—and kept his brown hair cut short, matching the simply cut jacket and pants he wore. The only thing that drew me was the slight intensity in his gaze.

I hadn't anticipated that it would be the exact same member of the Guild that I had dealt with before, but I had been hopeful. At least this way I could get some answers, or hope to get some. I wouldn't be surprised if he chose to remain taciturn.

He took a seat on the stage, pulled out his instrument, a strange stringed instrument that was not quite as large as the lutes that I'd seen other minstrels playing, and quickly set to work tuning it.

It didn't take long for him to strum into a familiar tune, and I was tapping along, listening. He was good. Skilled.

He didn't sing, at least not at first, but his playing style was lovely.

The woman brought the ale out and set it on the table. "The food will be a few moments."

"He's good," I said, nodding to the stage.

"He's been here a few times," she said. "Says he likes the soup."

"Oh?"

"He claims it's something that his mother once made." She snorted. "Not a lot of people care for it. They say it's got too much cheese in it. But I think the bacon goes well with that."

I smiled. "Sounds delightful."

"Oh, it is. Do you like music?"

"I'm somewhat particular about the type of music."

"Oh?"

"I like what he's playing."

"It's been my experience working here that you aren't likely to find too many people like him. Most have a little skill, but they can't take as many requests as Petran can."

I smiled. He used a different name. Maybe even Garridan wasn't his real name.

"Well, I would love to buy him a drink when he's done."

"Knowing him, he will gladly take it." She nodded.

She went away, veering off and stopping at a few more tables, and eventually, as she promised, my food did arrive. I ate, spooning up the soup, which was every bit as delicious as the waitress had promised, and then mopped up the residue with some of the bread and cheese. By the time the dessert came out, I was feeling satiated, and far more relaxed than I had anticipated when I had first come in here.

And that was when Garridan decided to take a break.

He strode through the tavern, straight toward me. He didn't go very far before the waitress handed him a mug of ale, pointing in my direction.

He grinned, taking the ale, and then dropped down to sit across from me. "You got the message."

I held out the note. "Figured that you'd want to see me, considering the way we left things on Erantor."

He looked around the tavern, and it seemed as if everything went still for just a moment. Quiet, even. It was unnerving. But then, having been around Garridan before, I was familiar with that unnerving sense. Did he have access to power? I certainly didn't feel it. If so, what kind of power could he use?

"I'm sorry about how we left things before. I couldn't have you destroying the aelith powder, as there are those who still need access to it. And I didn't need to get into an argument with you, so I just took it."

"Was that your plan all along?"

He frowned. "It wasn't. But when you revealed what had been going on, the way that the powder had been used, I knew that I couldn't leave it there. So I took it away. It seems as if you have dealt with the danger."

"Seems that way?"

"Yes."

"I'm assuming that you have heard of what happened."

He shrugged slightly. "I might have."

"The Guild has quite the extensive network of sources."

"We come to places like this," Garridan said, spreading his hands, "and people like to talk. People like yourself."

I frowned at that. "So is this you trying to use me as a source?"

"Would you be opposed to it?"

I wasn't sure. I had been irritated when he had taken the aelith powder, but I had also had the feeling that he was not going to misuse it. I still didn't know what he intended to do with it, but I assumed that it had something to do with fabrications, especially considering what I had come to learn about the Guild. And about him. Not only that, but Garridan *had* helped us deal with the situation on the Isle of Erantor. That wasn't the kind of thing that someone would do if they wanted to betray a person.

"I don't like being used," I said.

Garridan regarded me with amusement in his eyes,

and then he tipped his head in a nod. "And I can respect that. No one wants to be used. Perhaps we should phrase it differently. Not that you would be used so much as we could make an agreement. I provide information, and you provide information."

"Are you trying to get me to do anything that would violate my responsibilities to the Queen?"

"Would your Queen be offended if you were to share knowledge?"

"Probably not," I said. "But it really depends upon the kind of knowledge, and the purpose behind it."

"True. And I suppose the same can be said for anyone. But knowledge is really just knowledge."

"Knowledge is never just knowledge," I said.

Garridan watched me for a long moment. "Why don't I start, then? And you can decide what to make of the rest."

"Start as in you intend to share something?"

He offered a hint of a shrug. Something caught his attention, and he spun briefly, looking behind him. There was a strangeness in the air, a sense of power that struck me as the use of magic, though I didn't see anything. When he turned back to me, however, his demeanor was the same as it had been before.

What was he doing?

"Sorry about that," he said. "I was saying that it would be helpful for the two of us to share information, assuming that you would be open to such a thing."

"I could be interested."

Garridan started to smile. "Could you? Does that mean that you are not?"

"I said that I could be. But I would prefer you to be the one to start with the sharing."

"As would only be fair. I believe I do owe you, after all. You should know that I have received some information recently. I did not think it of much importance, but the nature of what I have uncovered is significant in a way that only one such as yourself would truly appreciate."

I frowned at him. "One such as myself? Somebody living in Busal City?"

"A Blade."

"What kind of dangerous power have you found?"

Garridan shook his head. "Not quite like that," he said. "At least, I don't believe so. And if there is a dangerous power, then you may need to leave it alone."

I shook my head. "Any sort of power that might harm the city is my responsibility."

"This is not one that would harm the city. At least, not directly. And not any longer. There were rumors that started to spread about a year or so ago," Garridan said, leaning back and glancing at the mug of ale that the waitress had brought him. He didn't lift it. I wasn't sure if he didn't want to drink or if he was waiting. "The kind of rumors that normally would draw my attention."

"Because of the Guild?"

"Indirectly. Something that runs the risk of needing the Guild's focus, only this was a little unusual. And for a long time, I wasn't sure whether to put much stock in the rumors."

"Are you going to tell me what you heard, or are you going to leave me guessing?"

"Directness. A useful trait."

"You have something that you want to tell me, so I figured that directness is probably for the best."

"It has to do with fabrications," he said. "But it isn't the reason that I came after the powder." He smiled tightly. "Just an element of fabrications that has proven to be troublesome. Do you understand the making of a fabrication?"

The shift in the conversation was a little jarring. "I understand fabrications store power."

"Simplistic, but true enough. They store power. They are not power."

"But they can create power, at least from what I've seen."

"Every fabricator has their own unique talent," Garridan said. "Some don't like to talk about their talent, or what it means, but they have one nonetheless."

I thought about Dara, and how she had the ability to manipulate metal. I didn't know much about Matherin and his ability, but I suspected that he had some unique ability as well.

"And with the right technique, the fabricator can place power into a fabrication. Or they can simply make a storage device." His gaze lingered on my blade.

"I get what you're saying."

"And there are various complexities to the making of

fabrications. I won't bother you with the intricacies, but some elements involved in the creation of a fabrication are more useful than others. But it was the storage that raised a curiosity in me."

"So?" I wasn't sure where Garridan was going with this. "Are you trying to warn me about a fabrication that might get used in my city? Because if you know of something, that would be knowledge that would be valuable to me. That would be the kind of knowledge that I would appreciate sharing."

"You've done a remarkable job so far. And that is not the reason that I called you here. I probably wouldn't have alerted you to my presence in your city, except that I found out more about those rumored fabrications, and their use. You see, there was a particular use case for them. I found a few that had not been used."

Garridan pulled out a small oblong item from his pocket and set it on the table. It didn't trigger any reaction in me, so I didn't think that it contained any power. Which meant that it had been deactivated.

"I haven't seen anything like that."

"No? A shame. Or perhaps it's for the best."

He started to put it away.

I reached for it, but he was quick. Faster than I would have expected. But he stopped.

"Just spit it out," I said.

"Knowledge for knowledge," he said. "That's how this will work."

I looked at it. Garridan knew something. And whatever he knew was significant for me. If it was about hunting fabrications, that wouldn't be much of a problem for me, because that was the kind of thing that I could very easily do. But this struck me as something else.

"As long as it doesn't violate my obligations to the Queen," I said.

"Fair enough."

"And as long as you can promise that the information you obtain will not be used to harm this city, or this realm."

He regarded me. "Harm?"

"I understand what the Guild is. I don't think that it's in the best interests of either of us for you or me to pretend we don't know what you do and the impact that you have. So just know that I'm not going to do anything that's going to harm anyone, and I don't want you to do anything that will harm anyone that I have vowed to protect."

"I suppose that is equally fair. Now, knowledge for knowledge. There is something that I would like to know about, and it involves one of your prisoners."

"A prisoner?"

"Yes."

My mind worked through various possibilities, quickly discarding them. I didn't think that he meant anybody in the city prison, though there was the possibility that he knew something about the Anvil operative that we had captured and who had killed himself, or who I had killed. But that didn't strike me as a reason for Garridan to come to me in particular. I figured that if he really wanted information about that, it would be a very easy thing for him to go to one of the constables, and he would probably be able to obtain any information he wanted without any difficulty. There were probably quite a few constables who would share knowledge with him for a quick coin, and considering that Garridan was a minstrel, and likely well paid, I doubted that he would have a hard time getting anybody to share anything with him.

So that meant someone else.

That meant Talina.

"Why?" I asked.

"Let's just say that I have an interest."

I frowned. "If you are asking about who I think you are, then you are asking a question that I can't answer."

"I didn't say that I would do anything."

I snorted. "You're looking for confirmation only?"

He nodded. "Confirmation only."

"Then yes. We have a woman by the name of Talina imprisoned."

Garridan said nothing. Then he set the item on the table. "Thank you. I just needed to know."

"Why?" I asked, grabbing for the item and testing briefly whether there was any magical residue lingering within it. There was a bit of power, but it didn't feel active.

"I'm afraid that is not information that I can share with you."

"She tried to kill the Queen," I said.

He was quiet for a moment. "Unfortunate."

"So, are you going to tell me why you needed to hear about Talina?"

"Knowledge for knowledge," he said.

"Isn't that what I'm asking?"

"It's the wrong question, Zaren."

"Well, what's the right question?"

"The right question is why that item was used to destroy your Blade training compound."

Chapter Twelve

If I had thought that Garridan would provide me with more information, I had been mistaken. He was true to his word. Knowledge for knowledge. He had told me that he had come to learn of fabrications being used to store power. But he had yet to learn anything more.

"Are you sure about this?" I asked him as he was getting ready to leave—presumably to play some more.

"I wouldn't have brought this to you if I weren't. There was some residue within it. I suspect that is what you detect." He watched me as he spoke, waiting for me to confirm. Was that what I was picking up on? The aelith powder was familiar to me. And if it was involved, then there would be an added potency.

"But Waleith believed that Talina was involved."

"This was not that kind of power," Garridan said.

"You know what kind of power she possesses?"

"Very well."

"Then what was it?"

"Dangerous. Destructive. The kind of power that has consequences. I would caution you against chasing down that lead, too, but I doubt you will have any difficulty with it."

"Why?"

"Simply because those that are responsible would not come here." He tapped on the table. "Thank you for the trade. I will visit with you the next time I have anything to offer."

I laughed, and Garridan frowned at me.

"What?" he asked.

"I doubt that you will be so concerned about what you have to offer. It will be more about what I have to offer. I'm going to assume that somebody in your position generally has something to offer."

He shrugged slightly.

He had taken two steps away from me when I called after him.

"One more thing. Do you know anything about the Anvil?"

"A nuisance," he said.

"That's it?"

"That's all that matters. They try to grasp at power but have been held in check."

"Let me guess. The Guild?"

"Among others."

"Could they be interested in getting out of check?"

He pressed his lips together in a tight frown. "Possibly. It's not something that I think you have any reason to fear, though. It is unlikely that they will be able to do anything here. The protections around the city, and the precautions that others have taken, would preclude that."

"We found some operatives," I said.

"Some is not enough."

"And there is something else. There was another with them."

He paused, looking at me. "Another?"

"Knowledge for knowledge," I said.

"It seems to me that you are asking for my help here."

"Maybe, but maybe not. We found something recently. It was strange, and honestly, I'm not sure what to make of it. I have some people who speculate that it was little more than a scare tactic, and I have others who believe that it is incredibly dangerous. Regardless, it raises some questions, and they are the kind of questions I don't have good answers to."

Garridan watched me for a few moments, as if trying to decide what to say.

"Have you heard of a magic related to the Daughters of Inkasa?"

Before I had even gotten half the name out, he had done something.

I had no idea what power Garridan had, though I had little doubt that he had some. The sudden change in his demeanor, and the sudden change around me, made everything go still. It was as if time had frozen in place.

He turned to me, took a step closer, and then lowered his voice.

"You need to be careful where you speak of such things."

"So you *have* heard of them?"

I looked around, but the tavern had gone hazy.

"Yes," he said. He flicked his gaze around him. "Meet me on the bridge. Give me ten minutes. If anybody follows you, I want you to continue across the bridge. Do you understand?"

"What is going on here?"

"Something that you should not get involved in." Garridan held my gaze for a long moment. "Do you understand what I am saying?"

"I understand."

With that, the sudden strangeness all around me faded, and everything went back to normal. Only it didn't feel normal. I had assumed that I had an ability to resist magic, yet here I was, quite certain that Garridan had just used some form of magic, and I had been unable to resist it. Whatever he had done had been powerful.

Who *was* this man?

He was far more powerful than anybody that I had ever been around, short of Talina, perhaps.

Could that be why Garridan was asking about her?

I left a stack of coins on the table and then headed out of the tavern while Garridan went to the counter. I waited for a moment, but he issued a quick apology and said that he was not feeling well before he stepped to the back of the tavern.

Once outside, in the night, I hesitated. A chill had fallen, and I felt something palpable within that chill. Something had significantly changed. What had happened here?

I had to be careful, because Garridan might possess dangerous knowledge, and perhaps I had done or said something that would potentially put me at risk. But then, everything I had heard about the Daughters of Inkasa suggested they were dangerous.

I weaved through the streets, testing whether I could sense anybody following me, and I was relieved to know that I had been left alone. By the time I neared the docks, I had started to relax, and I chided myself that perhaps I had overreacted.

It was then that I noticed a shadowy form following me.

Despite Garridan's suggestion that I ignore any follower and continue across the bridge, I was the Queen's Blade, and there was no reason for me to worry about some mysterious dark figure moving toward me in the shadows.

I grabbed for my blade, squeezed it, and immediately began to feel a faint energy tingling everywhere. It was subtle, enough that it was difficult for me to detect much within it. It was just a strange current of power.

And it was, most definitely, real.

I moved out into the open, near streetlights.

Once there, I hesitated a moment, and then the streetlights dimmed. It reminded me of Garridan's trick, only his had been a bright haze that had surrounded me. This was a darkness, as if the night itself were starting to engulf the streetlights. I turned in place, focusing on any power, and I drew upon that part of myself that gave me my ability. I didn't know how to control it, not fully, but I could feel the power inside myself. And the more I focused on it, the more I could control its directionality, and I guided some of it into my blade.

Into the fabrication.

The darkness continued to dim.

It was pressing down upon me. Pressing down around me.

I could barely feel anything.

And if I couldn't feel it, I wouldn't be able to counter it. It was just a shimmery weight that hung on me, little more than a wisp.

As if the shadows had grown tangible.

I focused.

Waleith had taught me how to use my focus and draw upon the magical energies that I could detect around me. I had not really expected to need anything quite like that here, but I could feel that energy building, and I needed to challenge what was coming and, if possible, counter it.

Otherwise, this was going to overpower me.

I felt somebody moving toward me.

I couldn't see them, though.

There was a fluttering, as if some part of myself, some deep and faint part, reacted to whatever was out there.

And then it all faded. The darkness dispersed.

And when it was gone, I saw a body lying on the ground, and Garridan standing over it, a strange curved blade in hand. He quickly wiped it, then slipped it into his sheath before shaking his head at me.

"I told you what to do," he said.

"What is going on here?"

He nudged the body. "Let's get moving before this one decides to cause more trouble for us."

"You killed him, right?"

"I did, but I suspect there will be others. Especially if what you said is true."

"What do we do with him?"

"What I'm going to say is going to sound a little ridiculous to you, but you must trust me."

I shrugged. "Knowledge for knowledge."

Garridan grunted. "We are past that, Zaren." He grabbed the man's legs. "Grab his arms. Beware of any Daughters of Inkasa you might come across."

"He's one of them? So a Son of Inkasa?"

"Not him. Just one who seeks to serve."

I pulled the man's sleeves down, just to make sure that I wouldn't touch anything that I wasn't supposed to. I didn't recognize him, though I wasn't sure whether he had been with the others outside the city.

We carried him over to the harbor, where Garridan motioned, and then we hurled the man into the sea, where he sank down with a splash. If anybody saw me doing this, I was quite certain there would be questions asked of me, the kind I wouldn't be able to answer. It would all get back to the Queen.

"Don't worry," Garridan said. "Some things can't be seen."

I laughed at him. "Oh?"

"Come. I will explain a little bit more. And then we need to talk about how you got involved."

He motioned for me to follow him onto the bridge. The bridge arched over the harbor, reaching its highest point about midway across, where Garridan stopped. He looked down at the water, and he gripped the stone railing. He breathed out heavily. "It's lovely out here at night. It reminds me of some of the places I've visited. The air is quiet, and you can almost imagine that you can find peace."

"What are you going on about?"

"I suppose I'm thinking of a song," he said. "But maybe not the right song." He looked over at me. "How is it that you know of them?"

"If I tell you, will you tell me what you know?"

"I think I must, because you are asking about the kind of power used in that fabrication," he said, nodding toward the pocket that held the fabrication that he had given me.

"What?"

"So now we are going to have to figure out why the Daughters of Inkasa have targeted your kind."

Chapter Thirteen

I filled Garridan in on what had happened. I didn't leave any details out. He had saved me, I presumed, so at this point, I didn't think that there was any reason to keep anything from him, and there was every reason to use the resources that I had available to me to try to find out more about what was going on. When I finished, he regarded me with curiosity.

"Interesting. What you may have interrupted the first time is a dangerous ceremony, though I don't know why it would have been done *here*."

"So what are they?"

"They connect to an ancient power, one very few know—or understand. It is a dangerous one, and it is not something that you should have been involved in. The Daughters of Inkasa don't use fabrications usually, so this element is unusual to me, and that is why I was surprised by the fabrication I uncovered at the training compound."

"Why would the Daughters of Inkasa want to destroy the Blades?"

"I don't know."

"Have they ever done anything like this before?"

"No."

There was a hesitation in this word, though, and it left me thinking that Garridan knew more than he was letting on.

My mind worked, trying to piece together everything that I now knew. It was getting difficult, though. The Daughters of Inkasa were present in Busal City, and their presence was tied to the attack on the Blades, and more than likely, it was tied to some greater plot. The idea that all these recent events were interrelated was difficult to accept, but it was even more difficult for me to feel I had no way to piece it all together.

Individually, each attack had been dangerous. But if each one was somehow connected, that would be even more dangerous.

"You were not surprised that Talina was in the city," I said, turning to Garridan.

"She has her ancient issues with your people," he said. "But she wouldn't be working with the Daughters of Inkasa."

"Are you sure of that?" I thought about the last time I had seen Talina, and the reaction that she'd had. She had known something.

"I'm sure."

"And what about the aelith powder?"

"I had not thought it tied together. When you spoke

of fabrications gaining strength, I had simply thought that it was a typical scheme to increase profit."

I chuckled. "Typical?"

"Typical for me," he said.

"And if the rest of this is all involved?"

"Then it becomes atypical."

"How do we stop them? You did something."

"You won't be able to do what I can do," he said simply.

"I could learn."

Garridan studied me for a moment. "Unfortunately, I don't think you have the time. And you have your own strengths."

"Obviously, those strengths will not be enough."

"Not with how you approached these people, but you will need to find your own technique. What you do has value, Zaren. How you do it has value. And it is unlikely that they will be able to counter you indefinitely."

Garridan sounded far more confident than he had before. He was concerned enough that he had wanted me to leave the tavern and not to speak of the Daughters of Inkasa.

"Why didn't you want to speak of them openly in the tavern, and why are we out here, where you clearly feel more comfortable with it? What changed?"

"Some places have a natural protective ability." He swept his hands around him. "Water is calming. Have you felt that way?"

"I suppose," I said. "But I fail to see how that has anything to do with what we are dealing with."

"Water," he said. "And it's not just that it is calming. It is how it calms."

"It works against magic?"

"Something like that. But it isn't a strict relationship, as you might think. It is just that water can be restorative."

"Restorative."

"The tattoos that they use are destructive. They take something, and they change something, and they eventually drain power. And it is unusual for there to be such a confluence of Daughters of Inkasa in one place." Garridan hesitated, and he watched me for a moment. "You knew the name."

"Yes. One of the..." I hesitated. He wanted information, and I had to be careful with him, because it seemed to me that for him, everything was a transaction for information. And I did not want to give up Matherin, because I was concerned that doing so would somehow release more information than was necessary. And I didn't want Garridan to go after Matherin. "Somebody I work with knew the term."

"I'm not going to harm this person," he said.

"No? An assassin wouldn't harm somebody?"

"I am much more than just an assassin," he said.

"Right. You are a minstrel as well."

"Yes."

I chuckled. "Anyway, I'm guessing that the term is not one that very many people know."

"It is not. It is rare that anybody has an opportunity to

learn of them before they are either forced to serve or are drawn into something more dangerous."

"A sacrifice," I said.

Garridan bowed his head slightly. "Exactly."

"All right. So what do I do?"

"You do nothing."

"That's not an option for me."

"I would encourage you to be careful. Unless they are coming after you, there is no reason for you to fear them."

"That last one certainly came after me."

"Because you spoke the name."

"They heard it?"

"Some things hang in the shadows, and in a place like that tavern, there are many shadows."

I didn't quite understand what he was getting at, but I also didn't think that he was going to explain any better than that. "All right. So now I wait?"

"I will provide you with a way of contacting me." Garridan reached into his pocket, and he pulled out a coin. He held it out for a moment and then hesitated, as if trying to decide whether he wanted to give it to me. Finally he let out a sigh. "I suppose that I should let you have this."

"You said you wanted me to have a way of contacting you."

"And I do. It is helpful, not just for you but for me."

"So what is the hesitation?"

"The hesitation is for..." He smiled tightly. "It doesn't matter."

"Are you afraid that I'm going to somehow misuse your coin? Don't worry. I'm not going to spend it."

Garridan chuckled. "I'm not concerned about you spending it. And I doubt that it has much value to anybody else, anyway." He handed it to me. "If you need me, please signal."

"And how do I do that?"

"The way that you would with a fabrication."

With that, he headed away, crossing the bridge.

I was left holding the coin, wondering what sort of fabrication it was and what sort of power was inside it. He had given me something, but now...

Now I felt I had more questions than I had answers. I was halfway across the bridge, and with my newfound knowledge, I felt I owed it to Asi to share with her what I had learned, because I couldn't help but feel she would want to know. If the situation were reversed, I would definitely want to know.

It didn't matter as much to me. Not that I wouldn't want to know what had happened to the training compound. It was just that I didn't have personal experience of it.

I looked out over the water, thinking about what Garridan had said about it. There was something about water itself that was stable, that would neutralize magic—at least, that was what I assumed. I debated going over to visit with Asi. But with everything that had been happening, she needed a warning, didn't she?

And until we had a better idea about what was

happening and how it was impacting us, I needed to try to help. And I needed to get Asi to help me.

So I made my way across the bridge. On the far side, I paused. I wasn't sure how to figure out where she had gone, but I wondered if I would even need to. It was entirely possible that she would detect my presence, the same way that she had detected my presence when I had come over here before.

I hadn't gone very far before I noticed movement in the shadows.

At first I couldn't help but feel it had to be Asi, that she was coming for me, but it wasn't her. It was a different movement. Not the same darkness that I had seen earlier, but there was a pressure, a presence, nonetheless.

It was potent. There was some aspect of it that called to me, some aspect that struck me as significant, some aspect that was trying to influence me.

I reached for my blade and squeezed it for a moment, turning in place as I attempted to make sense of what was here.

And then a shadow came toward me.

This was not at all like when the Daughter of Inkasa had come, but there was a presence, a pressure, that struck me as familiar.

It had a residual energy to it. I pushed against it, thinking that I might be able to resist whatever was building here, and perhaps try to counter that effect. And as it came, I turned in place.

"You're making a mistake," I said, sweeping around.

There were three people. I could see them as individual shadows, though they looked as if they were trying to stay better hidden. "I'm going to give you this one opportunity to change your plan here."

They didn't speak, and they kept coming at me. I hadn't really expected them to abandon their attack, but it would be nice if I didn't have to fight.

Then I heard a strange *snick*, a sound that I had heard before.

The woman who I had fought with outside the city stepped forward, making four of them here. She glanced past me, toward the others. She had her long staff in hand, and she spun it, the air starting to whistle.

"You," I said.

She tipped her head.

"Your friend is dead. And if you try to do anything, I'm going to—"

I didn't have an opportunity to finish. She moved toward me as if to move *through* me. She was quick. Fluid. And the spinning of her staff split the air, carrying with it a dangerous and violent whistle that carried into the night.

I moved to the side and nearly collided with the person standing by me. This was a smaller woman, and she had a similar staff in hand, though she didn't spin it with the same fluidity or grace.

I lunged at her, jabbing with my blade. I thought about what I had done when I had trained with Lijanna, and how I had needed to push myself through the dangers, risking injury, simply because it would give me an opportunity to overpower an attacker.

And when her staff struck my shoulder, it stung, but I was upon her quickly. I stabbed with my blade, catching her in the shoulder. She cried out and dropped her staff. I gave her a hard shove, sending her tumbling over and over until she collapsed. I had started to turn when somebody struck me from the side.

Then I straightened, shaking off the attack. This was a dark-robed man, and he didn't have a staff, but he did have a club. It hurt, but not nearly as much as the staff had.

The other woman had still not approached. It was only then that I realized she was engaged with someone else.

Asi?

Asi was moving quickly. And then she was darting toward the woman, her blade driving forward, catching the woman in the thigh, before she scurried back.

I guessed I didn't have to worry about her. I turned my attention solely to this man.

His club had hurt when he had struck me. He was strong, obviously, but it seemed to me that his attack should have hurt a lot more.

And there was a look of surprise in his eyes.

It was only then that I realized that my fabrication pin was protecting me. Of course it would be. I had known that it had that effect, and had taken advantage of it in training with Lijanna, but had never had an opportunity to truly test it like this.

I cracked my neck, and then I moved toward him. When I reached him, he tried to swing, but I grabbed for his wrist, twisted, and his arm broke.

"Now," I said.

But I didn't have an opportunity to finish.

Something changed.

Symbols began to work around him, through him, and along his skin.

It was odd, but I had seen it before.

One of the Anvil.

I didn't give him a chance to finish whatever transition he was going to make. I jammed my blade into his chest, and his eyes widened.

Blood bloomed around my hand.

I jerked back and shoved him away from me. He stumbled, catching the other woman with the staff, who leaned on it briefly before cartwheeling back. She glanced at me, then Asi, and then she bowed her head before disappearing into the shadows. I debated chasing her but figured it was probably for the best that I didn't, because at this point, I had no idea what was going on here, and I had no idea if I could even catch her. And I wanted answers.

"Well," Asi said, striding over to me. "This is quite the mess."

Chapter Fourteen

"Are you kidding me?" Asi asked as we dragged the man to the harbor. "We have to toss them into the water?"

I had filled her in on aspects of what had been going on, but not all the details. Surprisingly, she had not objected to the idea of tossing the man into the harbor.

"Apparently, it's the one way to prevent anything worse from happening."

She looked down. "You don't want to investigate this anymore?"

"What is there to investigate? The man is dead. We have stripped off anything he had on him, and we have the woman to interrogate."

She was bound behind us, injured but not dead. And there was no sign of any tattoos on her skin. We had one person. And I still didn't know if she was going to be enough for us to get answers from.

"Seems like this is a bit much," Asi said.

"Everything is starting to be a bit much," I muttered.

We heaved and tossed the man into the water. He splashed down, and then he descended into the depths.

I looked out into the darkened night, out over the water, and I breathed heavily. Why had Garridan just left me?

"Will you tell me why you brought this danger over here? Or maybe you're going to tell me that you weren't the one to bring it over here. That they were here, and you were drawn by them." Asi arched a brow at me as she made the accusation.

"Not that," I said. "I didn't expect to run into any difficulty when I came over here."

"No? You seemed awfully prepared for it."

"Well, I did have some problems earlier."

She grunted. "Let's take her someplace where we can talk."

"I know that you work with the constables," I said, "but maybe we shouldn't take her to the constable station."

"Where do you propose?"

"A place that she won't be able to escape, and that might mitigate any power she has."

Asi frowned, tipping her head to the side. "Mitigate?"

"Exactly," I said. "I don't really know what she might be able to do, but considering what we have seen with the others, there's a real possibility that she could present a serious threat."

Asi was shaking her head. "The palace prison? That's what you're getting at?"

"What? You don't think that we should take her there?"

"Well, I think that you can do so on your own."

"I need to talk to you, though. And if you help me, I can share what I've learned."

"Or you could share with me what you've learned, and we can go our separate ways."

"You're going to want to hear this."

I leaned down, hefted the woman, and slung her over my shoulder. We had already checked her for weapons, so I was confident that she didn't have anything on her, but I remained a little concerned that she might stir and try to attack again. I didn't know if she had any natural magical ability, but I didn't think so. If she had, I would have picked up on something during the fight.

Asi rubbed her hand across her face. "I don't particularly like that part of the city."

I paused as we neared the bridge. "What?"

"It's nothing," she said.

"Sounds like it isn't. Why don't you care for that part of the city?"

"Oh, it's just that I have never really felt welcome there. It's a me thing, so don't worry about it."

"I would love to hear more about it."

"I'm sure you would. Why don't you tell me what you know?"

We were making our way across the bridge. With the water around, I felt a bit more at ease to share with her what had been going on, even if I was wary of Garridan's warning that we needed to be careful with sharing this information. "This," I said. I reached into my pocket, pulled Garridan's oblong fabrication out, and handed it to her.

Asi took it. "What am I supposed to do with this?"

"Do you detect anything in it?"

"No. Should I? Is this some sort of test to see whether I'm still worthy to be a Blade?"

"No. Why would I do that?"

"I don't know. You've been spending an awful lot of time with Waleith, and it's the kind of thing that I would expect him to do."

"Did he do that sort of thing with you?"

"Not with me, but he apparently has a history of doing something along those lines. It's fine. What is it?"

"Apparently this fabrication, and others, were found around the training compound when it was destroyed."

Asi froze. She looked down at it. "What?"

"I have a source who brought it to me."

"A source? And you think that you can trust this source?"

"I know I can," I said. "Because they brought it to me knowing that I didn't really have anything to do with the compound, but they wanted me to have it because they understood that I would be intrigued by what had happened there."

"Maybe they intend to use you."

I shrugged. "It's possible."

She snorted. "You actually think that?"

"I'm not saying that's the case. Just that it's possible."

"So what is this?"

"The kind of power those people who attacked us were using is similar to what was in this."

Asi shook her head. "No." When I frowned, she glanced at the woman. "Think about what you're saying, Zaren. I realize that you don't understand what it was like at the training compound, what having that much natural resistance around you was like, but there was enough power there to mitigate any sort of threat. So no."

"You don't think that it's possible?"

"It's not just that I don't think it's possible. I know it's not possible. They wouldn't have been able to destroy the compound with the power we saw."

"And what if it was an even more powerful magic?"

"I suppose you're going to tell me that they have access to something stronger."

"Well, from what I saw, they probably do."

"All right," she said. "Assuming that is true, why would they destroy the training compound?"

"That's the part I don't understand. My source made it seem like it would be pretty odd for anything like that to happen."

"I would agree. First, they'd need to know how to find the compound. Then they would need to know what it was and the purpose behind it. And then they would have to know how to overpower the natural resistance of the people there. And then—"

"I get it. I do. I realize that it seems impossible to believe that anybody could do that, but I'm just telling you what I know."

Asi let out a sigh. "If this is real, this is significant."

"I know."

"You need to let Waleith know."

"I know. I don't know where he is, so..." I shrugged. "I'm starting to feel like I'm going to have to deal with these things on my own, and I worry about what's going to happen when he does finally return."

"And you don't have any way of sending word to him?"

"I tried asking about him at the palace. He doesn't tell me where he goes, but I figured that he might at least share with the Queen. But I couldn't get in to see her."

Asi started laughing.

"Why is that funny?"

"Because you are her Blade. I figured that you had access anytime you wanted it."

"Well, I'm sorry that I don't."

Asi was quiet for a moment. "All right. So the Queen doesn't know where he is."

"Like I said, I didn't get a chance to talk to her, but Prince Dorian didn't know."

Once we reached the far side of the bridge, I hesitated, because I remembered the strange darkness that had attacked me here. I found myself looking around warily, but I didn't see anything. However, I felt a strange energy. Nothing quite as potent as what had been here before.

Finally I spoke. "If you don't want to be here, you don't need to be. You could go back to your side."

"If this has to do with the Blades, then I'm going to be a part of it. I don't really understand how those people could have done it. I mean, the two of us took care of them pretty easily."

"What if there were more?"

"And you really think that the compound would have been surprised by more?"

I stared at her blankly.

"That's right. You don't know about the compound."

I shook my head. "I don't."

"A sizable army wouldn't have been able to sneak up on it. That suggests a single person. Or a small group."

I thought about when I had gone out to the ruins of the training compound with Waleith, and I had seen the emptiness around it. Asi was probably right. It would have been difficult to sneak up on it, especially if it had had magical protections. And considering that the Queen had fabricators working on her behalf, and fabricators who were making the Blades' blades themselves, I had a hard time thinking that there wouldn't have been some fabrications to defend the place.

Which meant that an assault would have been challenging.

And yet there were the shadows that the Daughters of Inkasa had used...

"It might be possible," I said.

"I don't like it," Asi said.

"Well, I don't like it, either. And probably for different reasons than you."

We veered through the streets, heading toward the palace. I took a direct path and found myself searching for anything that would signify that somebody was following us, as I didn't want to run into the same issue as before. I didn't see anything. There was no sign of the darkness, no faint stirring of energy, nothing.

And yet despite that nothing, I felt uncomfortable.

A figure started toward us, and Asi froze. I raised a hand, recognizing him.

"Hey, Blade." Lastin was skilled and had been with the Investigators for longer than I had been in Busal City. He had never really been opposed to the idea of my role in the city, and he took the fact that I was a Blade to mean that I was somehow his superior. And yet I had the feeling that Lastin had been serving for a long time. He had to be in his mid-forties, with a grizzled face and a scar over one eye that suggested that he had experienced his fair share of fights. "Got yourself a prisoner there, do you?"

"We do. Say, Lastin, can you do me a favor? Make sure that the Investigators are being extra cautious."

He frowned. "Something tied to that event the other night?"

"Something like that," I said.

"Anything that we need to be doing differently?"

"I don't know," I answered honestly. "I'm not even sure if there's anything that I need to be doing differently. But I just want you to be careful. I've got the constables looking as well, and I'm searching, but..."

Lastin nodded, flicking his gaze to Asi. He frowned before turning back to me. "Whatever you need, Blade."

He marched off, continuing his patrol.

"You really have them serving you well now, don't you?"

"It's not about serving."

Asi laughed. "You could've fooled me. Seems like they are perfectly happy to do whatever you want them to do."

"Let's just get her to the prison."

"Are you sure it will hold her?" Asi asked as we rounded a corner, bringing the palace into view. Her demeanor had stiffened a little.

I still wasn't entirely sure what issues she had with the palace, but I suspected that it was tied to how she had been trained. And in a way, it wasn't all that dissimilar to how I had been trained. My time in the army had given me a healthy respect for the Crown, enough that when I had first met the Queen, I had been a little overwhelmed by the experience. Honestly, I was still a little overwhelmed by the idea that I served her directly.

"You remember what I told you about the first thing that I dealt with when I came to the city?"

Asi frowned, then nodded.

"Well, the woman who was responsible for that incident is imprisoned there."

"And she is somehow magically enhanced?"

"Something like that."

We reached the palace grounds, where we were not stopped by the guards, though they did give me a strange look. I rounded the outside of the palace and headed over to the entrance to the prison, where I was finally stopped.

The guard there glanced at me, then Asi, before looking at the bound woman over my shoulder.

"I have somebody that needs to go in a cell," I said.

"At this time of night?"

"Is there any time that would be better?" Asi asked.

The guard regarded her, and then he shrank back.

I looked over and saw the intensity in her gaze, and I found myself laughing at it.

The guard stepped to the side, and I used my blade to open the door.

Asi watched, and then she nodded. "Would mine work?"

"I don't know."

"Can I try at the next one?"

I shrugged. "I think that the blades are all the same fabrication, aren't they?"

"Maybe initially, but we were taught that fabrications change over time. They sort of mold themselves to the people wielding them. I don't know if I believe that, but it does make a certain sort of sense."

"Interesting." I looked down at my blade. "I wonder why that would be."

"And I wonder why they gave you such a small blade."

"Small?"

She shrugged again. "Some wield swords."

I'd have to talk to Matherin about that the next time I saw him, though I wondered what he would tell me. He would probably tell me that my blade was enough, and under normal circumstances, the blade was enough. But if I had to continue to confront the Daughters of Inkasa, I couldn't help but wonder if I needed more—and I wondered if having a larger weapon would allow me to harness a greater measure of control in a fight.

Once inside, we descended into the bowels of the prison, and I felt a strange tension in the air that told me something was amiss.

I looked at Asi. "Be ready."

"Ready for what?"

"I don't know, but I doubt it'll be good."

Chapter Fifteen

There was a darkness in the prison. Some aspect of it pushed on me, reminding me all too much about what I had felt on the outskirts of the city. And yet it didn't feel quite as fuzzy as it had been there, making me think that I might be misinterpreting it. At least, I hoped that was the case.

I looked at the woman resting on my shoulder. "I'm going to set her down."

"Do whatever you want." Asi had drawn her blade and was clutching it tightly.

Was she nervous?

Of course she was. I had just filled her in on a deadly power that had killed the Blades at the compound, and here we were confronted by something similar.

We moved forward. Asi stayed close to me, but she didn't say anything. We neared the next level. There should have been a guard standing here, but there was not.

I focused on the energy that should be present, but I did not pick up on anything.

I nodded to the door. "Go ahead. Test your blade."

"Is now really the best time to do this?"

"You wanted to know, didn't you?"

Asi shook her head at me. "You can be difficult, can't you?"

"Sometimes," I agreed.

She brought her blade up to the door and pressed it into the lock. It opened.

Asi glanced at me, shrugged slightly, and then pushed the door open.

I darted forward. She stayed right behind me. The hall was dark, but not with the dangerous darkness that had found me on the street. This was a natural darkness. The faint lantern light that was usually here had been extinguished.

I moved carefully and found the first body. It was one of the guards. I moved on, came to Jasar's cell, glanced inside, and nearly gasped when I found it empty.

"Who is supposed to be in there?" Asi asked.

"Just somebody who was a little troublesome to me."

"And?"

"He's a little insane now, so I don't know what's going to happen. But the fact that he is out of his cell is a problem."

And I couldn't shake the fact that he was gone now, so shortly after I had shared with Garridan what was going on. What if I had misjudged Garridan? What if I had misjudged the entire situation?

But then I had seen him attacking the Daughter of Inkasa. That wasn't the kind of thing that somebody would do if they were working against me.

Or maybe it was, and Garridan was just doing such a good job that I would not know what he was doing.

I needed answers.

I looked at the other rows of cells, all of them closed. We could toss the woman in a cell, but the prison wasn't safe right now, so that wasn't the right strategy. We needed a better idea about what was going on here. I headed to Talina's cell. Trepidation rose in me as I grew increasingly concerned about what I would find, and whether she would still be there. If she wasn't, what would I do?

I paused at the door and found it slightly ajar.

Then I pushed it open.

As I suspected, Talina's cell was empty.

"This was where she was?" Asi asked.

I nodded. "She should've been here. It should've been impossible for her to break out."

"Impossible?"

"I would've said that it was impossible, but now I'm not so sure." How would she have managed to get out?

I looked around the cell for evidence of anything that Talina might have used to escape. I didn't see anything. There were a few markings on the wall, and I crouched down in front of one, holding my blade up to it. There was no sense of resistance, nothing to suggest that there was a power here, but there was something lingering in the cell. Whatever she had done had been subtle.

I looked over at Asi. "What are you picking up?"

"This entire place is radiating some vague sense. I don't know what it is."

"I'm feeling something as well," I said. I straightened, and I work my way around the cell, searching for the source. "Nothing obvious. Strange that there wouldn't be."

The chain was missing, which meant that somebody had taken it with them.

I went out to the main part of the prison. There was a quiet here.

"What do we do?" Asi asked.

"Well, we have to alert the palace."

"We?"

"Fine. *I* have to alert the palace. You can just return to your side of the city."

She let out a frustrated sigh. "You're going to make me help you, aren't you?"

"I'm not going to make you do anything."

"Seems like it. Let's get this over with. Let's see what is going on here, get to the palace, and..."

I looked over at her. She had turned to one of the cells.

The cell door, unlike some of the others, hung slightly ajar.

Asi glanced at me, then nodded as we both moved forward. She reached it first, and the moment that she did, I began to feel pressure from her blade as she pushed it up against the bars of the cell. It was odd that I would even be aware of it.

"You felt that," she said.

I nodded slowly. "I felt something."

"You felt what I was doing. I saw you stiffen."

I nodded again. "Why?"

"It's just unusual is all."

Unusual. Well, I couldn't help but feel that all of this was just a little bit unusual.

Asi stepped into the cell, and I noticed an undercurrent of energy that I had not detected before. Now I could, and it was distinct. The energy hovered around the cell, but I had not noticed it before we had entered.

"The cell is keeping this power inside?" Asi asked, confusion plain in her tone.

"Well, I can see how that would work, considering what the cells are supposed to do. I suppose I wouldn't expect the cell to do that with any sort of residual power."

Only why wouldn't it? It seemed sensible that it would. Why here, though?

"Something was here," Asi said. "Someone was here."

"The cell was empty," I told her.

"Are you sure? Is it possible that somebody else was imprisoned here?"

I shrugged. "It's possible. I was here not that long ago, however, and I would have been alerted to the presence of another prisoner."

However, there was no reason for that assumption. If there had been another prisoner here, the guards might not have reported it to me. I was just a Blade, after all. I had no authority over the prison.

"Look at this marking," Asi said, and I thought that

she was going to move over to the wall, but she didn't. Instead, she crouched down on the floor and began to trail her blade along the stone. A faint stirring spilled out and drifted around us. I could feel some of the power but could not identify the reason that I would be so aware of it. Whatever Asi was doing was drawing that power out of the floor. Strange, but it was also potent in a different way. "When I trace it, I can feel some of the residual power here."

"Whatever you're doing is disrupting something."

She looked up. "Of course it is."

"No," I said, and I looked to the walls, noticing how the bars seemed... different.

"I don't know what you're doing, but the cell itself is changing."

"What?" Asi stood, and then she cocked her head to the side. "Look at this. It is different here. The walls have expanded."

I followed where she was pointing. While she had been tracing the mark on the floor, the wall behind us had started to ripple. I wasn't sure that I would call it an expansion, but it certainly had changed, folding.

And now there was an outline that had not been there before. I moved over to it, holding my blade out, ready for anything. I couldn't shake the feeling that Garridan had used me. Irritation swelled in me with that thought, as it frustrated me that he would have done something like that after I had started to trust him to a certain extent. Maybe that had been my mistake. I had been too naive. Too trusting.

"What should we do?" Asi asked.

"Either we can keep disrupting the markings on the floor, or we can alert the Queen. I'm not sure which we need to do right now."

"You're her Blade. Aren't you supposed to be the one to make these decisions?"

I stood frozen, transfixed in a way. I needed Waleith here to help. That was the primary thought that came, as he would provide me with answers about what I should be doing, though I also wondered if anything he could tell me would make much of a difference here. The only thing that he might know was what was going on with the Anvil and the Daughters of Inkasa.

"We need to see what this door does," I said.

"And we should really look to see if some of the other cells have one like it. If there's one here, it's possible that there are others."

Asi made sense.

She returned to the indentation on the ground and used her blade to disrupt its power. I didn't know if it was a fabrication mark, but it didn't strike me as typical for a fabrication. It seemed like rune-based magic. I had not seen anything quite like it before. Maybe Waleith had, or perhaps even Asi had.

"Did you learn anything about this kind of power at the compound?"

She shook her head. "We learned about different powers at the compound, but most of the time, we focused on fabrications. That was considered the greatest threat to the realm. There were other kinds of power, and we were expected to be able to identify them, but beyond that, we weren't asked to do much."

"So you don't recognize this?"

"This looks old, Zaren. It almost looks like it was part of the original building." She straightened. "But if that's the case, then why would these kinds of markings be in the prison?"

"Maybe it wasn't always a prison," I suggested.

The bars had been added later, I suspected. But if it hadn't been a prison, then it would have been some kind of open space used for something else. But what?

None of that really mattered, though. Not now.

"Let's keep working," I said. "See what you can disrupt, and then we can look for answers."

"These aren't the answers I want to look for."

"I know," I said. And I did. But more than that, I realized that I needed to focus more on the captive that we did have, to see if we could learn anything from her. That would help us know more about what was taking place. I paused. "All right. Here's what we should do. We stop interrupting this power, because it's not going to change much. We go and alert the Crown. And then we interrogate the woman."

"There's a lot of 'we' in this plan," Asi said.

"You don't want to be a part of this?"

She crouched for a moment, and I could see the hesitation that flickered through her as she attempted to decide what to do. I didn't want to force her to make a decision, because what we needed to do was going to entail significant danger, I suspected. But it was more than just that. I needed to ensure that the strange power that I had now encountered throughout the city wasn't going to cause additional problems for us.

"I want to be a part of it," Asi said, "and I suspect that I need to be a part of it, to a certain extent. But that leaves my side of the harbor unprotected."

"Are there threats there?"

"There are always threats, Zaren."

"How about this? I will assign several Investigators to work on your side while we are working together."

"Would they do that?"

There were several Investigators that would probably be opposed to the idea, but there were just as many that would jump at the chance to do what I asked. So I shrugged. "I suspect that we won't have too much objection."

"I'm not talking about from your Investigators. I'm talking about whether the Queen would permit it."

"The Queen gives me permission to do what I feel is necessary."

"It must be nice," Asi said.

"Don't do that," I said.

She smiled innocently. "Do what?"

"Let's talk to our prisoner."

Chapter Sixteen

We bound the woman in Talina's previous cell. If she did have some innate magical ability, I wanted to be careful with her, though I didn't really expect that she did. Still, the mere possibility that she might find a way to escape was enough to make me ensure that she couldn't break free while we were trying to get answers.

We didn't have chains, but the chains had only been a secondary aspect of the protections for Talina. The cell itself had been the primary counter to anything that Talina might have been able to do. As far as I knew, the chains, and the fabrication marks worked into the metal, had only been assisting in keeping her incarcerated.

I still wondered how she had managed to escape. That was going to be a question, and a problem, for another time, but it was most definitely a problem.

"What if she doesn't talk?" Asi asked.

"She'll talk."

"She's got a knife wound to the shoulder."

"That was me."

"I realize that," Asi said, shooting me a hard look. "But what if she chooses not to talk because she's injured? What if she can't? What if you severed—"

"It's to her right shoulder, not her heart. I might've punctured a lung, but given the way that she's breathing, I doubt it. If I had, she would've been gasping for breath, and would not have been able to sit here so comfortably. In fact, considering the way that she is resting, I would argue that she's awake and just feigning unconsciousness."

Asi frowned and turned to the woman before heading over to her and nudging her. "Is that right? Are you awake?"

The woman didn't react.

"Seems like she's not," Asi said.

"Watch her."

"Is she going to use some sort of trick?"

"Maybe. But if she does have any power, she's going to quickly find that this room mitigates it. There are certain protections here that will ensure that she can't escape, and that she can't use whatever devices she might have on her, or in her."

Asi regarded me with a curious look before turning her attention back to the woman. "You think this is a Daughter of Inkasa?"

"I think it's possible. Maybe even probable. I haven't seen any sign of the ink, but I don't know if that's just because she hasn't displayed her particular talents."

Asi regarded the woman again. Then she brought out her blade, strode over to her, and jammed it into the existing wound.

This was an interesting technique.

The woman reacted. She gasped, immediately opened her eyes, and tried to squirm away.

"I guess you were right," Asi said, yet she held the woman down. For someone her size, she was incredibly strong. She was also quick, so I wasn't terribly concerned when the woman tried to swing at her, though she had her arms bound and wouldn't be able to even reach Asi.

Asi brought her free hand up and chopped the woman on the shoulder, which sagged as if she had shattered a bone, or maybe just incapacitated some nerve there.

Maybe I had been going about my training the wrong way. I had paired up with Lijanna to try to improve my fighting style, but I had somebody else that I could train with if I were so inclined. Then again, there was no guarantee that Asi would even work with me.

"Care to tell us what you were doing over there?" Asi asked. "In my part of the city?"

The woman regarded her with a darkness in her eyes.

"Looks like she doesn't want to talk," Asi said.

"Looks like it. Maybe you should shove your blade a little deeper. Whatever ink she might have, that should be a pretty easy way for you to incapacitate her. Then again, I doubt that she will appreciate it."

"I might appreciate burying my knife in the other

shoulder," Asi said. She started to move, and the woman struggled again.

"You can't stop this," she said. Her voice was high-pitched, anxious, and I didn't recognize the accent.

Asi, however, did.

"Okarsan? Really?" She grabbed the woman's uninjured arm, and with a deft touch, she sliced her blade up along the sleeve, revealing a line of tattoos.

"What is it?" I asked.

"If she's from Okarsan, these markings will indicate house and rank."

"Nobility?"

"They wish," she said. "It's not nobility so much as it is a status within the city. A caste system. I don't know how to interpret the markings, but one should indicate which house she belongs to, another should indicate rank, and others should indicate…" She shook her head. "I don't know. I'm sure there are people in Busal City who can help with this. But Okarsan is far enough away that we almost never encounter anybody from it."

"How is it that you know anything about it?"

"This wasn't my first assignment," Asi said, but she didn't elaborate.

Every time Asi made comments like that, I was left wondering just what she had done before she had come to Busal City. It probably had something to do with the reason that she didn't want to serve as the Queen's Blade, but it might be something that I would need to be aware of, especially given the predilections that she seemed to have.

"This doesn't seem to be the same sort of ink as the others had."

"It doesn't," Asi said. "But did you look?"

I thought about the man that I'd had in the constable station, and how his markings had started to change. But I had not pulled up his sleeve and had not bothered to look for any other type of ink. Because I wouldn't have recognized the accent.

"No."

"And we tossed the other ones into the harbor. I suppose we could fish them out, but..."

"Probably unlikely that we will find him," I said.

"Probably," Asi agreed. "So, what do you want to do?"

"We need to know what's going on, and we need to know what she knows."

"We will soon take our rightful place here," the woman said. "You can't stop it."

"I think that we can," Asi said. She kept leaning on the woman, her knee arresting. "And I think that you're going to talk about it."

"You have made a terrible mistake."

Asi looked back at me. "*We* have made a mistake? Look at her. What mistake does she think we've made?"

I started to grow more concerned. Something about the ink on her arm started to change, rippling, reminding me of the wall that had changed in ripples.

"Asi," I started, "you might want to back away."

"Back away?"

"Look at her arm."

Asi turned her attention to the woman's arm. The ink was shifting.

Where it had been a series of symbols, triangles and circles and squiggly lines, now it was taking on a very different appearance. I had never seen a tattoo move like that. Well, I had seen tattoos suddenly appear, especially recently, but I had never seen ink that appeared to be alive. It was flowing and re-forming.

And extending from somewhere higher on her arm.

"She's using blood," I said. "She's doing something with it."

"I don't even feel anything," Asi said.

Without hesitation, Asi drew her blade across the woman's tattoos, gritting her teeth as she did, and then she stood over her. For a moment, the tattoos stopped moving. But only for a moment. It was very much the same as what had happened in the cell with the man.

"If this is the same thing, we should be careful here, as it will eventually begin to flow into more markings."

"What do we do to her? I don't feel anything, Zaren."

"I don't, either."

And it was the inability to detect anything she was doing that troubled me the most. There should be something there for me to pick up, and the fact that I could not identify anything left me even more concerned. It should not have been possible.

But then, there had to be powers that I could not detect. Unless it was the tattoo itself that shielded her. And shielded something else.

"Check her other arm," I said.

Asi swept her blade across the other arm, carving through the clothing, revealing another set of tattoos. These were like the first, ink that had started to swirl and change.

"How many would she have?" I asked.

"I don't know. I only learned about the house and rank from someone who'd had a little too much to drink," Asi said. "And I might have gotten him naked in the process." She shrugged slightly. "And traced my fingers over them while we were—"

"I don't need all the details," I said.

"You asked."

The woman was still bound, but now I was starting to detect something. As the tattoos changed, rippling, there was a faint, hazy energy. It was subtle, but it was definitely there. And not only that, but the dim light of the prison cell started to fade even more. It got to the point where I couldn't discern any detail, and I sensed that whatever she intended to do here was going to be powerful in a way that would allow her the opportunity to get free.

And if she did, what could I do?

Nothing, I knew. Short of killing her.

And we needed answers.

"We have to figure out some way of negating the tattoos," I said. "We have to use the..."

We'd have to use something that would store the power, wouldn't we?

But it seemed to be tied to blood, from what I had seen.

I reached into my pocket, grabbing for the spherical item that I had taken off the pillar. I didn't know if it would even work, but the other pillar that I had seen had been filled with blood, and I wondered if this would do something similar.

But what I pulled out wasn't that object.

This was the one that Garridan had given me.

And now it was vibrating.

I had not noticed it while it was in my pocket, so the fact that I could feel it now was surprising, but the reaction from the woman was even more surprising.

"You should not have that," she said.

"What is this?" I asked, bringing it down to her. I pressed it to her shoulder. I didn't know if it would do anything, but the idea that it was trembling in response to something that she was doing suggested to me that whatever power was within it could be used here.

She cried out.

I watched the woman's arms, waiting. She didn't do anything. The ink was still swirling, but even that had started to change, becoming somewhat less vigorous.

"Is that fabrication some sort of key?" Asi asked, crouching down.

Now that I looked at it, there was something familiar to it. It reminded me of the orb I had found on the pillar outside the city. "And if they had something like this, it makes me wonder if they were using it to either add this marking or strengthen it in a way."

"Or change it," Asi said. "Activate it, even? Maybe

this fabrication—assuming this is a fabrication—somehow deactivates it."

It was a distinct and realistic possibility.

"Take it away," the woman said.

"I will," I said while holding it in place, "but you're going to talk. We have some questions that need some answers. Considering that we have you here now, I think that it is a perfect time for you to tell us what you were doing."

"We only came to collect what is ours," she said.

"We? And by 'we,' are you implying the Anvil, or are you talking about the Daughters of Inkasa?"

She glowered at me. "You cannot understand. The price must be paid."

"The price. So you came for something, or someone?"

"The price must be paid."

She suddenly started thrashing.

The fabrication vibrated in my hand, as if the power within it was growing even more intense. It left my hand aching, and I wanted to release it, but I feared that if I were to do so, this woman would regain whatever talent she had from the ink and might be able to escape. More than anything, I wanted to ensure that we did not release somebody who had some strange power that would harm us.

"If you keep that up, I don't think you're going to get the answers that you want," Asi said. "I'm all for tormenting her. I mean, she attacked my side of the harbor, so I'm not going to claim that she doesn't deserve it, but you want answers."

"I think we have to get them," I said.

The woman continued to shake. Now it was violent.

I didn't have much choice in the matter, so I withdrew the fabrication, holding it tightly, and then waited. I half expected that whatever was happening to her would ease, but it didn't. She kept shaking, just as violently as before.

"What did you do?" Asi asked.

"I thought I had released it," I said.

The woman was now convulsing. Foam came to her lips, and blood burbled in her throat.

"Be careful," Asi said. "I feel—"

Before she had an opportunity to tell me what she felt, I began to feel something.

Power.

It was unbridled, uncontrolled, and it was radiating up from the woman. I had never felt anything quite like this before. It was a strange, unique kind of power, and it was one that struck me as nearly overwhelming. The power continued to build, spilling outward. I held out my blade, feeling clueless and a little ridiculous as I attempted to counter the power, but there was nothing I could do to stop this pain, this strangeness. And more than that, the convulsing persisted in a way that was overwhelming.

Then I noticed the darkness around her starting to change.

It had been a haze at first, but now the darkness had fallen around us in the way that it had when I had been attacked in the street while with Garridan.

"We have to cut through that," I said. "I don't know what she's doing, and I don't know if she's released some additional power, but we have to cut through it."

"Cut?"

"Use your blade," I said.

I leaned forward, and then I started slashing. I felt like a madman, carving at shadows, but strangely—and perhaps surprisingly—I noticed some resistance to my blade as I was cutting through them.

Asi grunted, suggesting to me that she detected the same sort of resistance. As we worked, the resistance started to fade, and then the shadows began to ease. Finally the darkness relented altogether.

And it looked like ribbons of black scattered across the ground.

"Is that her *tattoo*?" I asked.

Asi stepped forward and nudged the woman, who was now unmoving—and presumably dead. She shoved her sleeve up, which revealed that while there was blood on her arm, there was no sign of the tattoo that had been there before.

"Looks like it," Asi said.

"Some sort of living tattoo? Or maybe a fabrication?"

"Is that like any fabrication you've ever seen before?"

"Honestly, I'm not particularly aware of different fabrications like you are. I don't have that same training."

"Sorry," she said. "You're right. I haven't seen anything like that before. And it's not like anything that we were trained on. So if it's a fabrication, it's a unique one."

"Then we need to talk to a fabricator."

"Do you know somebody who can make a fabrication like that?"

"I don't need somebody to make one. I just need to know if something like that is even possible."

And if so, would Matherin even share that information? That was the key, after all. I needed to know. And until I had that answer, what could I do? The activity in the city was more advanced, and violent, than I was prepared to handle. More advanced and violent than Asi was prepared to handle.

Would Waleith even know anything?

Maybe Garridan had been right. Maybe this was the kind of thing that I needed to avoid. Assuming he wasn't involved.

"What are you doing?" I asked as Asi scraped at the black ribbons of ink on the ground.

"I'm just testing something," she said. "Don't get all agitated."

When she scratched at the ground with her blade, the blackness flowed, and there was something strange about it. It started to move again. She jammed her blade down into the stone.

"What was that about?" I asked.

"I don't know. I felt like there was something there."

I was still holding the strange fabrication, and on a whim, I dropped it onto the ground.

There was a rippling.

That was the only way that I could describe it. But as it rippled, the dark ink began to flow, moving toward the fabrication as if drawn into it. There was an increase in the vibration, though I was no longer holding it. Considering that the strange ink was smeared across the ground around the woman's fallen body, I didn't really want to, either.

It wasn't long before all the ink disappeared, drawn into the fabrication, leaving me with an odd sensation that flowed through me.

Once it was done, Asi just stared. I did the same.

"Well," she said. "What do we do with that now?"

I licked my lips. What *did* we do with that?

"Throw it into the harbor," I said.

"And release it there?"

"You might be right. Until I know if I can trust... well, my source," I went on, catching myself before revealing too much, which elicited a sharp glare from Asi, "we should make sure that it's safe to do that."

"So what do you want to do with it?"

"Not touch it. That's for sure," I said.

"We have to make sure that it's safe somehow. I don't know if it's going to be safe to leave it here. Talina obviously managed to escape, so it's possible that somebody else could break in, assuming they wanted it."

"They'd have to know that it was here."

"True," I said.

"And then they would have to know how to use it."

"I suppose that is also true."

"So it's agreed. We leave it here."

"We do. But maybe we don't keep it so close to the woman."

"She's dead, Zaren."

"I know. But…"

But I thought about what Garridan had said about the dead. And while I had been concerned about the actual dead, maybe that wasn't the concern. Maybe he was concerned about the tattoos.

"I think it's time for us to understand the Daughters of Inkasa more."

I just didn't know how to find that information or even who to ask.

Chapter Seventeen

After ensuring that the prison was secured—which had taken more time than I had intended, mostly because the guards were terrified of the idea that Talina had managed to escape and concerned about what she had done in her escape—I went over to Matherin's shop. It was late enough now that I didn't think the strange man was even going to be there, and yet I had a rising hope that he would be, mostly because if he wasn't, I didn't know what we were going to do. I needed information, and it felt like there were increasingly few resources that I could approach for that information.

"I've never been here before," Asi said as I stood in front of the door.

"Even when you got your blade?"

"My blade was given to me at the compound."

"I wonder if Matherin made it or if somebody else did."

I pounded on the door. The grounds of the palace

were awash with activity now, especially after the attack and the escape from the prison. Every so often, a pair of guards on patrol would make their way toward me before realizing who I was—which surprised me, because given my size, I should be quite recognizable from a distance—and then heading back onto their patrol.

There was no answer.

"You know where he sleeps?" Asi asked.

"No. And even if I did, I'm not so sure that I would go and bother him there."

"We need answers, right? People should be awake. The city should be awake. You saw that—"

"I saw it," I said.

And I understood that Asi was concerned. *I* was concerned. But I had a growing resolve that I needed to do something here.

I started to piece together what I knew, which unfortunately was not enough. We had seen the strange pillar—or at least, I had seen the strange pillar—and had then found one that was filled with blood. I hadn't understood that. I still didn't. Maybe there had been something about the spherical device that had activated the first pillar, and it had perhaps given power to others. Maybe that had been part of the process.

"There's not much that most within the city can do. This is our job, Asi. We are to protect the city from things that it can't handle."

I had known my responsibility when I had first come to the city. I had been told by Waleith what I needed to do, and when the Queen had been attacked, I had felt a sense of responsibility to offer as much protection as I could to ensure that nothing happened to her. It was my job, after all. And with my natural ability, I couldn't help but feel this role was a calling. But I had never felt ownership of it. Not even when I had dealt with the aelith powder, investigating how it had been used in Busal City, had I really felt it was an obligation.

But this...

This changed things for me. It was strange to feel that way, but there were not many people who were equipped to handle this kind of threat in the city. And without knowing what it was, I had to be careful, but I also had to try to ensure that anything that happened here could be dealt with. It needed to be, after all.

I pounded again.

"We should keep moving," Asi said. "We should try to figure out what the next step is, and we should go to talk to..."

When she trailed off, I looked over. "Talk to who? Who do you use when you don't know something?"

"Now?" she asked. "I don't know. There was a time when I would have sent word to the compound. There were scholars that researched such things and could provide information to us active Blades. I haven't encountered anything quite like this since the compound fell."

"I'm sorry," I said.

"Why? It's not your fault."

"I know that it's not my fault, but I'm still sorry. And I also wish that I had an answer about who to go to. I just don't know."

"Which is why you are staying here."

"We need to understand the storage device. Fabrication? I don't know what it is. But we need to understand that first. And Matherin did mention the Daughter of Inkasa, so I have to see what he knows."

And if he didn't know anything, then it would come back down to trying to find other information, but the challenge that I had with digging into that other information was I wasn't sure how to find Garridan, but he was the next person on my very short list of people that I could go to in order to dig into what had happened.

But it wasn't even just finding that information.

I glanced back toward the prison. I still needed to find Talina and Jasar. They were out there, somewhere, and their presence in the city—especially Talina's—posed a danger to me and the Queen. I didn't know what Talina would do. All I knew was that she had wanted to kill the Queen. And there was no reason to believe that she wouldn't try again.

I pounded again. I felt ridiculous, because at this point, I didn't know if Matherin would even answer the door, so it was a surprise when it opened, with Matherin wearing a weary look on his face, his hair standing wild, and only a robe covering him.

"What is it?" He frowned, looking up at me, and then immediately turned to Asi. "Two Blades?" He cocked his head, and then he sniffed. "Something is wrong."

"It is. I need to talk to you. And I have some very specific questions about something that we talked about before."

"Dangerous," Matherin said, making the connection immediately. "Especially with what I'm smelling."

"What *are* you smelling?" Asi asked.

"Death." He took a deep breath. "Who died? Prisoners?" He pointed. "It seems the prison is a little active, so if you are responsible for that, you know that the Queen is going to be displeased."

"Not responsible. At least, not responsible directly. A couple of the prisoners managed to escape. I'm not sure where they are going, but that's not the reason I'm here."

Unless Matherin had some way of tracking that kind of power. The right kind of fabrication could be helpful. And as I thought about it, I started to wonder if Matherin could detect the storage fabrication. That had been tied to death, hadn't it? It could certainly absorb some aspect of power that was tied to death.

But I didn't know if it was even safe to talk here. And if not, then where could we go?

That was the key here, after all. We needed to ensure our safety, especially with all the recent events around the city.

Matherin was the key, however. He was the one who knew things, and short of getting in touch with Garridan —and I couldn't help but feel I still needed to do that—I did not know if he could uncover anything whatsoever.

I looked over at Asi, who was quiet.

Behind me, I still heard the commotion. I would need to get to the Queen, or even to Prince Dorian, assuming that they were available. But for now, this was where I needed to be.

"When I was here before, you mentioned a dangerous organization concerning what I had described. I think we found something tied to them. But I don't think it is in the way that we would've expected."

Matherin regarded me for a moment. "How so?"

"I am not entirely sure, but I do think that I need to show you, assuming that you would be willing to come with me."

"It is late, Zaren."

"And that is the time when dangers tend to strike."

He inhaled slowly. "I will come with you. Let me gather a few items, so I can ensure that I have whatever I might need."

"Good."

He stepped into the shop, and I followed, with Asi following tentatively.

She looked at me as we got inside, her mouth twisted into a frown.

"You haven't been here before," I said.

"No."

"Well, this is where the magic happens."

Matherin glanced at me at the comment, shaking his head slowly. "Believing it to be magic devalues what it is, and it devalues what you are. Both of you, I suppose."

He pulled open a cabinet, grabbed a few instruments, including a shimmering metallic pouch, before tucking them all into a leather satchel. Once he was done, he turned to me and nodded. "Ready."

"Say," I said, looking around the shop, "I do have a question."

"And?"

"It's about this," I said, holding up my blade. "I don't suppose that you would have something a little larger?"

Asi mentioning that some at the compound had wielded swords had gotten me thinking. That might be useful for me.

"Larger than that?"

"Right. I'm a big guy. I need something with a little bit more reach. It doesn't matter if it weighs more."

"When it comes to the blade, it is not the size of the fabrication that makes a difference."

"When it comes to the size of the weapon, however, it does."

A hint of a smile curled his lips, which surprised me. I hadn't expected him to react quite like that.

"I had thought that you might request something along those lines." He reached under another cabinet and rummaged around for a moment. "I asked Waleith if you would be interested, but he made it seem unlikely." He shrugged. "Perhaps he was mistaken." He held out a scabbarded blade.

I took it and squeezed it for a moment, and I immediately felt something different about it. For one, it vibrated in my hand.

"What you are feeling is a raw fabrication," Matherin began. "And it will take time to attune to you, and for you to find it as valuable as the blade that you have been carrying. So do not rely upon that one exclusively."

"See," Asi said.

I nodded. "So I have to make it useful to me."

"You have to *use* it, and the *blade* has to welcome it."

"So the blade is somehow alive?"

"It's not so much that the blade is alive as it is that the blade carries a measure of potential, and what you do will reach into that potential and activate it. It is a combination of both the fabrication and the person wielding it—in this case, the Blade."

I nodded slowly and carefully. "All right. So the blade is alive, and I have to turn it on somehow."

Matherin just snorted. "So stubborn."

"Sometimes," I admitted.

"A useful trait. But I would say that it might respond to you better, since you are taking it in a raw form."

"Because I wasn't given a raw blade before?"

"Your previous fabrication had been activated."

"I didn't realize."

"Very few Blades begin with one such as that," he said, motioning to the sword. "Until a Blade has control over their potential, it is far too dangerous to wield such a thing."

Asi was frowning. "What about me?"

Matherin regarded her for a long moment. "Are you in need of a new weapon?"

"I'd like mine a little more... functional. Look at this thing," she said, drawing her own blade. "It's nice—"

"Nice?" Matherin asked.

"I got this when I left the compound. But like you said, it was activated. I've been using it for years, but..."

"I can make you something specifically," he said. "Assuming that would be preferable. All I have is weapons similar in size and style to the one that you carry. That is a standard-issue blade for a Blade. But you strike me as someone who has something else in mind."

"I might. How about I meet with you later?"

"That would be fine." Matherin nodded to me. "Now, if you don't mind, do you want to show me?"

We headed out, and Matherin did something to secure his fabrication shop. I felt a strange tingling and a hint of resistance that suggested to me that whatever he was doing was tied to another fabrication, probably locking up his fabrication shop so that nobody else could enter it and get into any sort of trouble. That was likely for the best, as I could easily imagine somebody wanting to break in and see all the items that the Queen had her chief fabricator making. Once we were on the grounds, heading toward the prison, Matherin watched me. I was still squeezing the hilt of the longer sword and had already begun to feel something about it changing. The vibration had shifted. It was not nearly as potent as it had been before. It seemed it had settled, which felt a little odd.

"Are you already controlling it?" Matherin asked.

"What do you mean by 'controlling it'?"

"I have had many Blades describe it as a tingling when they first hold a raw blade."

"It was more like a vibration, but I know what you mean," I said.

"Vibration. A stronger sense, then." He frowned and then nodded. "That would make sense with someone like yourself. So you have a vibration, and it is reacting to you."

"I suppose. But now it seems to be fading. Am I just getting used to it? I don't want to overpower it, do I? Or deactivate it."

"No. It's not like that, nor do I think that you would even be able to do that. I suspect that would be dangerous for you to even attempt, because it would probably tear free some of the natural ability that your blade will provide."

"So I have to just tame it?" I asked, frowning at the concept.

"Something like that," Matherin said. "But it surprises me that you would do so this rapidly."

"Well, I don't exactly know that I am taming it. I just feel that there is some part of it that is easing."

And if that was all it took to tame it, then maybe the blade would be useful sooner rather than later. And for that matter, it was nice having a sword again. It felt like a more appropriate weapon for a person my size, especially if I got into difficulty with someone who I didn't want to have to get close to. The smaller blade had been useful, but I might be drawn into a fight where my size and strength would not be as useful.

We reached the prison, passing some guards who glanced at us but then gave us space, and came to the cell at the end. I looked through the door, and then my breath caught.

The storage fabrication was gone.

Chapter Eighteen

"If what you are describing is true, then it is quite dangerous that it is gone." Matherin seemed agitated, and he shifted his stance, as if trying to get into a comfortable position. He had taken out several small fabrications from his leather satchel and had placed some of them into his pockets, and there was one—a small band of silver—that he had placed around his wrist. I was curious about what he was doing, whether any of his fabrications would offer him—and therefore us—a measure of protection, but that didn't seem to be the case. "Are you sure of what you saw?"

When we had arrived here, I had pulled the door open and slipped my gaze around. I had expected some sign of the fabrication, but there had been nothing. So I had described it to Matherin, thinking that that cell, and whatever natural protections were on it, would offer a way to speak about such things without needing to worry about the dangers inherent in the process.

"I am quite certain about what we saw."

Matherin looked at Asi, who nodded.

"It is unusual," he said carefully.

"That's it? Just unusual?"

"I do not know how to describe it in any other way. It is not something that should've been found here. There are defenses that generally prevent such activity so close to the city."

I knew that there were some natural defenses around the city, and I had come to discover more of them, such as what could be found in this cell, in the constable station, and on other buildings scattered all throughout the city, but I didn't know the extent of them.

"And you don't know anything more about the Daughters of Inkasa?" I asked.

"Only that they wield a great power," he said, his voice a whisper. "I don't even like to speak about it."

"Somebody told me that we could do so over water," I said.

Matherin frowned, and then his expression softened before he tilted his head to the side and turned toward the harbor. "Water. I suppose if the water is vast enough, it could work. Strange."

"Wait," Asi said. "Are you telling me that he's not making this up?"

"About water or about this threat?"

"I saw the threat," she said. "I'm talking about the water. We tossed a body into the harbor."

"Two, actually," I said.

"So you have two of these bodies in the harbor?" Matherin asked. "And you think that should be enough?"

"I don't know if it's going to be enough, because I don't know if the harbor, and whatever power the water there has, is going to be enough. I just did what I was told."

"You keep talking about this source you have," Asi said.

"Just let it go," I said.

"I don't know if I can. I don't even know if I should. With everything that's been going on, and now this, I think it's time we talked."

"And I think that it's time I tried to figure out what more he knows," I said. "Why don't you come with me?"

Asi was quiet for a moment, and then she nodded. "I'm open to that. Besides, it's late enough now, and you've already taken me away from my side of the city."

"I believe I made some arrangements to help protect your side of the city."

"So you claim," she said.

"You know that it's true."

Asi grinned. "Maybe. Anyway, let's get going."

Matherin still looked a little off.

"Should we stay with you?" I asked.

He seemed distracted. "No. You don't need to do that. But you should, however, describe the fabrication that you used to contain this strange ink, assuming that was what it was."

"You don't think that it was ink?"

"I do not know," he said.

"So if it's not ink, then what do you think it is?"

"Again, I do not know."

But his hesitation as he spoke suggested otherwise. He might not know exactly what it was, but he had his suspicions.

"If it's going to help us in any way, don't you think that you should tell me?"

He looked around. "If what you have said is true, I'm not so sure that here is the right place."

"We could go out to the harbor, if that would make you feel better, or—"

"I have a place," he said, and he motioned for us to follow.

We went back to Matherin's shop, where he triggered the lock fabrication—leaving me wondering if my own fabricated blade would be enough to do the same thing—and then to a door leading into a back room. The back room was small. Only a few paces in either direction, and cluttered with hunks of metal, some broken tools, and a wagon that I had no idea how he had even gotten here. He pushed the wagon to the side, revealing a section of the floor, and he crouched down, placed another fabrication on the visible flagstone, and then an outline began to form on the floor itself.

"That's like in the prison," Asi said.

Matherin looked over. "You saw something like this?"

"We saw something in the prison," she said. "One of the cells had a marking on the floor. I caused it to move, but not completely."

He breathed in slowly and then turned his attention

back to the floor. He pushed the fabrication down into it until it popped open, causing the stone to slide to one side, and revealed a staircase that led downward.

"These grounds are ancient," Matherin said. "We do not truly know the origin of them. Some claim that the fae once lived here, though that is unlikely. More likely, though still unprovable, is that those who served the fae—the Inarak—once lived here. And if they did, it would explain some of the potency found here."

I knew next to nothing about the Inarak, and absolutely nothing about the fae. There were some who claimed that the fae would cross over from their realm, passing through some mysterious gates that would bring them to our world, but I had always found such claims to be fanciful stories and nothing more. After hearing Matherin—somebody who I had come to believe understood aspects of the world in ways that I did not—speak about them in terms that made them seem real, I wasn't sure quite what to say.

We went down the stairs. Matherin went first, and Asi and I followed, until we arrived in a simple closed chamber. Matherin looked up and then whispered a mild swear under his breath before he crawled up the stairs and pressed something up against the stone, which closed the entrance off once more. Once he was done, he came back to rest next to us. He pulled out an arcane lantern, and it glowed with a pale blue light, reminding me of the night when I had encountered the strange bloody pillar in the alley.

"I'm sorry that my accommodations here are not more exciting."

"This is it?" I asked.

"This is all that I'm going to show you," Matherin said.

I shared a look with Asi. His choice of words suggested that there was more here, but what? How far did this network of underground channels go?

Could it lead to the prison? Could this have been how Talina and Jasar had managed to escape? Could somebody—even Talina—have gone back through a similar pathway in order to find the fabrication that we had left behind?

"Why all the precautions?" I asked.

"This leads to a place that is a little better protected," he said. "The protections are distinct and will hopefully hold. Theoretically, they should be as potent as using the harbor, assuming that was effective."

"Assuming," Asi asked.

"As I said, I can only speculate on the efficacy of such things, though the theory sounds as if it should work. But a place like this is equally effective."

"So why all of these precautions?" I asked. "You didn't make it sound as if you knew all that much about the Daughters of Inkasa."

"And I don't," Matherin said. "Or at least, I don't believe that I do, though there is the possibility that what has been happening, and unfortunately, what's happening here, is all interconnected."

That had been my feeling as well, though at this point, I had no idea how it was all interconnected.

"Describe again what you saw," Matherin said.

The light bounced off the walls, causing the shadows to move. It left me uncomfortable, reminding me far too much of the prison cell and how the ink had flowed.

I had to force my mind back. The chamber itself was small enough that the top of my head was brushing the ceiling, but only in sections. Other parts of it were higher overhead, giving me more clearance. I leaned up against one of the walls, and I questioned whether there was some presence here, as I felt a bit of magical resistance behind me. Which suggested that there was a doorway here. If I had more time, I could test where that doorway led, assuming that there was one present.

"I told you what we saw," I said. "I can't describe it any differently than I already did. If there is something about the ink that you are concerned about, please share it. This is serious."

"Oh, it's quite serious," Matherin said. "And it might be more serious than we know. I will look into it on my end, but I want you to be aware of it as well. There are stories." His voice took on a different tone, one that was a bit edgy but almost professorial. "Stories of strange powers. Powers that can infest, and powers that can control."

"You're talking about some sort of magic that can control someone else?" I asked.

"That doesn't exist," Asi said.

"Perhaps not in the form spoken of in stories," he

agreed. "And I'm not trying to get us to talk about folktales. In fact, I think those are dangerous, though there are some who find such stories to be useful, only because they carry the elements that might provide hints of historical facts. But this infestation magic is somewhat similar to fabrications." He nodded to the hand in which I was holding my blade. "What do you feel with that sword?"

Since going to prison, I hadn't been paying that much attention to what I could pick up from the blade. The vibration had eased completely. Now there was nothing left of it. It was just still. Strangely, I felt as if it wanted me to know that it was waiting. And that left me thinking that I was imagining it, as I couldn't believe that the blade actually wanted anything from me.

"It's quiet," I said.

"Which is impressive," Matherin said. "And unusual. Most who have experience with such items find that it is not so quick. But you felt a vibration. You felt something that was active within it, correct?"

"In a way."

"And that is how many of the more complicated fabrications work. The power itself must be tamed. The fabricator is the primary one to do so. The taming is done so through the container that holds the fabrication. But the user, depending upon certain fabrications, must also be capable of containing that power. Do you understand what I'm saying?"

"You're saying that I had to be capable of using the sword."

"Exactly," he went on, nodding his head vigorously.

"Had I given that blade to a different Blade"—he glanced at Asi—"it is quite possible that they would not have been able to tame it. That is not to disparage them, or any other Blade of their potential. Quite the opposite, in fact. Most such things are attuned in a specific way, depending upon the design."

And then I understood. "You designed this blade for me. You thought that I was going to come asking for something like this."

"I said you were capable. That was when I decided that you might benefit from a blade meant for you. You have a history with the army, and you are a large man. Quite large," he said, pressing his lips together in a frown as he regarded me.

I wondered how much he knew about my background, especially considering that he knew about the aelith powder that had brought me some information about my family.

"So I thought that perhaps in the matter of sheer size, you would benefit from something more significant. But then you displayed considerable potential with what Waleith had you doing. And so I knew that I had to give you something that would share in that considerable potential. It would not be functional for somebody like Asi, and that is not to say that she does not have considerable skill."

"So you're saying he's more stubborn," Asi said.

Matherin smiled slightly. "Somewhat. But back to the topic at hand. The fabrication requires someone to have the ability to control it. To tame it. According to the stories I've heard, the same can be said about that ink."

"So it's just a fabrication," Asi said. "And if it is, then we should be able to destroy it."

"I don't know if it is only a fabrication."

"Well, what else could it be?"

"There are stories, and I don't know if I believe in them, but considering your description, I think that they warrant further investigation. The ink used by the Daughters of Inkasa is more than just some magical potential. There are stories that it is alive."

I considered what we had seen. It hadn't seemed alive, but it had seemed aware somehow. It had known that we were there, and it figured out a way of avoiding us, until we—well, *I*—had used the strange fabrication to hold it. And there had been the odd sense that I had as the ink had flowed into it.

Was it even possible that something about the ink was alive?

The whole concept struck me as impossible, but there were so many other impossible things that I had experienced since coming to Busal City. So many things that I had once thought were not real that had proven to be very much the case. And in my short time in the city, I had come to realize that the world was far more complicated than I had ever known.

It was easy enough for me to think about fabrications. That was a kind of magic that I could understand, even if I couldn't control it. But it was far more difficult for me to fathom the kind of power that I had started to see and feel around the city, the kind of power that had obviously had an influence, and could be used in destructive ways.

"I don't know," I said. "That could be true."

Asi regarded me. "You're buying into this?"

"I don't know if it's a matter of buying into it so much as trying to understand what we have been dealing with, and whether some of the things that we have been seeing are real. You know what it was like when we were facing that ink."

"Facing that ink. You make it sound like we were battling some monster, but we were just trying to mop it up."

"And we left it, and now…" I shrugged. "I don't even know."

"I will look into other answers," Matherin said. "As I told you, I think it is possible that I will find something more, but it will take time. If the Daughters of Inkasa are using this magic in the city, it is possible that we will not have the necessary time."

"It would be easier if we were just dealing with the Anvil," I muttered, shaking my head.

"Maybe that is all we are dealing with," Asi suggested. "I mean, the Anvil are known to play with power, aren't they?" She looked at us. "There's another possibility, and that it is the Anvil are *using* the Daughters of Inkasa. Maybe they hired them or have somehow negotiated with them. I don't know."

I didn't really know either. At this point, I was well out of my depth, even though I was a Blade.

"Let's see what we can uncover," I said. "And if nothing, then we switch our focus to the things that we can control." My mind started to turn, coming up with answers that were difficult but potentially key. "We have to make sure that Talina doesn't try anything. She attacked the Queen once, and it's possible that she will use this opportunity to do so again. Especially if she somehow has access to your little hidden network," I said to Matherin.

"She would not be able to access the palace this way," he said.

"Are you certain of that?"

He was quiet. "Mostly."

I snorted. "Well, mostly isn't good enough. And while I believe that Talina fought her way out, used some power to batter her way past the guards, there's also the possibility that she didn't do it that way, and she was just using that as a distraction. So if she is in the walls somewhere, find her, and make sure that she doesn't harm the Crown. Can I leave that task with you, at least?"

Matherin seemed to consider it for a moment, as if he didn't want to acknowledge that he had any sort of obligation, but he finally nodded. "I can take that responsibility on myself."

"Oh, good. And here I was concerned that you would tell me no." I turned to Asi. "We are going to do our jobs. We are Blades, after all, and there is dangerous magic in the city."

"I have my side of the harbor to focus on," she said.

"You do, but maybe not just now."

"I thought we both agreed that you don't command me."

"I'm not trying to command you. I'm trying to ask you to help."

She arched a brow at me, and I just shrugged. "We are both Blades. And at this point, the greatest threat is the one that we must both deal with. I know that Blades were taught to work on their own, in isolation, to a certain extent, but I don't think that is how we are going to stop what is happening here. I think we need to work together, at least until Waleith appears."

And even after that, I didn't say.

That was the one lesson that I had gleaned on my own. Waleith had not been the one to teach me that. He was too tied to the old ways of the Blades, wanting to do everything on his own. But from what I had experienced in the city, handling such dangers on my own was not safe, nor would it lead us to the answers we needed to find.

"Fine, but if anyone takes the blame for this, it's going to be you."

"The blame from the Queen?"

"Oh, no," she said, shaking her head. "I'm not at all concerned about the Queen." From the way that she said this, however, I wasn't convinced that was true. I knew that she had some issue with the Queen. But I wasn't going to push her on it. "I'm talking about Waleith. If anybody takes the blame from him, it's going to be you."

I laughed. "I think that's a fair trade."

Chapter Nineteen

I poked my head into the tavern and paused for a moment. I swept my gaze around, not really getting my hopes up. At this point, I had started to believe that Garridan had simply disappeared. He'd left me a coin to try to reach him, but there was a trick to using it that I hadn't learned, so I resorted to searching the old-fashioned way. I had looked into several taverns and grown increasingly frustrated that I hadn't found him. I wanted to inquire as to what he knew about the ink, and about whether it was truly alive. If it were, I would have expected him to warn me.

But then, the more I thought about it, the more I believed that he *had* attempted to warn me. Either I had not listened, or I had been so preoccupied that I had not been in the position to fully understand what he had been trying to tell me. Given what we had seen, however, I needed to find him.

And it was not just about the ink, and the fabrications, and the bodies.

No. I needed to see if he was somehow responsible for Talina's escape.

I didn't like to think that he was, but then, he had asked about her. And then she had simply disappeared.

There weren't many ways in which someone like her would have been able to escape. The only way that I thought possible was if she had outside help, and though I didn't think that the Guild would want to anger the Queen, there was a distinct possibility that Talina had had help from them, and for a reason that I didn't know.

Asi had returned to her part of Busal City, mostly to make preparations, as she claimed. I wanted to tell her that I needed her help, but I didn't have any right to tell her what to do, and I had to be patient. She was willing to help, so I had to take that help in whatever form she was willing to provide it.

At this point, that help was in the form of a willingness after she had made a few preparations.

She had been more than happy to take on the help of the Investigators, but that wasn't the only preparations that she had wanted to make. She believed that there were other issues that she needed to attend to, and I knew better than to challenge her. Besides, I could hunt the taverns, wander the city, and detect anything that would suggest Talina's presence without her.

At least, that was what I told myself, but so far, I hadn't been able to find anything whatsoever.

"Come on in," a man at a nearby table said, slurring

his words lightly. He waved a mug in my direction. "Ale is warm, tastes like piss, but can't be too picky around these parts."

I offered a nod, surprised that somebody would just randomly talk to me, especially considering the greeting that I normally received.

"Just looking for a friend," I said.

The man got up, took my arm, and tried to pull me inside the tavern.

I resisted and checked that he wasn't a threat. I found myself testing for magical resistance coming off him, not expecting it, but I had certainly been surprised before, and I had to be careful not to be surprised again.

"Oh, big guy, just come in and have a drink. I'll buy the first round." He grinned. "You have the looks of someone who can handle a few rounds."

"Any minstrels here?" I asked.

"You looking for music? Not so much here. We like our dancing and all, but if you want music, you'd best go to the Battered Burdan or the Hairy Snip. Both places tend to get their minstrels in and, if you ask me, tend to be a little snooty."

The names of two taverns. That was useful.

"Here," I said, grabbing a copper penny out of my pocket and flipping it to the man. "This round is on me."

The man held it up against the lantern light before he stumbled away.

I stepped out into the street, looking around. I didn't know the location of either of those taverns, but at least having some names helped me in my search, and I had to hope that I could get a better idea of Garridan's whereabouts in either establishment. Finding one minstrel might allow me to track down others.

I worked my way along the dock taverns—of which there were many. I found more drunk men trying to wave me in, some trying to get me to play games, and a few prostitutes who thought to seduce me. I ignored all of them, checking on minstrels but finding none. There were a few singers. I didn't know if the singers were part of the Guild, and even if I found a minstrel, there was no guarantee that they would be a part of the Guild.

There had been no sign of anybody.

My quest grew increasingly frustrating.

At one point, as the time drew closer to midnight—and it had been late when I had started this process—I felt a flash of power in the distance.

I turned and jogged along the street, pushing past several people, who paused to look at me, as I hurried toward what I had detected. It was nothing like what had drawn me out of Busal City. That power that had been tied to my first experience with the Anvil—and possibly even the Daughters of Inkasa. But it *was* power.

And to a certain extent, this power struck me as familiar. It reminded me of Talina. I had only a passing experience with her, the kind of magic that she was able to wield. I didn't know what she could do, especially untethered and unbound. I hadn't been very far along in my training at that point. Ever since she had been captured, I had continued to progress in my ability, but it was difficult to know.

I didn't find anything, though.

No sign of Talina. No sign of magic. The sense of it had faded.

What had it been, then?

I was getting tired. It was difficult to stay alert for as long as I had, to remain active after working for a long time. And if there was one thing that I had learned in the army, it was that fatigue could easily lead to mistakes.

I had to be careful that I did not make a mistake here.

I made a circle around the city once again. I didn't feel any power, and I even paused at a few taverns, testing for any sign that would lead me back to Garridan. When I found nothing, I eventually ended up back in my home and collapsed on the bed.

* * *

I woke up far earlier than I wanted to.

Rubbing the sleep out of my eyes, I sat up on the edge of my bed and felt better, and worse. The threats in the city were significant. And yet there was the possibility that the threats weren't necessarily *for* the city, just present in it.

That didn't change what I needed to do. And considering some of the attacks that had taken place, and the fact that somebody had escaped from the palace prison, I knew that I needed to act quickly, but at least there had been no sign of any real danger. Not yet, at least.

That wasn't to say that something serious wasn't coming.

I pulled the door to my home open and stood out in the street. It was sunny, and with the early morning sunshine along with the benefit of some sleep, everything felt a little better. Perhaps that meant I had more time.

I started toward the constable station, intending to talk to Harent. He deserved a warning about what we were dealing with, because if there was something dangerously magical, I wanted to ensure that the constables didn't try to investigate. I wasn't even sure that I wanted the Investigators looking into it. This might be too much for them as well.

As I neared the station, somebody came jogging up toward me.

"There you are, Blade," Kurn said.

"What is it?"

His Investigator jacket was slightly ajar, and his eyes were bloodshot, as if he had not gotten much sleep. "Jos wanted me to get you. Said that you needed to see what he's found."

"And?"

I glanced toward the constable station, wondering if I needed to involve the constables in this. There had been a little activity coming in and out of the constable station, though not as much now as there would be later. The time of day mattered.

"I don't know. They kept me out of it. Made me stay up on the shift overnight, though."

"Why?"

During my patrol, I hadn't come across any Investigators, so if they had been out last night, why wouldn't they have found me?

"Don't know. They said that it wasn't ready yet."

I groaned. "How long have you been looking for me?"

"Not long. Well, I haven't been looking for you that long, but I think that they went looking for you last night, but you weren't at home." Kurn shrugged. "Either that, or you wouldn't wake up." He regarded me as if trying to decide which it was.

"I had a long night," I said.

"Hear you were stopping in some taverns," he said.

"You heard that, did you?"

"Word gets around. A large man like you, wearing the mark of the Queen, we get reports."

"I wasn't drinking, if that's your concern."

"Oh, no," he said hurriedly, waving his hands. He motioned for me to follow him. "I didn't think that you were drinking. Everybody said that you were just stopping into taverns. You're looking for some sort of musician? A friend of yours, maybe?"

I had to be careful. Too many people getting word around that I was looking for a minstrel could reveal too much of what was going on, and that was not something that I wanted. And not only that, but I didn't want people to avoid me.

If there was one downside to my size, it was how easy I was to recognize.

"Show me what you need me to see."

"I was supposed to bring you back to the station. Then we can go from there. Or maybe you can go from there. I think I'm supposed to be done with my shift." He blinked, and I saw the fatigue washing through him. "I can stay, if you need me."

"I'm sure we do, but I'm also sure that you need to get your rest. If there's one thing I know, it's that fatigue can kill."

Kurn's eyes widened. "It can *what*?"

"Not directly," I said, laughing softly. He was young, inexperienced, but he had a good head on his shoulders. "It can prevent you from paying attention to the things that you should be. So I want to make sure that you get the rest you need in order to stay alert. Does that make sense? It's why I went to bed last night. Otherwise, I would've stayed up all night searching."

"What were you searching for?"

"Something dangerous," I said.

Kurn looked as if he was waiting for me to go on, but I was not going to share with him. I didn't want the Investigators involved in the Daughters of Inkasa if I could avoid it. And I didn't know if I could even avoid it, but I needed to try to keep them out of it as much as possible.

We weaved through the streets, passing shops that were just awakening for the early morning, and merchants setting up carts and stands, with a sense of normality beginning to build all around us.

It was reassuring.

And the fact that there was nothing here that was obviously dangerous gave me further reassurance.

That put everything into a different light for me. It certainly made me feel a lot better about things. As I had been navigating through the city the night before, everything had started to strike me as strange and dangerous, and perhaps that had been a mistake. There was nothing strange and dangerous this morning.

I breathed out, feeling a wave of relaxation washing over me.

And maybe a little less urgency filling me as well.

By the time we got to the Investigator station, I was starting to feel pretty good about the time that I had to dig into the Anvil and the Daughters of Inkasa, and whatever it was that they were responsible for. That was until I entered the station.

Most of the time, the work the Investigators did was calm. There was a certain relaxation to the type of work that they did, partly because they didn't have to handle more complex issues. They were trained to search for magical items, to deal with some of them, but anything more complex required them to call in a Blade—and in most of the cases, that involved me.

But today was chaotic.

Jos stepped out of the back room, and he caught my eye. "There you are. Sacred Souls. You would not believe what we have been dealing with."

"I'm here now," I said.

"All right. I guess it's time to show you."

"Show me what?"

He looked over at Kurn. "I told you to find him and then get back to work."

"Let him go to bed," I said.

Jos frowned at me. "Let him do what?"

"Look at the boy. I don't know how long you had him working yesterday, but it had to have been most of the day, and overnight."

Jos nodded. "With what was going on, we thought that it was necessary. And it's an all-hands-on-deck kind of situation."

What was going on here?

"Even if it is, he still needs to get some sleep."

"Wait till you see this," Jos said. "And then you can tell me how you feel about it."

"I doubt it's going to change how I feel."

"Oh? Well, maybe it won't, but let's just take a look first."

I hesitated and then followed him, heading into the warehouse.

The smell hit me first.

It was the smell of rot, decay, and death.

And I immediately knew why they were concerned.

Chapter Twenty

They had arranged the bodies in the back of the warehouse, along a section that was devoid of any magical items. I didn't know if that was intentional, because they were concerned about what would happen with the bodies, or if it was because that was the place that was less likely to stink up the rest of the warehouse. If only they had a way of partitioning this area off so that we wouldn't have to smell it throughout the whole warehouse, but it didn't seem that was possible.

There were three of them, the same number of bodies I had encountered in the alley with the blood pillar. All of them were pale, and all of them looked as if they had been bled dry.

"Where did you find them?" I asked Jos.

"You don't look surprised," he said.

"Where did you find them?"

"South side of the city. In an abandoned section."

"Inside a building?"

"No," he said. "That's a strange thing, isn't it? If you're going to do something like this, why do it out in the open?"

"Maybe they needed to be exposed," I said. "I honestly don't know."

"But you've seen this before. This is what you were describing."

"This is what I was concerned about," I said. "And this is what I have the constables on the lookout for. And you, for that matter."

"You didn't tell me it was going to look like this," Jos said, with anger flashing in his tone. He looked up at me, and then he softened. "Sorry about that, Blade."

I ignored the apology. There was no need for it. "I should have shared with you more about what was going on here. I didn't know that you were going to get involved in it. Had I known, I would have..."

What would I have done? I wasn't even sure that I would have shared anything with them regardless. Having come to know more and more about the Daughters of Inkasa, I couldn't help but feel the Investigators were far out of their depth here.

Much like I was out of my depth.

"Did you find a pillar?" I asked.

"Like what we found outside of the city?"

I nodded.

"No. I didn't see anything. And you think that is tied to it? Some sort of fabrication?"

I breathed out heavily. "Honestly, I am having a hard time finding out."

I crouched down in front of one of the bodies and found the same long incision along the neck. This was an older man, with graying hair and a scraggly beard. There was no staining of blood around where the incision had been made. It seemed impossible that somebody would be able to cut him like that without dropping any blood, so they must have gone to extreme pains to ensure that they didn't spill any. Either that, or doing so was dangerous in whatever ritual they had carried out.

I moved on to the next. Another man, this one with the same long incision, and with the same lack of droplets of blood on him.

The third person was a woman.

I thought about what we had interrupted outside the city with Jos. Had that been the same? We hadn't had enough time to piece that together.

"What is it, Blade?" Jos asked.

"It's just that I saw something similar elsewhere in the city," I said, and I explained what I had seen, and my concern about whether the ratio of men to women was somehow significant.

"Maybe it's just chance," he said.

When it came to magic, I wasn't sure anything was chance.

I wondered how many more of these bodies we were going to uncover, and whether these pillars were active throughout the city.

Questions.

And what was worse was the fact that I had not detected anything. The fact that there was power in the city that I couldn't even pick up on was troublesome to me.

I straightened, looking at Jos. "All right," I said. "We need to search the city for anything else like this. Be as detailed as you can and careful as you approach. If you find anybody maneuvering one of those pillars, stay away from it. Get me first."

"We haven't seen anything like that," Jos said. "And honestly, I would've expected to have. If there were something going on here, shouldn't we have picked up on it? The idea that there is no way for us to see these being moved around the city is surprising."

"Unless they have them in a wagon," I suggested.

"Maybe, but considering the weight that is involved, the wagon would be heavily burdened, and it shouldn't even be able to get into certain areas. Didn't you say that the second pillar you found was in a section of the city without easy access?"

I frowned. "Maybe there is some other way of transporting these things. Or perhaps they make them on-site."

"Or maybe it's a fabrication that can change," Kurn suggested.

I looked over at him. I had thought that he was going to go home, but he had stayed. And I was glad that he had. "What was that?"

Jos shot him a look, as if to silence him, but Kurn held

his gaze on me. "It's just that we've come across a few fabrications that change. I'm sure you have as well, Blade. With the right kind of power, they can be modified. There has to be a way for some of them to expand, right?"

"Maybe," I said. "So if that's the case, then they could start off smaller."

That might explain why we hadn't come across anybody maneuvering pillars throughout the city. They could have just set up the portable fabrication, activated it, and then used it for whatever ritual they needed to do in order to draw in the blood, and then...

Well, and then came the part that I didn't fully understand. It had to be tied to the storage fabrications.

Assuming that was what they were.

If they were fabrications, then they were the kind of fabrications that Matherin did not know about.

Once I was done with the Investigators, I was going to need to go back to Matherin and talk to him about what we had been finding. I needed answers.

"Here's the thing, Blade," Jos said. "We didn't notice anything."

"What do you mean?"

"We have these fabrications," he said, "but we didn't notice anything. And maybe the power is subtle enough that we wouldn't, but I thought that we had powerful enough fabrications that we could pick up on something like this, assuming that it is some sort of power."

"I'm still assuming that it is," I said.

"So if it is incredibly powerful, as we believe, then shouldn't we have detected something?"

He wasn't wrong, as I was incredibly troubled by the fact that I had not been able to pick up on anything.

"We need to keep searching," I said. "And I can talk to the Queen's fabricator to see if there are other forms of fabrications that we can find."

"You would do that?"

"We need to work together, Jos. This is on all of us to investigate."

He regarded me for a long moment, as if trying to decide whether he wanted to say anything more, before he nodded. "We would appreciate it."

"Of course," I said.

It was a strange reaction, but then, maybe it was tied to the fact that others, including Waleith, had not been the most forthcoming about fabrications for the Investigators.

I let out a sigh. "I guess this is my patrol for the day."

"You can take some of us with you," Jos suggested.

"Continue your usual patrols, but just keep an eye out. I'm going to continue mine, and if I see anything or uncover anything, I will let you know."

Jos nodded.

"Have you found anything else?"

"Nothing. Why?"

"Oh, I just figured that now would be the right time for somebody to slip something else into the city. We have all the Investigators and me distracted, and if there were going to be some attempt on the city, it would be easy for somebody to try that now."

"That sounds devious," Jos said.

I shrugged. "It does, but it's the kind of thing that I wouldn't put past a careful planner."

"We haven't found anything."

Maybe I needed to have Asi investigating that sort of thing rather than searching with me, especially since I had the Investigators hunting, and it was very likely that we wouldn't even pick up on any sort of power, anyway.

What would I ask her to do, though?

I already had her helping me find Talina, and I still had to deal with Jasar and whatever he was up to.

After making a few more plans, I headed out of the Investigator station and then stood in the street.

I needed answers. That was the thought that lingered within me. I needed answers, and unfortunately, I didn't know how I was going to find them. Somehow I had to come up with what was going on here, and who was ultimately responsible for it. And what was worse, I felt as if I was truly out of my element with this.

Checking taverns had been relatively useless. Hunting for Talina had not gotten any results, either. There was an undercurrent of magic within the city, and even though I was attuned to it, I had not picked up on anything to suggest that there was anything, or anyone, here to be concerned about.

It all seemed to be tied to Garridan, however.

How was I supposed to find any member of the Guild?

The situation reminded me of the very first days that I had been in Busal City, when I had been training with Waleith, and how he had tasked me with trying to uncover different sorts of magic. I had felt helpless, but for a very different reason. I'd felt helpless because I had not known how to do the one thing that he had asked me to do. He had asked me to track down power, to hunt it in a way that would allow me to find anything that was askance in the city. Using that connection to magic should have given me a way to find out what was going on now, but it didn't seem to be working for me.

Maybe it was the fact that I had spent so much time in the city, and I had a different understanding of the power here. When I had first come, I had not known that so much magical energy flowed around here. I had believed that the Queen had wanted to ensure that there was no magic. I had not known that she would welcome some, and perhaps even use some.

But I had come to realize that the power within the city was all around. It was perpetual. It was potent in a way that I could not ignore.

But that meant that it was difficult for me to find distinct energies within it. Energies like Talina's, assuming she was using her power.

And the only way that I would pick up on anything significant would be if she were to use it.

My path led me past Dara's shop.

I didn't know if I had come here intentionally, to see her. As I approached, I felt the familiar and distinct sense of her power from the shop. I didn't feel anything else, which suggested that her employer was not there. That was probably for the best. I didn't want to deal with him.

I pulled open the door and stepped inside. The sense

of her power washed over me, familiar, potent, and comforting in a way.

Had I been able to ignore my responsibility to the Queen, it would have been far easier for me to have a relationship with Dara. I suspected that she wanted the same, but I also knew that she was concerned about my role in the city, and whether I would eventually come to betray her. I didn't intend to, but I also knew that if it came down to it, my obligations to the Queen would outweigh my affection for her.

But I did feel a growing affection for Dara.

"I know you're there, Zaren, so just come up here," Dara said.

Could she detect me?

I headed up to the counter, frowning as I did.

"Mirrors," she said, pointing behind me.

I glanced back. There were a couple of mirrors angled so that she could see the doorway behind the shelves. "Well, I suppose you always knew when I came in here."

"Of course," she said. "We can't have people surprising us. The items in the shop are too valuable."

She looked at me defiantly, as if to challenge the assertion. I wasn't going to.

"Have you uncovered anything about the Anvil?" Dara said this a little bit more carefully, and there was an edge in her tone.

"Not really," I said.

"You look troubled."

"I am."

"Anything you want to talk about?"

"I don't think it's safe to do so here," I said.

"He's not here, if that's what you're asking about," she said. "Even if he were, I doubt that you would have anything to fear from him. It's more likely the opposite, as you know."

"That's not it," I said. "It's just that..."

I wasn't sure what it just was. It was just an uncertainty, and uneasy sensation, and I was wary of talking about the Daughters of Inkasa out in the open, because they clearly had some way of observing those who did. I thought about Matherin's concern, as well as Garridan's, and the shared unease from the two made me feel cautious.

As I suspected I should be.

"Go on," Dara said.

"It's not just the Anvil," I said. "I don't know who else is involved. Can you tell me more about your brother's involvement with them?"

She sighed, looking around as if she was afraid to say anything. "I don't know all the details about what he went through. Just that he got pulled in. He... had some talent."

"Like yours?"

She looked as if she wanted to hold back and then hesitated. "Not like mine. More. He always had more. That's why they wanted him. But they forced him to do things. I don't know what they were, so don't ask, but the last time I saw him, he warned me to stay away. He said they were looking for powers they couldn't control."

Could that be what this was about?

"Anything you know will help. There are other threats active in the city."

Dara frowned at me. "Other threats?"

I nodded. "Again, I don't know all the details, but these other threats are making it difficult for me to appropriately investigate."

She started to smile. "It sounds like you have someone who is outmaneuvering you."

"You ever get a job that you don't think that you are fully equipped to handle?"

"What?" Dara asked.

"Here." I waved my hand around. "Do you ever get a job that you don't feel you can fully handle? Something that somebody is asking about," I went on, trying to avoid talking about fabrications, but we both knew that was what I was implying, "that you just can't make as well as you wish that you could."

"That happens from time to time," she said, seemingly choosing her words carefully. "Why? What sort of job have you had to take that you aren't fully equipped to handle? That's what this is about, right? Something happened, and somebody wants something, or is after something, and you don't know how to deal with it."

"It's something in the city," I said. "At least, I think it is. And people are getting hurt. I don't know if I'm the right person for the job, but I also don't know who else could do the job."

"It's not like you to be this hesitant," Dara said.

"I don't even know if I'm hesitant," I said. "It's just a

matter of trying to figure out who can help me the best. Help the city."

"Did you come here thinking that I was going to help the Queen?" she asked, setting her hands on the counter. I noticed that she had a small, slender piece of metal in hand, and she was probing at her project.

"No," I said. "I just came because..."

Why *had* I come?

Had I come because I wanted to talk to her, or had I come because I wanted to see her, or had I come because there was something that I thought she might offer me? She was one of the people who knew something about the Anvil, though.

"I guess I just came because I wanted to see you."

"You know, you could just ask to see me."

I tensed. "What?"

"You could just ask. You act like I'm not willing to see you. I'm not sure how I feel about what you are," she went on, "but I still like you, Zaren. And I think you've got a good heart. So I guess I'm concerned that you haven't thought that you could ask to see me."

I licked my lips. "I thought that you didn't want to."

"When did I ever give you that idea?"

"I suppose you didn't," I went on. And it made me feel even more ridiculous than I already did. "I'm sorry."

Dara laughed. "Sorry. 'Sorry' doesn't really change anything here, Zaren, but I do appreciate the honesty. For a hulking man like yourself, I would've thought that you would be a bit more... well, *more*." She shrugged. "Anyway, why don't we plan dinner? You can tell me about what you're dealing with, if you want, and I can tell you about my projects, if I want. Does that sound acceptable to you?"

"That does," I said.

"Good. Now, if you don't mind, I really need to keep working."

"Anything that would help me with my job?"

She regarded me for a long moment as if trying to decide whether she wanted to answer. Then she shook her head. "No. I don't think so, at least. And even if I did, I don't think that I can be the person to report what you're looking for."

"I understand."

"Do you? Because I think that we have to make sure that we both understand each other, especially when it comes to this, Zaren. I don't want to betray what I'm doing, much like I don't think that you would betray what you need to do."

"No," I agreed. "I don't want that for either of us."

"I do know that this is licensed work," she said.

I didn't think it was, but I didn't want to challenge Dara on that. The fact that the Investigators had not bothered her suggested that whatever she was doing, and whoever she was working with, wasn't going to cause a problem here.

"Of course," I said.

Dara nodded.

"When you're done with all of this?" she asked.

"That sounds great," I said.

"I don't know what you're dealing with, but if it gets

bad, just send word to me. Can you do that? I don't want to be worrying about you."

The idea that she'd worry actually brought a smile to my face. "I will send word."

"I'm glad you came in, Zaren," she said.

I stood straighter. "I am as well."

Chapter Twenty-One

Outside the shop, I paused. I became immediately aware of a strange energy in the air. I didn't think it came from Dara, but I could have suddenly picked up on some aspect of her work. Typically when I left her shop, however, I felt her fabrications, but this was far more distinct. And this was far more familiar to me.

This was a Blade.

Could it be Asi?

If she had returned to this side of the city, I would have expected her to look for me at the Investigator station, as that was where I had told her to get word. Either there or at my home, or even the palace. But we had agreed on a time and place to meet, so I didn't think that it was Asi.

Which meant only one other possibility.

Waleith.

Could he really be here?

I stepped down the street and focused on the Blade

energy, tracking the sense of him. If I could find where he was going, and what he was doing, I could get some answers. Answers were what I needed, after all. Answers were—

"There you are," a familiar voice said from behind me.

I spun. I hadn't even noticed him coming up behind me, though he had snuck out of an alleyway. I resisted the urge to look back at Dara's shop, not wanting him to know where I had been, but I suspected that he already did. I didn't know the extent of Waleith's ability with his innate talents, but I believed that it was at least the same as mine, perhaps stronger. Or maybe not stronger but different.

"You're back," I said. "I'm glad."

He flicked his gaze around. There was an edge to him that there wasn't usually. "I'm back, but I don't know for how long."

"Were you looking for me?"

"Of course I was looking for you. What else do you think I would be doing out in this part of the city?"

"You could've just left word for me."

"Where's the fun in that?" Waleith asked, cocking his head to the side. "I want to make sure that I can still find you, and it seems I can." He grinned. "Did you know I was here?"

"I detected you," I said.

"Good. I would hate to see your skill dwindling in my absence. Why don't we find a good place to talk?"

"Where are you thinking?"

"The garden."

And with that suggestion, I knew that what he had to say was likely significant, and probably dangerous. The Queen's garden had its own natural defenses, which I didn't fully understand, but they were likely fabrications, or perhaps another kind of magic, that allowed open conversation in the heart of it. I had not spent much time in the garden. I had gone there with Waleith, and once with Dara, simply because she had wanted to see it. Without Waleith, though, I almost never went to the garden. There was no purpose behind it for me.

We made a direct line toward it.

"Anything interesting happening in the city?" Waleith asked.

There was a slight edge to the question, which suggested to me that he either knew or suspected something. And maybe he was testing me. I would not put it past Waleith to try to determine if I had been faithful to my obligations.

"Have you been to the palace since your return?" I asked.

"Not yet, but I intend to do so after we talk. Why?"

"I assume that you are asking because you know."

He shrugged. "No. I don't know. I was hopeful that you would share with me."

"Not here," I said, glancing around me. I still hadn't picked up on anything, but there was something that I could talk about that I didn't have to worry about. And maybe that was where I should start. "There's been an incident."

Waleith arched a brow.

"At the palace. Prisoners have escaped."

He froze and immediately reached for his blade, his face screwing up in concentration as he looked around. "Prisoners? More than just Talina?"

He said her name openly, which suggested a lack of concern about whether she would identify his presence.

"Both her and Jasar."

"Really? Interesting. I wonder why she took him?"

"You're assuming she did?"

"There's not going to be a prison break that doesn't have a connection," he said. "If she managed to escape, the real question is how, and why she took Jasar with her."

"Honestly, I'm not even sure if she escaped or if she had help."

"Why is that?"

"We can talk about that once we get to the garden."

"I don't like the way that this is going," Waleith said.

"And I'm sorry. I don't know what to tell you."

He took a deep breath and then released his hold on his blade.

He was tense, though. Much more so than I usually was. Waleith tended to be uptight on the best of days, and I wasn't surprised that he was now, especially considering what I had told him, but this was distinct, and this suggested to me that whatever had brought him back to the city was significant. Maybe he had learned about the Anvil and the Daughters of Inkasa.

If he had, maybe he knew more.

We reached the garden. It was surrounded by a wall about ten feet high, with an ornate iron gate that blocked access to it. Waleith approached quickly, drew his blade, and slipped it into the lock, which clicked open. It occurred to me that I didn't have my sword. I had not even thought to strap it on, though I had carried it last night when I had been out patrolling. I had been thinking about what Matherin had said about needing to tame it. I didn't know if I had managed to tame the power within the blade, but it certainly felt as if the blade had reacted to me, connected to me. I still had my normal blade. That had been instinctive to grab. And it felt instinctive to have it with me.

Once inside the garden, Waleith swung the gate closed, and it locked behind us. A trembling of power washed over me as it did, leaving me all too aware of the kind of energy that existed within the garden. Perhaps this place would protect us.

Maybe it was not at all dissimilar to the underground chamber that Matherin had taken us to.

"Let's get to the heart of the garden. Then you can fill me in," Waleith said.

"You don't want to fill me in on what you have been doing?"

"I think that what you are dealing with takes precedence, especially if we have escaped prisoners." He breathed out. "Well, maybe not."

"Why?"

"Let us get to the heart."

We moved past the hedgerow, passed a few trees, and

then entered the fragrant, flowering garden with a central square. Waleith took a seat and then made a motion for me to sit by him. We had come here so that I could learn about power and practice, and yet this felt a little different now. We had come here to have a protected space to converse.

"When I left you, I went looking for the Guild," Waleith said. "Well, I went looking for Garridan in particular, but the Guild in general. I had hoped that I might find more activity concerning them, and after learning that they were minstrels, I thought that I had an easy way to uncover what they might be involved in."

The fact that he had gone looking for the Guild made me wonder if perhaps what he had uncovered would be helpful in what I was dealing with.

"What did you find?"

"Unfortunately, I didn't find anything. Did you know that not all minstrels are part of the Guild?"

"I did assume that," I said. "They couldn't all be."

"No," he said. "You can't imagine how many people I questioned."

It was my turn to arch a brow at him.

"I didn't reveal the purpose behind my questioning. Or at least, I tried not to reveal it too openly. And I only asked questions of people who had a certain look about them."

I started to smile. "Did you really think that Garridan had a certain look about him?"

Waleith's brow furrowed. "Actually, no. That is a

good point. The man looked too young to be some deadly assassin, didn't he?"

"Too young, and he didn't look like anybody I would consider dangerous."

He grunted. "Perhaps I need to revisit my investigation. Later, of course. But I didn't find any evidence of the Guild. Plenty of minstrels. Some with skill, some without. Some who travel as a troupe, others who travel by themselves. And none who obviously have any sort of power that we need to be concerned about."

It was that part that I suspected he was most curious about.

My experience with Garridan in Busal City had suggested to me that he had considerable power, even if it was the kind of power that I didn't really understand. Until we had a better way of identifying what kind of power he had, I knew that I needed to be careful. I had not even really felt anything when he had been using his power, which suggested to me that he had some ability to mask his power.

"And?" I prompted.

"And they're quiet. I haven't been able to find them, and I certainly haven't been able to find Garridan. The trail has gone cold. So eventually I began to look into the aelith powder. Considering his interest in it, I suspected that there would be a trail of powder that I could track down, to try to understand where they had gone and what purpose they had for it. I assumed that it was related to fabrications, but I haven't gotten any reports of considerable fabrication manufacture." He shook his head. "So, as you can imagine, none of this makes all that much sense to me."

"What if the Guild isn't manufacturing fabrications?"

"Then why would they have wanted all that aelith powder?"

"I don't know. They might've wanted it to prevent somebody else from making fabrications, or perhaps they wanted it for some other purpose altogether."

Waleith clenched his jaw. "Perhaps."

He was anxious. I had not seen Waleith quite like this before. It was strange, to be honest. Maybe it was more a matter of frustration. He was probably accustomed to being able to find the answers that he wanted, and in this case, he had been outsmarted and outmaneuvered. Then again, I'd had the same experience as I had hunted for Garridan, and others of the Guild, in Busal City.

"I think the Guild finds you. You don't find them," I went on.

Waleith looked up. "Why would you say that?"

"Because they found me."

I didn't know why, but I chose to keep from Waleith that Garridan had been the one to find me. There was just something to his look that had me a little alarmed. It was a wildness. Or maybe it was the fact that I knew that he was angry about what had happened when we had traveled to the Isle of Erantor, but whatever it was, I hesitated to reveal the identity of the Guild member who had found me.

Still, I felt as if I needed to inform him that the Guild had been here.

"And?"

"And I think you are right. Not all minstrels are in the Guild."

"That's not the question."

"They were asking to trade information," I said.

Waleith frowned. "Trade?"

"And I wouldn't have been compelled were it not so important," I went on. I had to admit what I had done, even though it would likely upset Waleith.

More than that, it might get back to the Queen, and get me into trouble.

"There was an attack," I said, and then I began to fill Waleith in on what had happened in the last few days.

I shared with him how I had tracked power outside the city, how I had interrupted a ritual, and then how there had been the bodies found around the pillars. And when I was done, I looked up at him. "So I need information. There are no sources for that kind of thing in the city. When I was called to meet with the Guild, and I was made an offer, I took it."

"What did they want?"

"They wanted confirmation of our prisoner."

"And you just gave it to them?"

"I didn't think they were going to break her out."

"But you shared with them who we had?"

"They already knew."

"Did they?"

"They knew." Even as I said this, I had to wonder if they had. Maybe I had been manipulated.

I didn't think so, though. Garridan had known about Talina. And because of that, there had been no reason to hold that information back, had there?

And yet she had escaped.

"I don't think that he had anything to do with what happened in the prison."

"You say 'he.' It was Garridan, wasn't it?"

"It was," I said.

"And why did you think to keep this from me?"

"I'm sharing it with you now," I said, facing him. "I am serving as the Queen's Blade. I am doing what I need to do in order to serve the Queen as best I can. And in this case, that entailed me sharing information that I thought would provide me with some insight into an organization that I did not know how to confront."

I held his gaze. For whatever reason, Waleith intimidated me. I think at first it had been the fact that he served the Queen, but now that we both did, the intimidation was due to the fact that he understood what it meant to be a Blade better than I did. I was getting better, but I still did not know the things that he knew.

"If you end up being responsible for what happened..."

He left the threat of the Queen hanging in the air, but I fully understood what he was getting at. And I also knew that he wasn't wrong. If I was responsible, then there would be consequences.

"I get it," I said. "Truly, I do. But I did what was necessary."

"Don't do this," Waleith said. "You are too clever for that."

"Too clever for what?" I asked.

"Too clever to fail to see the consequences." He shook his head. "And you would know that there were consequences."

I understood, but I had done what I had needed to at the time.

"And you have never made any mistakes?" I asked Waleith.

"Everyone makes mistakes, Zaren. The challenge is undoing those mistakes." He got to his feet. "Well, now that we're all caught up, I think I should take a look at what has been going on."

"I can go with you," I said.

"That's not necessary," he said. "You have done more than enough."

He strode away, leaving me in the garden by myself.

And I couldn't help but feel I had done more than just disappoint Waleith.

Maybe I really had made a mistake that would have the wrong kind of consequences. I needed to deal with this, and quickly.

Chapter Twenty-Two

"More bodies?" I asked Jos as I strode with him through the streets.

"You told me to get you when we found them," he said.

"I know," I said. "I just didn't think it would be so soon."

"I've been thinking about that," he said, turning a corner and pausing. We were near the western edge of the city. From here, one of the roads led away from the city, stretching toward distant mountains. "Whoever is doing this obviously isn't concerned about us finding them, right?"

"Obviously," I said. "And it makes you wonder, doesn't it?"

Jos quickened his steps before pausing near an older section of the city. Most of the homes here were more run-down, some of them crumbling, weeds growing up around the cobblestones, though there was an old temple not far from here. It loomed over much of this area. I could easily imagine what it would have been like in its grandeur. In a way, it was actually a little disappointing that it had fallen into such a state of disrepair.

"It makes you wonder about what?"

"They don't care that you find them, so they obviously aren't concerned about the bodies. And they aren't concerned about being discovered."

"I sort of gathered that already," I said.

"But the first time that we dealt with this was outside the city, right?"

"It was."

"The rest of them have been in the city."

"And you think that is somehow significant?"

"I don't know what sort of training you had when you became a Blade." Jos shot me a smirk, because I had shared with him, and the other Investigators, how I had received a nontraditional education, though I had not gone into an extensive report of what that had looked like, nor had I shared with them everything about Waleith's training techniques. "But when I first became an Investigator, I learned to look for patterns. Sometimes the patterns don't make sense, and sometimes they do. But when it comes to dealing with magical items, if there is an increasing trend, it suggests that something more dangerous is taking place."

I snorted, noticing the bodies not far from where we were standing. There was a single Investigator there, a man by the name of Henry, who had been working with the Investigators since before my time with them. He nodded as we approached, rubbing a hand through his reddish hair.

"What sort of trend are you seeing here, then? I think seeing so many bodies would suggest that something nefarious is afoot."

Jos shrugged. "I'm not saying that we need to find anything different here, I'm just saying..." He shook his head. "Oh, I don't know what I'm saying. But it seems these incidents are starting to get more frequent, right?"

"What do you mean by that?"

"There were a few days in between the first one and the second one, and then a little bit less time, and now..." He shrugged. "Now look at it."

Jos wasn't wrong.

"So the time. You think we are running out of time."

"I do."

"Well," I said, "I guess we have to be a bit more on edge, then." I wasn't sure how that would be possible, because at this point, I was plenty on edge. I turned to Henry. "Anything?"

"Just the same as the others," he said.

I crouched down to look at them. The Investigators had not moved them, but they hadn't needed to. They were lined up the same way as the others had been.

Three bodies, the same as the last few times. No blood. Just long incisions along the necks. "I really need to get Waleith," I mused.

"He's back?" Jos said.

"He is. He came back... Well, I don't know when he came back. But I saw him yesterday."

"He hasn't come back to see us," Jos said.

I wasn't surprised. Waleith didn't have the best rapport with the Investigators, though I wondered whether that was just his stubborn personality or whether he did not see the benefit to working with them. Either way, I didn't want Waleith to disrupt the work that I had done with them. Not that I would expect him to, but I was making inroads with the Investigators, along with the constables, that I didn't want to see thwarted.

"We need to examine one of these further," I decided.

"How so?" Henry asked.

"I don't know. They have all been drained of blood, and it seems to me that is significant. So we need to bring them to someone who might help us understand more about what happened here."

"You mean more than just that they were killed?" Jos asked.

"It's some sort of ritual. And if we can learn more about what happened here, maybe we can get a better idea about the purpose of the ritual."

"You're going to do this?"

"I have somebody in mind."

"Oh?" Jos said. "Somebody who wants to examine a body for some sort of magical injury? Didn't think that we had people like that in the city."

"Oh, he's not going to be pleased with me, but I think he will do it."

I gave directions to Henry and Jos and then made my way to the palace. I still had time before they brought the body over. I tried to speak to the Queen, but Hobell once again told me that she was incapacitated.

"I can get the prince for you, if you would like," he said, "but he has been a bit preoccupied. It is my understanding that you are the one responsible for what happened the other night."

"I wouldn't say that I'm responsible for it," I said. "But I did alert the guards to what had happened."

"Quite the disruption. An attack like that on the palace grounds." He shook his head, making a small tutting noise as he did. "Things have really been quite disruptive since you came."

"Thanks," I said. "I appreciate the comment."

"I'm just making an observation, Mr. Joha."

I smiled tightly. An observation. And of course, I wasn't terribly surprised about the observation that he had chosen to make, but I didn't think the prisoners' escape was my fault. And in fact, I thought that my arrival in Busal City had been helpful in uncovering some of the dangerous activity that had been taking place here. But Hobell wasn't the first one to have expressed such an implication.

"I don't suppose you've seen Waleith here?" I asked.

"The other Blade has returned to the city?" Hobell frowned. "No. I have not seen him."

"Well, if you do, let him know that I would like to speak with him."

"Of course. If there is anything else that I can do to be your servant," he went on, sarcasm dripping from his words.

"I'm a part of the household," I said. I felt the need to remind him of that. "And I am simply doing what I have been asked to do. If the Queen were available, I wouldn't have to go through that with you."

"Now you're blaming the Queen for her lack of availability?"

"Again…" I replied, before just getting frustrated and holding my hands up. "Fine. Thank you for your help today, Hobell."

He tipped his head slightly. "I am always happy to be of service."

I shook my head as I departed the palace, and then I made my way over to Jamie's workshop and arrived just in time to see Henry and Liash, another Investigator, carrying one of the bodies, though Jamie refused to let them set the body down.

"This is your doing, isn't it?" Jamie said, turning to me, hands on his hips. "I'm not an undertaker, as you are well aware. I serve the Queen—"

"I'm just looking for some assistance. I realize you're not an undertaker, and I realize that you don't necessarily have expertise in examining dead bodies, but I am hopeful that you might know something that could help us."

"All right," he said, exasperation filling his words. "Set that one on the table in the back." He glanced at me. "Are you going to wait around, or do I have time to handle whatever must be done?"

"I think I need to wait around," I said.

Jamie let out a frustrated sigh and then flicked his gaze to the two Investigators. "The two of you can go."

Henry waited on me, as if hoping for permission. I nodded. Then he and Liash slipped out of the door.

"You really have them trained," Jamie said, twisting the lock on the door.

I frowned at that. "Trained?"

"Well, I wasn't expecting a pair of Investigators to come carrying a corpse in, as it is not the kind of thing that would have previously happened."

"I keep hearing that," I said.

"It's not a bad thing, Zaren. Well, bringing a corpse to my office is not a good thing." Jamie made his way over to the metal table that the two Investigators had set the body on. "Care to tell me what is going on?"

"Do you want the full details, or do you want the summarized version?"

He looked up, frowning. "Full details. Always."

"You know what that might mean."

"That you will tell me about all of the strange and dangerous magic that you have been dealing with? Of course I know what that means, Zaren. I serve the Queen, no differently than you. Well, I suppose I do serve the Queen differently than you, but I still serve the Queen."

"I've been trying to see her to talk about what's happening in the city."

Jamie's expression darkened. "Yes."

"Nothing that you can talk about?"

"What's there to say? She's been unwell. I have given

her several restoratives, and they are helping, but this is now the third such illness this year. Unfortunately, I fear that the Queen's constitution is just susceptible to affliction."

"I'm sorry to hear that," I said.

"As am I."

"Does she blame you?"

It was a difficult question to ask, but I felt it was also a necessary one, especially as *I* had been blamed for what was happening in the city. Maybe Jamie would understand what I had been dealing with.

"Thankfully, no. She does not blame me. Nor do others in the household. Though I do suspect that they have been looking for alternative forms of therapy. Not that I would blame them for that, and I have actually encouraged them to look beyond the type of healing that I can offer. She expresses great faith in my abilities, however, for which I am quite thankful, but I do fear that there might be others who could help her more than I can." He shook his head. "Anyway, that is not why you are here."

"I'm here because of the Queen," I said. "And I haven't been able to get in to see her, so I suppose that is actually helpful to know."

"And yet I doubt that it changes anything for you."

It didn't, and so I shrugged.

"Now, fill me in."

I didn't really know how much Jamie wanted to learn. I had grown to know the man better and better in the time that I had been spending in Busal City, though I didn't know how he felt about magic. He was the person who had helped me understand the aelith powder, or he had at least set me on the right path to understanding the powder, so I owed him a debt of gratitude, but then, he was constantly irritated with me, and with the fact that I was bringing work to him.

Knowing about the Queen's illness actually made me feel this was perhaps a mistake.

"Maybe the timing isn't right for me to be asking this of you," I said.

"You mean because I have to help care for the Queen?"

When I nodded, Jamie shook his head.

"No. The timing isn't an issue. I have given the Queen what she needs, and she is on the mend. So I do have time. I did not think that I was going to have time for this," he said, waving his hand above the body. "Somebody who has clearly been drained of blood. The incision along the artery is quite skillfully done."

"That's about the only injury that we see."

"Is there anything special about this person?"

"Only that this is one of now nine bodies that we have found like this."

Jamie froze. "Nine? Well, at least I understand why you have decided to look into it."

"It's more complicated than that."

He got to work, rapidly stripping clothing off the body, which was a little disconcerting for me, but it didn't seem to bother him whatsoever. The man was even paler fully nude, but then, he had been completely drained of blood. Jamie continued his examination, lifting the man's arms, his legs, and rolling him from side to side as he worked.

"Go on," he said.

"Sorry," I said. "I've not seen you work."

"You've seen me work."

"On me."

"Right. So you've seen me work."

I began to fill him in on what had been going on, keeping some of the details limited, but not at all when it came to talking about these bodies, and the blood in the pillar, and even my concern about fabrications.

When I got to talking about ink, and alluded to the Daughters of Inkasa, I watched him with a bit more curiosity, wondering if he might recognize the name, but he didn't. Then again, I wasn't terribly surprised, as he was simply a physicker, after all.

"I think you're leaving something out," Jamie said, pausing in separating the man's toes.

"What do you mean?"

"When you are telling the story, you tend to pause. There's something that you didn't want to tell me, or perhaps something that you didn't think was significant."

"Did I mention the Anvil?"

"The what?"

I wasn't surprised Jamie didn't recognize that name, either.

"Apparently, the Anvil are—"

"I know what the Anvil are," he said, his voice dropping to a soft whisper.

"What?" That actually surprised me. "How?"

"I haven't always served in the city, Zaren. And with my skills, unfortunately, I have been exposed to people of wealth and power." He spoke without any hint of arrogance, just stating a fact about his talent. "Sometimes that involved people who were involved in things that I did not want to hear about."

"Such as the Anvil?"

"Yes."

"Where?"

"It was about five years ago. I was stationed in Prelin, a large town along the coast, and was continuing my education. I was already being groomed to come back to Busal City, though I suppose I didn't really know the details of that. And honestly, it's not the kind of thing that I had anticipated, though an opportunity to serve the Crown had obvious appeal. There was a man in that town, someone of some importance, who was brought to me with a series of injuries that looked as if he'd been attacked by a wolf." Jamie shook his head. "Lacerations here," he said, miming marks across the chest, "and additional injuries along his thighs."

"You said that it looked like a wolf attack. Not that it was."

"Oh, I think that it was designed to look natural, but the wounds were far too clean." He looked over at the body. "Not clean like that. But clean, nonetheless. He was alive. And I was forced to heal him as well as I could."

"What do you mean, you were forced?"

"Just like I said. I was forced to help him. I didn't know much about power in the world at that time. Still don't," he said, looking toward me, "but all I heard was that they had been looking into something they shouldn't have been. Didn't know what it was at the time, but now I think it was a power they were trying to use. That's why they call themselves the Anvil, you know. They want to reforge power." He sighed. "When this man recovered, he was quite effusive with his praise and paid me well, but unfortunately, others started to come. Not the same kinds of injuries, thankfully, but injuries nonetheless."

"And these were all tied to the Anvil?"

"I don't know if they were all connected, but I came to know that the first man was. I didn't ask him outright, and he didn't tell me outright, but men tend to talk in their sleep when they are injured." Jamie gave me a pointed look. It left me wondering what I had said when I had been delirious from my injuries, while he had healed me. "I did a bit of careful questioning to try to divine more information about the Anvil, and everything that I heard suggested that I did not want to ask those questions. So I stopped."

"So you have heard a bit about them, but you don't know anything more."

"I know they are dangerous individuals," he said. "If they are involved in this, then it is a dangerous situation."

"But everything that I've learned about the Anvil tells me that they do not involve themselves in magic like this. Perhaps fabrications, but this is something different."

"Perhaps it is somebody claiming to be a part of the Anvil."

"Maybe. I'm not entirely sure. But that is what I have to find out."

"Well," Jamie went on, motioning to the body, "back to your original question. You asked about markings. There are subtle marks on this man's flesh. It is as if there were some marks, but they are now gone. Here, and here," he said, pointing to the forearms. "But it is possible that there were others."

"Marks?"

"I can't say, as the indentations are subtle, but there was something here."

Strange. I wondered what that had been.

"Can you see if you can figure it out? If there is anything that is tied to what's happening, that will be helpful."

"And you think that this is all somehow connected?"

"I do. I just don't know how."

"I will do what I can. Just don't bring me any more corpses."

"I'm not going to make any promises."

Chapter Twenty-Three

Asi found me along the docks after I had left Jamie and started back toward the Investigators. If there had been a change in the time frame that we were dealing with, I wanted to be ready for it. She came charging toward me, her head tilted to the side as she regarded me, frowning.

"Where's the sword?"

I looked down. "I keep forgetting," I muttered.

She laughed. "After all you went through to get it?"

"I didn't do all that much to get it. I just asked."

Asi looked past me, in the direction of the palace, and I knew what she was thinking.

"You can talk to Matherin. I bet he has your blade ready."

"I don't know if he does," she said. "He said that it will take time to make, and even once he makes it, he's going to need to ensure that it is attuned in the right way, or whatever it is that he does with them."

"Still," I said.

I really needed to get back to him as well. There were things that could be done with fabrications that would be useful for others in the city, including the constables and the Investigators.

Asi shrugged again. "Anything new?"

"More bodies."

Her eyes narrowed. "The same as before?"

I nodded.

"Nothing like that in my part of the city. I wonder why."

"I'm not sure, but one of the Investigators made a suggestion about the decreasing time between the killings. Said that there might be a pattern to it."

"He could be right. If that's true, then you probably don't have much time before another lot comes."

"But I don't know why."

"Well, think about what Matherin said. What if that ink is alive?"

"So?"

"If it's alive, then maybe it is feeding somehow."

"Feeding on blood, or feeding on these people, or what?"

"I don't really know," she said, shrugging. "I figure that if we don't have anybody to ask, we won't be able to solve this mystery. And unless we have somebody who knows things, we are stuck, aren't we?"

"Waleith's back," I said. "And he doesn't know anything about it."

"He is?"

I nodded.

"I suppose that's good. I was concerned about why he was gone so long."

"He was acting a little strange," I said.

"How so?"

"He seemed a little jumpy."

"I think he's taking the loss of the training compound hard, Zaren. Most of us Blades are, but he spent a lot of time there."

"I didn't realize that."

"He taught at the compound for little while. I'm not sure that he always enjoyed it, but he was decent."

I arched a brow.

"I know how that sounds, and it's sort of damning praise, but he was a decent instructor. Not the best one that I had when I was there, and not the worst. Many of us had a hard life before we ended up as Blades, but rumors about him were that his was especially hard. Orphaned young, forced to move from everything he knew, and then he ends up as a Blade. Most say he was happy to serve and have a purpose."

"So why did he leave?"

"I think he was always angling for a greater role. Don't know all the details, but I think he wanted the opportunity to serve the Queen more directly."

"When we went out to the compound during his investigation, he seemed irritated and upset, but I didn't really understand the gravity of what he was dealing with."

Asi was quiet for a moment, glancing along the street.

"You know, I've wondered about that. I've considered what it might be like if I were to go out and see the remains of the compound. I don't know if I could learn anything. If Waleith didn't, then I certainly wouldn't. But I suppose it would be a way of remembering what I went through." She looked over. "You could go, too. You could show me what Waleith was investigating."

"I don't know if I should leave the city without justification."

"Well, not right now," she said. "But at some point in the future. You have the Investigators working quite well. Honestly, Zaren, I am surprised at just how effective they have been. Did you know that they uncovered several troves of fabrications on my side of the harbor? I hadn't even uncovered them." She shook her head. "It's hard, though. I have some limitations being the only person on that side."

"Why have you not used the Investigators before?"

"I asked about them when I first came to the city, and when I was taking over my position here, but I was told that I didn't need that kind of help. I was a Blade, and because I was a Blade, I needed to manage my responsibilities on my own," Asi said, sounding as if she was repeating something that she had been told. "I wasn't going to make it sound like I couldn't function by myself, and so I never said anything. But..." She shrugged again. "I wouldn't mind help."

"I think having a little more presence across the harbor wouldn't be bad, anyway. The Investigators can work together and communicate their findings, and hopefully, figure out any trends. I think the constables do that already."

"To a certain extent," she said. "It's just that we Blades have always been isolated. It's just sort of how we have been."

"I don't like it," I admitted.

"So you're just going to change it."

"I'm changing how I function. I can't change how you do your job, but I'm happy to help you."

Asi laughed, and I was going to say something else when I saw a flash of a figure. He lingered for a moment before slipping down an alleyway. The instrument strapped to the man's back was clear.

"I think I'm getting summoned," I said, motioning ahead of me. "You can come along. I think it would help me."

Asi frowned but then shrugged, and we made our way down the street and into the alley. We hadn't gone very far before I started to feel the strange pressure and resistance that I had felt around Garridan before.

Light bloomed around us, faint, pale, and yet enough to clearly see Garridan.

He grinned at me. "You didn't come alone," he said, glancing at Asi. "Another Blade, I'm presuming."

"This is Asi. Asi, this is Garridan."

"This is your source," she said.

I shrugged slightly. "He is."

"A bard?"

"I prefer the term *minstrel*," Garridan said, tipping his head in a slight nod.

"What did you do here? You've obviously used some fabrication. I can feel it, but I don't know what it is." Asi looked around before her gaze settled on me. "What did he do?"

"I'm not exactly sure," I said, my attention on Garridan. "He has some talent."

"Why, thank you," Garridan said. "Most minstrels love to be told that they have some talent." He flashed a smile.

"You came to find me."

"I did. I thought that it would be helpful. Especially with what you have been dealing with."

"You mean the increasing number of bodies."

His brow furrowed. "Yes. I had thought that we could resolve the issue, but unfortunately, the situation has become more problematic."

"And how was Talina connected to it?"

"She should not be."

"You did something. You went after her."

"I did not," he said.

"And I'm not sure that I believe that. We went to drop off another prisoner and found she was missing and quite a few guards had been attacked."

Garridan was quiet for a moment. "I did not attack anyone."

"Why would you be concerned about a minstrel?" Asi asked me.

"Because he's not just a minstrel," I said. "He's part of some guild of assassins—"

"He's *what*?" She lunged forward.

Before she even had a chance to get to Garridan, he simply held a hand out, and Asi froze in place.

I had no idea what he had done, but this was a power that I had never seen before. I hadn't even felt anything.

"That is quite enough," Garridan said, his voice soft.

"The Guild is responsible for killing Arin," Asi said.

"Your mentor?" I asked, remembering the only time she'd brought him up with me.

Garridan hesitated for a moment, his frown deepening. "I'm not familiar with that name."

"And you would be?"

"Yes."

"If it wasn't the Guild, then who?"

"As I said, I'm not familiar with that name. I can look into it if you'd like, but—"

"But you are implying that it would involve exchanging information. Is that correct?"

"Yes. That is how it works. Information for information. As you are quite well aware, Zaren."

Asi relaxed, suddenly released from whatever hold Garridan had had on her. She looked at me. "You can't trust somebody from the Guild."

"Oh, I'm aware of *that*," I said. I turned my attention back to Garridan, as he was truly the real threat, because I didn't know what he might do. "I understand that Waleith has been tracking you."

Garridan smiled slightly, a smirk, really. "I can be difficult to track," he said. "And I find that some who try to follow me end up going down a rabbit hole, following leads that go nowhere."

"So you knew."

He shrugged again. "I did."

"And the aelith powder?"

"Do we need to address this again, or should we focus on the issue at hand?"

"Well, I'd like to know more about what you are doing with the powder, and why you had to take it. It wasn't just about fabrications, was it?"

"No. As you undoubtedly saw when visiting Erantor, that powder can augment the function of many fabrications. Had you been raised there, like your father, you would have known all the ways in which it can be quite damaging and destructive. There are times when that is useful, but only a few times."

"So you needed it for the Guild? It's not some sort of poison?"

Garridan regarded me. "You are asking very good questions, and unfortunately, I don't have the answers that I know you deserve. There are certain things that I can share only within the Guild. Now, if you would have an interest in joining the Guild, I might be able to provide you with a little more detail."

I didn't know if that was a sincere invitation or not. And if it was, how would I feel about it? "I don't want to be a part of the Guild."

"If you change your mind, we can talk more."

"Why did you come find us?" I asked. "Obviously, either you think that I can help you, or you are looking for something. Did you want more information, or did you only come because you wanted to see if I was interested in your offer?"

"I came to ask you to stand back."

I frowned at him. "Stand back?"

"There are aspects of what you are dealing with that are beyond your capability. You do not have the necessary skills to deal with them."

"You mean the—"

I caught myself before mentioning the Daughters of Inkasa by name, as I didn't know if it was safe, despite the protection he had obviously placed around us. Instead, I made a motion toward my arm, indicating the tattoos I'd seen, and watched him as I did.

"I do mean them. This is beyond what a Blade, or perhaps even a pair of Blades, can manage."

"And what about three Blades?"

"He has returned," Garridan said. He frowned. "Interesting."

"Why is that interesting?"

"It's just interesting."

"Explain," I said.

"No," Garridan said. "Unless you know how long he has been back in the city."

"Not particularly. I saw him the other day, but it's possible that he's been here longer."

There was more at play here than I knew, and I wondered what more Garridan was keeping from me. It bothered me, partly because I had started to question whether I would learn anything from him, but partly because he was talking about Waleith as if he was concerned about something.

"Regardless," Garridan said, "as I said, this is beyond what you can manage. I have done my best to work around you and your people, but I see far too much activity."

"You mean the Investigators," I said. "Or the constables?"

He nodded. "I mean both. There is far too much activity with them, and it is becoming a problem. I do not want them to get caught in my plans."

I hesitated a moment, trying to decide what I wanted to say here. I couldn't just stand aside and do nothing.

"This is my city. I am the Blade here."

"And if you do not stand aside, it is possible—and probable—that your people will get caught in what must be done."

"And what must be done?" Asi asked. "I'm asking because I want to know what the Guild is going to do to the Investigators and the constables. Is it the same thing that happened to—"

"Easy," I said, holding my hand up. "Let's hear him out."

"I have said what I needed to say. This is a warning that I do not give often, or lightly."

"Sort of like the warning you gave me when we went to the Isle of Erantor. And when you decided to take the powder. And when you decided to slip away, abandoning us."

He held my gaze. There was a vibrant and dangerous intensity there. Even though he was smaller than me, he gave me the feeling that it would be a very simple matter for him to deal with me effectively. Seeing as he had simply held Asi in place, I couldn't help but feel he very much could do that.

I licked my lips. "We can't be kept out of it."

Garridan squeezed his eyes shut for a moment, and then when he opened them, he nodded, though it seemed he was deciding something. "There are elements to this that you might be useful for, though I don't like involving others not of the Guild."

"What sort of elements?"

"You have mentioned the Anvil."

"I have," I agreed. "Are they involved because they want the power of the... other organization?"

"There are some among them who have made a play for power. It is something that I've been tracking for some time but has not been much of a concern. At least, not until recently. It seems as if some among the Anvil have decided that they want greater influence than they have already achieved."

"So they are using these markings?" Asi asked.

"No. At least, they should not have been. These markings," he said, tipping his head as if appreciating that we were being somewhat careful with our words, "represent an ancient power."

"Something alive?" I asked.

"Why would you say that?"

"Something that I saw," I said.

"What do you mean, something you *saw*?" He turned

the intensity of his gaze fully upon me. I didn't care for that.

"Just that," I said. "There was somebody in the city that we dealt with. She had some markings," I went on, looking at Asi before turning back to Garridan, "and we brought her to the prison with the intention of holding her and interrogating her."

"And that is when you noticed Talina was missing." He frowned. "That fits."

"It fits what?" I asked.

"The timing. I'm not entirely sure if it will make much of a difference, but perhaps you can help. If the Anvil are, as I believe, attempting to obtain an ancient power that they are not equipped to contain, then I will deal with this aspect, while you deal with the Anvil."

"What do you mean, they aren't equipped to contain it?" Asi asked. "This thing *is* alive?"

"It is an ancient entity. I believe that what you have found is evidence of its presence in the city, but it is surprising, nonetheless. And with that presence in the city, the likelihood is that the Anvil has been trying to keep it controlled, though they are failing. Few other than true Daughters of Inkasa can control that power."

I surprised me that he would be so willing to speak that aloud. What had changed that he would do so now?

"Control? How so?" I started thinking about what we had seen, the bodies, wondering how that worked.

"Until it is placated," Garridan went on, as if still trying to choose his words carefully, "it must feed."

"Is there some sort of ritual involved?"

"Yes."

"So that's what we've been dealing with. A ritual to placate this entity."

"Placate? No. Call upon. Summon. And perhaps use. But it is doubtful that they will be able to control it. So as I said, this is beyond you. It may be beyond me." There was a real concern in his tone. "But I am going to ensure that it is dealt with." He inhaled deeply. "And you ensure that you deal with those who attempt to placate it."

"The Anvil."

"Yes."

"Then help me understand how to unmask whatever they are hiding from me."

"What do you mean?" Garridan seemed honestly surprised by that request.

"It's just that I haven't been able to uncover what they are doing. It's like my natural ability has been blocked."

"It shouldn't be that way," he said. "Your potential is unique, and I have not heard of the Anvil possessing that ability. These others, however"—he waved his hand over his arm—"have an innate ability to conceal themselves from all who have power. So I would not expect you to be fully aware of their power. Unless you had trained to be so."

"And you have?"

He nodded. "I have trained in many such things."

"Any suggestions on what I can do to unmask what they are doing?"

Garridan looked down at my blade. "Find a raw fabrication. Use your talent, focusing on the people you are looking for. That should trigger the fabrication to reset. But your blade has already been tempered, and it is likely that there is no other way to handle what you must. I would offer to help with the fabrication myself, but unfortunately, that would take considerable time. And it might be beyond my skill."

"It's fine," I said. "I have something in mind that I can use."

"Excellent. Now, unfortunately, it does seem as if we are running low on time. I again caution you to stay out of this, but it seems you will not."

I shook my head.

"Then if you see me again, I warn you to avoid me."

I snorted. "Of course."

I glanced at Asi and then turned back to Garridan, but he was gone.

"Well," she said. "He's something, isn't he?"

Chapter Twenty-Four

I couldn't get what Garridan had set out of my head. I wasn't sure what it was going to take to discover what the Anvil and the Daughters of Inkasa were doing, but increasingly I felt it would involve figuring out a way to draw on my magical connection, at least in some way.

"What did he mean when he was talking about the powder?" Asi asked.

I looked over. We'd been hurrying through the streets toward my home, which inevitably brought us closer to the palace, and made Asi more uncomfortable. "Apparently, my father was from Erantor, and he left the island." I shrugged. "I didn't learn much more about him than that."

"Did you want to?"

It was a strange question, but one whose answer I probably needed to devote some time to working through. "I never knew that side of him. He was a farmer and a soldier, both of which he taught me to be. I don't know why he left Erantor, and I'm not sure it matters. He's gone now, anyway."

"Sorry," she said.

"It's fine. He's been gone a long time now. My mother, too."

We rounded a corner, heading uphill toward my home.

"You'd have fit in with the Blades. All of us were orphans, of a sort. Most were just taken from our families, but some had truly lost them."

"Is that why you have the reaction to the Crown you do?" I asked, flicking my gaze toward the palace, which rose above the rest of the city skyline.

She shrugged. "I serve. I know I have an ability others don't. I won't complain about that. But there are times when I wonder what it might have been like to have a normal childhood. Had you trained like I did—"

"Like a normal Blade?" I asked.

Asi sighed. "That's not what I meant. But it makes you harder. During the training, I didn't think about it. And I probably never would have had I been stationed anywhere else. But here... I get to see the palace every day. Kind of hard not to. Sometimes I get irritated. Just sometimes." Her defiant look practically dared me to question her more. "You want to tell me why you wanted to come home?"

"I was curious about what I could find here," I said, understanding her need to change the direction of the conversation. "And I am coming for the sword."

"You really believe what Garridan had to say?"

"I have plenty of reason to think he might double-cross me." Again, I didn't add.

"So the sword will help you?"

When we stopped at my home, I stepped inside. Asi waited outside for me.

"I don't really know," I said. "If defending myself is somehow tied to a raw fabrication, and if I can figure out how to access the connection in some way, maybe turning it from a raw fabrication into something usable, then shouldn't I?"

"I suppose, but do you think that it will work?"

"Honestly? I have no idea."

I grabbed the sword and brought it back to Asi. Strangely, the vibration I had felt when I had first been given it by Matherin remained. There was something odd about that.

"What is it?" Asi asked.

"I thought that I had tuned it. I don't think I have, though. When I was carrying it around the first night, I felt the blade had started to adjust to me, but now it feels like… well, like it did when I first picked it up."

"That's not surprising," she said. When I frowned at her, she went on. "When we are first learning to connect to the power of the blade, we have to use it over and over again in order for the blade to function properly."

"But your blades are already attuned."

"Mostly," she said. "And maybe entirely, for that matter. But our training requires us to continue to work with them, because over time, we get to harness some of that power." She shrugged. "It's all very complicated. And honestly, I'm not an expert."

"But you understood what was involved?"

"I did. But because it was taught to me at the compound."

"Where Waleith was," I said.

"Right. But he hasn't been there for a while."

"But he would understand the attunement?"

Asi shrugged. "Probably. He was one of the instructors. I trained with him. Even had Prince Dorian watch me one time. Figured I'd get a good placement after that, but never thought it would be *here*. What are you getting at?"

Prince Dorian had been to the training compound? Why did that surprise me?

"It was just something that Garridan suggested."

"You're going to take the opinion of a member of the Guild over Waleith?"

"I'm not taking the opinion of anyone. I'm trying to find my own information and answers here, and if power has been used in the wrong way, then I want to make sure that it is dealt with. Shouldn't I?"

"You should," she said, letting out a sigh. "What are you going to do now?"

I looked at the blade. "I need to attune this to me. And I need to see if what Garridan said was true. And..." I looked around, thinking what might work. "I could try something else."

"What?"

"Come with me."

"Where are we going now?"

"The palace."

"Great," Asi said.

"What is your issue with going to the palace?"

"I serve, don't I? I can be a little annoyed with certain aspects of the role."

"I'm not debating the fact that you serve. I'm just curious about what is driving this reaction. I would've thought that you would be happy to go to the palace."

"'Happy' might be a stretch. I am perfectly content going where I must go, but I also recognize that there are things there that I don't necessarily want—or need—to find. Is that a reasonable response?"

I shrugged. "I suppose. And I'm not judging."

She frowned at me. "Seems like you are judging a little bit."

"I'm not judging much."

She snorted. "No. It seems you are not."

We set off, and once we got to the palace grounds, I veered off toward Jamie's workshop. I ignored Asi's pointed expression, and when I got to the door, I knocked and waited for a moment. I squeezed the hilt of the sword, having been focusing on it ever since lifting it again. If it needed to be tamed, then it would certainly take time, but I also wanted to have some measure of control over the blade so that I could feel the power flowing through it. I needed to know whether it was a power that I could use.

"No one here?"

"He's here," I said. "Either he's here, or he's up in the palace again."

"This is the physicker you were telling me about."

I nodded.

I knocked again, and when there was no answer, I tried the door, found it locked, and then slid my blade into the lock, testing whether it would work. I was pleasantly surprised to see the door swing open.

"He's going to be quite displeased with me," I muttered.

"Are you really worried about him?"

"I'm concerned about what he might say. And I'm a little concerned about angering him."

"Because of breaking into a physicker's workshop? Doesn't seem to be a good reason to be upset."

"You don't know him, though," I said.

There was a strange, medicinal smell inside the building. I wrinkled my nose and strode toward the covered metal table in the back, while Asi gagged softly.

"It doesn't seem like he's any good at his job," she said. "Smells like death in here."

"There is death in here," I said. "I brought a body here. One of the people used in the ritual. I figured that Jamie might learn something from it."

"And did he?"

"He said that there had been some marking on the skin that had faded. He wasn't entirely sure what it was, but I wonder if it was evidence of the ink fading."

"That shouldn't be possible," Asi said.

"I realize that."

"All of this is really quite strange."

"It really is."

I stood over the body. It was covered with a blanket, exposing only the face. And as I stood there, focusing through the blade, I concentrated on that part of me that was attuned to magic. I had only some training with it, and not nearly as much training as I needed to handle this situation.

I looked over at Asi. "What can you tell me about how you access that part of you that makes you a Blade?"

"Why? Didn't Waleith teach you?"

"I think he assumed that I had some innate knowledge. And he just sort of took advantage of it."

"That makes sense. Most of us learn to access that part of ourselves when we are training. It takes a long time. For some, it takes weeks, and for others, it can take months. There were some stories of people taking a year or more."

"And you?" I asked.

"Is that your way of testing what sort of potential I have?"

"Not particularly," I said. "It is more about curiosity. I want to know what you went through. My experience was different."

"Well, I would say that I was on the quicker end of the scale, but I wasn't as fast as some." She shrugged. "I had some potential, but I wasn't as capable as some of the very best Blades."

"I didn't realize there was a ranking to them."

"You would've had something similar in the army, I'm sure."

"I suppose," I said. "But I didn't think about it with Blades."

"This position—your position—is considered one of the most important. Somebody has to have considerable potential to be chosen as a Blade to serve the Queen. Not only that, but they have to have the Queen's blessing. And they also have to have the blessing of the previous Blade."

"So in my case, Waleith."

Asi nodded.

"What about Waleith?"

"Well, the Blade that served before him..." She shrugged. "Honestly, I don't know what happened, but I think he died. It was before my time."

"And which is the most important? The Queen's blessing or the previous Blade's?"

"The Queen's. Always. That's what makes you the Queen's Blade."

I thought about my experience with the Queen, and how she had interacted with me. I wondered if she knew about the full extent of different magical powers, and if that was what had helped her make a choice.

"What are you doing there, anyway?" Asi asked.

"I'm holding on to the connection I have, but I'm also trying to see if I can pick up on another power."

"If you are trying to control it, that's a very different technique. It's considered fairly advanced, but then, considering some of the things that you have done, I would anticipate that you have some advanced skill, probably innately as well. Focus on just feeling yourself. Feeling around you." Asi's tone took on something more directive. "You have been able to detect magic used around you in the city, so focus on that now. But also focus on what you feel inside. There should be a distinct connection between the two."

I frowned. "I haven't been asked to do that before."

"It's probably not necessary for most of what you do, but in this case, you are looking to have some express control over it. And what I'm asking you to think about is how things feel to you. That's where you start."

"Wouldn't it be easier to do this someplace else?"

"Probably. But it's not like there isn't anything here."

I realized that she was right. There were other items in this workshop that I could take advantage of. There had to be several fabrications here, though I didn't know the purpose of them, but I could feel them. I could feel that strange resistance around me. It wasn't uncomfortable. That was one of the things that Waleith had taught me to detect, so that I could concentrate on what was dangerous and what was not.

"Once you have a sense of the energies around you, start to draw them in. It's going to be strange. Eventually, you will be able to draw energy in quite a bit more effectively, and you can start to focus on yourself. It's a skill that usually takes a few weeks of practice, though maybe you can do it faster."

Draw it in. I thought about the extent of the energies I felt around me, and then I began to pull inward. Doing so was strange. I noticed some gradient of power as I did so, and then there was an undercurrent of resistance, but there was also an absence of it.

And maybe having Asi with me helped me understand that. Asi had power, and I was able to detect it—the same way that I could detect Waleith's power—but she also had a strange emptiness around her.

And that strange emptiness was the same thing that I had around myself.

That was what I could follow and track of my own connection to power.

"All right," I whispered. "I can feel it as something of a void."

"Really? I don't feel it like that. Mine feels like a vibration. When you were describing the raw fabrication, I thought that it was similar."

"Waleith said that everybody feels things a little differently."

"That's what we were taught as well. And some of my instructors like to claim that it was tied to potency, but others thought that it wasn't. It was just a distinctness. An individual connection. And I guess it's probably a combination of both. Some people are stronger, and so they feel things differently, and other people have their own unique signature to what they can detect and how they can use it." She shrugged. "So it sort of all works together."

That made sense. "So I can take this emptiness and do what?"

"Well, if it's an emptiness, then you can try to

maneuver it, if that makes sense. You can push it directly. If you have enough control over it, you might even be able to push it into the sword, as the entire purpose of the fabrication is to store your connection."

Could I do that?

I thought about what Waleith had taught me about disrupting magic, though. And in the lessons that he had given me, I had needed to train so that I could disrupt magic, but it had been more than just training to disrupt magic. It had been training so that I could overpower magic, and so that I could find the dangers and carve through them. Why couldn't I do so now?

I concentrated on that technique. I could use some of what Waleith had taught me, some of what Asi was teaching me, and I could blend the two. And if I did it well enough, I had to believe that there would be some way to draw through my connection and store power in the blade as the fabrication.

Slowly I pushed, thinking about the fabrication not as something that I had to overpower but as something that I wanted to simply extend part of myself into. And when I did, the vibration within the blade began to still. Maybe having carried it only a short time had also done something, but it hadn't tamed it the way that Matherin had claimed I would need do. The only way that I could tame it was continuing to push that power out. And as I did that...

I felt more. There was no other way to describe it. Just that there was more in the blade. And it felt as if it was storing, concentrating, and... reacting.

"I feel something," I said.

"Do you? You're probably feeling me, and I'm guessing that any good physicker would have plenty of fabrications around him." Asi pointed to a few implements that were hanging on the walls. "I see two here, and there was the arcane lantern when we first came in, so that would have its own energy as well. And—"

"Not that," I said. Then again, I did feel her, and I was aware of fabrications, but I didn't think that was the source of what I was picking up on. No. What I had picked up on was the body in front of me. "I feel something here. With him."

"You do?" Asi stepped forward, and she drew her blade to hold it out over the body. "I don't. Maybe the sword is better at it, or maybe it's because it was truly raw when you took it and you connected to it yourself. Or maybe you're just stronger than me. I mean, you were chosen as the Queen's Blade, so I can't be too upset if you end up being stronger than me. A little disappointed—mostly in myself." She offered a faint smile.

"So if I can feel something here, maybe I can try it on some of the others."

"How many bodies have you kept around?"

"Well, the Investigators have a couple of them, though I don't know if they have left them where they found them."

I should have asked what they planned on doing with them.

"Let's go. Test this. And if you can track those bodies,

then hopefully you can track others, and maybe even intervene."

For the first time in a little while, I had a bit of hope.

Even if it was going to be difficult, maybe I could still do this job.

The door swung open, and Jamie paused, glancing from me to Asi, and then shook his head. "Didn't figure I'd see you here. I suppose I shouldn't be terribly surprised. You broke in?"

I motioned to my blade sheathed at my side. "Used the universal key."

He grunted. "I suppose that's to be expected. Waleith never did that, but then again, he didn't really come around here. Anyway, I tried to get word to you. I figured out something about our friend here."

"What?" I asked. I figured that Jamie was going to tell me something about the marks that he had detected, or maybe what had been drained off, or something along those lines.

"A name."

"What do you mean, a name?"

"The man is local. I went through his belongings. Honestly, Zaren, I would've figured that you would've done that yourself. He had a small medallion in his throat. Looked like he was trying to swallow it. I recognized it." Jamie went over to his desk and flipped the medallion over to me. "Recognize it?"

"No. But then I'm not from Busal City."

"It's a guild marker for the masons. They use it to mark their work," Asi said.

"Exactly. So I started asking around. Had a constable checking on it for me. Looking to see if anybody was missing, and that sort of thing. Figured you wouldn't mind." He watched me expectantly, as if to try to determine if I was upset.

I shook my head.

"And they got word. One of their men was missing. No word from him, but..." Jamie shrugged. "There you have it. Somebody local."

"I didn't think that the Anvil had anybody working locally," I said.

"He's not part of it."

"Or was he trying to be?" Asi suggested.

I frowned, staring at the dead man. "I guess I should have been looking into the identity of the others."

"You haven't been doing that?" Jamie asked.

"I've been a little preoccupied."

"Then let the constables do their job, Zaren. That's what they are for."

"I guess it's time to go see Harent. Want to come?" I asked Asi.

"I think I probably should."

Chapter Twenty-Five

We hadn't gone very far before I caught sight of Lijanna coming toward the palace. I hesitated and motioned to Asi to wait with me. She watched, frowning as she did, and then started to smirk.

"What?" I asked.

"It's just you. The look in your eyes. Someone you care about?"

"A colleague, of a sort."

"She's a little old for you, but I can see the appeal."

"A little old?" Lijanna might only be about five years older than me at most.

Asi laughed.

When Lijanna caught up to us, she nodded to me, then looked at Asi as if sizing her up. "I was sent to find you, Joha."

"You were sent?" I had wondered if she was coming to discuss training again, as I really needed to continue to work on my fighting skills, but the suddenness of her appearance and her slight agitation suggested that there was something else. "Let me guess. More bodies?"

She offered a hint of a shrug. "You guessed right."

"Three?"

"Exactly." Lijanna turned to Asi, sticking her hand out. "We haven't met. Lijanna Holins."

"And I'm Asi Lano."

"Another Blade?" Lijanna frowned. "Interesting. Well, seems Joha has decided that he needs a little extra help."

"Men," Asi said.

"You were saying?" I said, interrupting the two in the middle of their banter. "More bodies?"

"That's right. Harent wanted me to bring you. He's waiting."

"Good. I have to talk to him, anyway."

"He's not in any trouble, is he?"

"No. You seemed almost hopeful, though."

"Not hopeful. I wouldn't mind if you give him a hard time, though." She turned serious. "This has started to become a problem. We keep finding bodies, and there is no evidence of who killed them or how they killed them. And they are all the same. It's got people within the constabulary worked up, as you can imagine. We don't usually deal with this kind of thing. This is the domain of the Blades. But even then, we aren't accustomed to running into this sort of problem." She breathed out heavily. "How are you keeping calm?"

"I'm trying not to overreact," I said.

We headed north and slightly east. I had been trying

to figure out if there was a pattern around the city, but it seemed random.

When I said as much to Lijanna, she nodded. "The Captain thought the same thing. Started looking into it, even going so far as to pull out a map to record where these bodies have been found. He figured that he could help you." She grunted. "Now you have him chasing shadows on your behalf."

"Not exactly shadows," Asi said.

"Whatever is doing this is a shadow," Lijanna said. "So regardless, he has us jumping at shadows." She let out a sigh. "We don't much care for this, Zaren."

I understood what she was getting at.

Deal with it. And not just deal with it, but deal with it quickly.

"I'm going to resolve this," I said. "Has Harent picked up on anything?"

"Such as?"

I filled her in on how one of the most recent victims was a local.

Lijanna frowned. "No. But they didn't really have anything on them that we could use to identify them, and short of searching through any missing person reports—and that's not the sort of thing that we get a lot of—we wouldn't really have a way of tracking them down."

"We were lucky with one," I said. "He had a guild marker on him."

"Strange that he managed to keep that."

"Apparently, it was in his mouth," Asi said.

Lijanna was quiet for a moment. "You think he put it there to try to alert someone?"

I shrugged. "None of the other victims had any identifying features. They were all about the same. Dressed pretty similarly, plainly, and all had the same type of injury. None had any personal belongings on them."

"You're starting to sound like a constable," Lijanna said. "Careful. Harent might try to pull you into the constabulary."

"I think I'm serving as I need to." At least she wasn't accusing me of being responsible for this, so there was that.

We kept going, and I started to focus on the sword. I was curious. Having started to test whether I could detect anything, I had begun to recognize a faint sensation around the last body. Would I be able to do the same thing with these new bodies? If so, I might be able to identify the power—and perhaps even track it.

Doing that could give me a chance to interrupt another attack.

A chance, but only that.

Asi glanced over. "We are really going to need to pull Waleith in. You need to try to reach him some way."

That had been my concern, but ever since Waleith had found me, there had been no evidence of him. It was as if he had disappeared again, though I sincerely doubted that he would have disappeared one more time, especially considering the threats that were now present in the city. He might trust that I could serve as the Queen's Blade, but he also would—or at least, should—

feel a sense of obligation to Busal City, and to ensuring that the threats were dealt with.

"I can go back to the palace," I said. "Try to get word out to him. I did once, but I don't know where he is. He's probably conducting his own investigation."

"Sounds like him," Asi said. "But in this case, I think there is strength in numbers."

"You're starting to see things my way," I said.

"I can see the appeal," she admitted. "It's not easy."

"Would the two of you just stop?" Lijanna said. "We're getting close."

I drew my blade and squeezed the hilt. That elicited a strange reaction from Lijanna, but her expression changed when Asi drew her blade.

"Something going on here?" Lijanna asked, starting to reach for her own weapon.

"I'm testing something," I said. "I don't detect anything, but I want to see if I can."

"That's right," Lijanna said, nodding, mostly to herself. "You weren't able to detect anything before. Has that changed? I see you carrying a sword, which is new for you."

"I am hopeful that the sword will permit me to detect things that I wouldn't have been able to detect otherwise. I don't know, though."

"Just give me enough of a heads-up if I need to be ready," she said.

"I think that by the time the bodies appear, the threat has passed."

Lijanna relaxed. "That's what we thought as well, but then you go reaching for your weapon, and..." She shook. It was strange seeing Lijanna shivering like that, especially given how strong a person she was. "Like I said, it has us all shaken a bit."

I really had to deal with this quickly.

I didn't know how many more times people were going to be slaughtered, nor did I know the purpose behind the increasing frequency, but whatever was happening was starting to intensify.

We turned a corner, and the street was empty for this time of day. There were quite a few constables stationed along the street, so it wouldn't take much to dissuade people from traveling through here. And there was something else. At first I just thought that it was the humidity of the day, though it wasn't really a hot day. Gradually I began to detect the undercurrent and started to feel how this energy was beginning to build, pressing inward, as if it were going to push upon me. That was strange, but stranger still was the fact that it seemed to echo within my blade.

"I can feel it," I said.

Asi looked over. "Good. Keep testing it."

"You detect something?" Lijanna asked. "Anything that we need to be concerned about?"

"I don't think so. I think I'm actually detecting what happened here."

She was quiet.

We ended up in a small courtyard between three

buildings. Most of the buildings were newer around here, except for on this street. These buildings were a bit more run-down, with the stone cracking, but there was some other undercurrent that lingered within the stone itself that left me with a very different awareness here. I could feel the stone pushing on me, as if it were warning me.

That was odd, but not nearly as odd as the way that my blade had started to vibrate.

It was quite different from how the blade had vibrated when I had first acquired it as a raw fabrication. This seemed to be reacting to me in a way, and it seemed to be building. I wasn't exactly sure how, but I detected some element to it that I had not detected in the past.

The bodies were as I had seen before. Three of them, lined up in a row, and this time there was no pillar. There was, however, a small stone, which made me wonder if it was serving as the pillar.

"Something is different here," I said. "They don't have the same fabrication." I made my way around the courtyard until I saw Harent waiting. He approached me. "How long ago did you detect them?"

"We didn't detect them," he said. "They were reported."

"Anybody see anything?"

He glanced from me to Asi and then back down at the bodies. "No one saw anything. That's the disturbing thing about all of this, isn't it? It's one thing for nobody to see anything at night. I can deal with that. But for nobody to see anything during the daytime—and I have to believe that this happened in the daylight—is another thing altogether. Can you imagine the kind of power that would be involved in that?"

And the way that he said "power" suggested to me the exact kind of power that I was well aware of. Magic.

"I can," Asi said.

"I still don't think Garridan is involved in this," I said.

"You don't think so, but what if he's using you to find targets?"

I frowned. I didn't think Garridan was involved in this like that. It had seemed to me that he had wanted to help, but there was a possibility that he would betray me, as he had on Erantor.

I turned my attention to the three bodies, still holding my blade. Strangely, as I swept around the courtyard, I felt that undercurrent of power, but I felt it more strongly near the stone that was situated at the center of this space. I approached it and rested my blade on top of it.

"What are you detecting?" Asi asked.

"Something is here."

"Just don't go shattering anything again, Zaren," Harent said. "We don't need to have blood exploding all over the place."

I started to smile. "I don't intend to. I'm just testing."

"Well, be careful with how you test."

He wasn't wrong. I did need to be careful here.

There was a pressure against me, a heaviness that lingered in the air, but there was also a faint emptiness here as I approached the stone. It reminded me of the emptiness inside myself. Odd, but it was unique, and it felt familiar.

"Why don't you see if you can detect something here as well?" I said to Asi.

Rather than shattering the stone, I tested the bodies, holding the blade just above them, but not attempting to push down into them. Even standing, I could tell that they had the same injuries, the incisions along the neck, and there was probably no blood in them, either.

"Lijanna says you identified one of the victims," Harent said, getting close.

"Just one. A local. Makes you think that maybe they are all local."

"Well, you have been working with the belief that this was all tied to some sort of ritual, right?"

"Something along those lines," I said. "But I also think that there has to be more to it. I just don't know what."

Harent snorted. "How many bodies is this now?"

"In total? Let's see. There were the three that we found—or you brought me to. There were three that the Investigators found. Another three that the Investigators found. These three. That puts us up to twelve. And then there was whatever was happening outside the city that we interrupted. One of them was dead, but I think he was a part of the group performing the ritual."

"Thirteen bodies. The number is starting to get a little high."

I didn't want to say that people died in the city all the time, and the constables didn't get quite as excited about them. Most of the time, when people died, there wasn't some supernatural element to it. And I understood. Harent was uneasy, the same way that Lijanna was uneasy, and this was Harent's way of telling me to deal with things.

"The frequency is increasing," I said. "But I'm hopeful that we have a plan in place."

"A plan? That's where we are? Come on, Joha. We have to do more than just have a plan."

"I can barely detect what is happening here. And up until not that long ago, I couldn't detect it. So you'll have to give me a little grace here."

Harent was quiet. "Sacred Souls. I'm trying to give grace, but what do we know that they are even doing?"

"I don't know."

"Exactly. We don't know what they are doing. So what happens if this becomes an even more dangerous attack, and they start hitting people a little more renowned? I mean, we've dealt with some crazy things here lately, but this one is making me far more uncomfortable than some of the others."

I didn't want to tell him that the others had involved him, not directly. I had gotten him drawn into the arrest of the councilor, but that was it. I had been the one to deal with the aelith powder. I had been the one to deal with Talina. I had been the Blade.

And now what was I?

I was failing.

And I was starting to question why things had started to fall apart ever since I had come to the city. I understood that was coincidence, but it was still a strange, and dangerous, coincidence. And I didn't like it.

"I'm going to get this resolved, Harent."

"I hope so. And I hope you do it before too many more people have to die."

Chapter Twenty-Six

Time was starting to run short. That was the thought that kept marching through my head. So I patrolled the city.

I was exhausted, having spent every bit of my waking time marching through the city, testing for anything that would remind me of the Daughter of Inkasa power, keeping my blade mostly in its sheath, not wanting to startle or scare anybody, but every so often, I would need to unsheathe it, because I would need to have the benefit that the blade could offer.

But I had not found anything.

Asi had returned, though I sensed her own uncertainty.

Both of us had been looking for Garridan while also hunting for anything that might be unusual. There had been no further attack. But then, it had been less than a day since the last one.

I was starting to think that the time might not be

quite such an issue as I had initially believed when I detected something.

I had reached the harbor. It was quiet, and I enjoyed looking out at the water, watching the ships as they moved in and out, and just having the opportunity to detect the flow and potential of power that came in through the city. Not only that, but there was something about the harbor that struck me as peaceful. Maybe that was why Garridan had said to go to the water, that it was calming. Maybe he knew that I would need something like that. That would surprise me, if so. I still couldn't shake the feeling that he was not involved directly, but there was that possibility that he had done something, especially with what I had seen from him, what I had felt from him.

I couldn't deny that kind of magic, especially given that the kind of magic that he had was something that I simply could not explain.

So I focused on that part of me that gave me the ability of a Blade. I was testing and detecting the energies around me, and trying to extend my senses outward as Asi had instructed, when I noticed a faint ripple.

That was the only way that I could describe it. A ripple.

In a way, it reminded me of what I detected when I was around Asi, but it also reminded me of what I had felt near that stone. I hadn't been attuned to anything when it came to the pillars, so I didn't know if it was the same sensation. I didn't think so, however.

But now there was something.

And the timing...

I couldn't just stand by. I couldn't just do nothing.

Which meant that I was going to need to chase this down.

But chasing it down could be difficult, not to mention risky. At least, it would be risky doing so alone.

I didn't know if I would have time to track down Asi, but did I need to?

She had proven to me that she had the ability to detect what I could. She could detect the power of a Blade. And if she could do that, then that was what I needed to take advantage of.

I focused, drawing on my blade, drawing on the power that I could feel, and then there was nothing.

Emptiness.

I waited, but I continued to probe. I still focused on the rippling, but I did not detect it as I had before.

But I knew where it had been. I could still feel it.

I looked across the bridge. I didn't want to linger. But I wanted Asi's help. Not only that, but I thought that I was going to need it, as I had no idea how dangerous this was going to be, or if I could handle this on my own.

I was a Blade, wasn't I?

That didn't mean that I had to work alone, though.

I started toward the strange sensation. I moved carefully, but I paused at the Investigator station, opened the door, and caught Byron, who immediately jumped to his feet.

"Something's happening, so gather the others, and be

ready. I don't know what you might need to do, but I want us to be prepared."

"Should I come with you?"

"Not right now. This is something that I need to do as the Queen's Blade, but I do want to make sure that you are ready. Can you do that for me?"

"Of course, Blade," he said, and then he almost saluted.

I hurried on. I hadn't gone very far before I caught sight of a constable. He was a younger man, paired up with another, who was a little bit older than him, both of them wearing their crisp constable uniforms, short swords at their sides, and they eyed me suspiciously as I approached.

"My name is Zaren—"

"We know who you are, Blade," the nearest of them said. "The Captain told us to keep an eye out for you. Said you might need help."

I nodded. "I don't know what's going on, but I detected something. And I want you to send word to the Captain. Keep your people away until I tell you that it's safe."

"You want the constables to stay clear?"

"If it is what I'm afraid it is, then I think you need to."

He nodded. Then he looked at his partner, and the two of them hurried away.

That was all that I could do. At least for now.

I still had to hope, though. I had to hope that I was right. I didn't want to be right, but I needed to be. I couldn't let this keep going. The sensation was not there any longer, but somehow I knew exactly where it was drawing me.

Another older section of the city. The remains of a temple were nearby, crumbling and faded, set off to the side and left to fall into disrepair, though no one had any interest in removing those remains. There weren't too many who followed that faith any longer, but it was considered bad luck—and probably sacrilege—to risk interfering with the ruins.

This was where I had detected something.

As I got closer, I started to focus, holding out my blade.

And then I detected the strange buzzing once again.

It was as if the blade was reacting to me, as if it knew what I wanted to find, and it was trying to show me how to get there. That was new for me.

Then I heard a grunt.

I had started forward when someone called my name from behind.

I spun, swinging my blade up, and for a moment, given the strange void of resistance that I detected, I thought that it might be Waleith. It was not.

It was Asi.

She was racing toward me, blade outstretched.

"I felt what you did," she said. "It was strange. It was like you were trying to signal something. I figured that couldn't be coincidental, so I came looking for you, but then you were gone. And now here you are."

I raised a finger to my lips, cutting her off.

I pointed to the temple. "I felt something. Don't know

what it is, but we might have gotten here in time. All the other places where these rituals have taken place have been old," I said, realizing it then. Even the very first one had been like that.

"We were taught at the compound that certain places hold power. Maybe that's the reason." Asi took a breath as she looked around. "So it's just going to be the two of us?"

"We don't know what's here."

"You know that it might be them. Do you think that you are ready for it? Should you try to call Waleith?"

I shrugged. "Haven't seen him much, though I've tried. And since you detected what I did, I have to believe that he would have as well."

She was quiet for a long moment. "Sacred Souls," she muttered.

"Ready?"

"I suppose."

We stepped forward and reached the low, moss-covered wall that surrounded the temple grounds.

I rested my hand on the wall, felt a faint undercurrent of trembling energy within it, leading me to think that there was some residual power in the wall itself. I looked for an entrance. But if there was an entrance, somebody would be watching it, I suspected.

So I jumped, grabbing for the top of the wall. Then I heaved myself up.

"A hand," Asi called up to me.

I reached down while craning my neck to look over the

other side. The temple grounds were overgrown, like so many other places in the city were. There were weeds, vines, and even a few scraggly trees. Once Asi had reached the top of the wall, she crouched there for a moment before jumping down on the other side. I followed her with a much louder thud on the hard-packed ground than she had made.

"Anything?"

"I feel something in the wall," I mused.

"Like I said, these old places have power."

"I think I need to know more about these places. And other magic. When this is over, maybe we can start to put ourselves through our own kind of training."

"I'd like that."

And I would as well. I enjoyed working with Asi. There was a practicality to her.

"Which way?" she asked.

I swept my blade forward, keeping it low, keeping myself crouched down, as I carved through the tall grass. I felt the grass react to the blade, which left me wondering how much power was actually here. But then I felt the same emptiness, along with the ripple that I had detected. It was far more acute now than it had been. I pointed. We moved forward, and once again I heard a grunt.

In a small clearing just up ahead, there were three people. The sacrifices, I suspected, given their clothing. I didn't see a pillar, or the stone fabrication they had to use, but there was something else present. I noticed the shadowy shapes of five others, and two of them were near us, with their backs turned away, but they were swaying around.

But I had heard something.

"Anvil," I said, pointing forward. "The ritual."

Asi pressed her lips together into a tight frown. "So, what do we do?"

"Let's take them down, and then we can move forward."

She nodded.

Asi branched off, going to the other figure, while I crept forward. The man facing away from me must have had a fabrication on him, because he radiated a bit of power. He was oblivious to my presence, and I grabbed him by the legs and yanked quickly, pushing his face down so that he couldn't shout. I rolled his head to the side, and his eyes widened ever so slightly.

I held him down until he stopped fighting. Then I checked him over for fabrications, but I didn't find anything. Nothing. That was odd.

It had felt like he had had something.

I pulled up his sleeve, looking for tattoos, and I noticed marks similar to those on the woman that we had captured.

Interesting. Tattoos, but he didn't strike me as a Daughter of Inkasa.

I dragged him back. Asi reached me, having dragged her victim back as well.

"Anvil," I said, "but he has markings like those of a Daughter of Inkasa."

"Same with this one."

"So maybe they're working together."

"Maybe. It still doesn't make a lot of sense. Something doesn't feel quite right."

"I get it. I don't know why, but I get it."

I crawled forward again. The three sacrifices—and that was how I thought of them—remained where they were.

Then I heard a familiar voice.

"Just release them, and we can make this easy."

Waleith?

I motioned to Asi, who frowned, but she followed me as we kept moving forward. If Waleith was here, then we didn't need to be quite as concerned.

I crawled forward. I saw Waleith facing someone who I couldn't see but who was dressed in a familiar dark cloak, with a familiar slender staff.

The woman.

Wasn't she one of the Anvil? Or was she a Daughter of Inkasa?

Something didn't feel quite right.

"Let's take out the others," I said. "Then we can figure out what else is going on here. Waleith can keep her occupied."

Asi nodded.

We crawled around the perimeter of the clearing, staying low, while feeling for the strange energy that was here. I couldn't help but feel there was more at play here than I had known.

What was going on, and how had Waleith found this?

Because he was a true Blade, and I was still learning what that meant.

I reached the next Anvil operative who was standing guard. I dragged the man down, but he was better prepared. He was strong, and he started to struggle, making too much noise. I drove my elbow into his throat and then dropped my weight down on him, crushing him.

But he had already sounded something of an alarm.

I crouched, looking around.

And then half a dozen other Anvil guards started crawling forward, moving through the shrubs. I didn't have to test them to know that they probably all had the same markings that this one had, and they all probably had some power that they could wield.

I just hoped that Asi could handle them well.

Chapter Twenty-Seven

Everything seemed to lurch forward all at once.

The other Anvil guards were moving forward, and the woman swung her staff in place, creating a soft, steady whistle that rippled outward. That wasn't what I had detected, was it? I had felt something different.

And she stood in front of the three sacrifices almost protectively.

That was odd as well. All of this was strange.

Somewhere nearby, I could hear Asi fighting.

And then I decided to take it upon myself to just step forward. I might as well draw attention and get this over with.

I did so, and Waleith flicked his gaze to me, shaking his head.

"Can't let you have all the fun," I said.

Several Anvil guards converged on me.

They were large, strong, fast—faster than I had expected.

But now that I had the sword, I felt far more comfortable than I had been when fighting with the shorter blade. I suspected that Waleith would be displeased that I needed a sword to feel more confident in my fighting style, but there was simply something to be said about having that weapon.

One of the men lunged, but I brought the blade up, slicing him through the belly, and he crumpled. Another came from behind me, and I brought the blade down, swinging in a sharp, controlled strike that caught him in the leg, and he collapsed. I darted forward, heading toward the next Anvil guard, but Asi was already there, her blade a blur as she jumped, striking straight at his chest, and drove it into him.

Then I turned.

The woman with the staff was spinning it with a ferocity. She darted toward Waleith, and he deflected her attack, once, twice, and then a third time as he managed to keep her from getting too close. Each blow seemed stronger, faster than the last.

And then she caught him on the leg.

I knew how much a strike like that hurt. I had felt it myself.

He stumbled, and then he let out a strangled grunt.

The woman was there, driving the staff down.

I jumped.

I still wasn't exactly sure of the nature of her power, but it had to be considerable.

I felt something this time. When she spun, there was a strange, uneasy pressure against my blade. It caused the blade to vibrate. I swept my weapon from low to high, thinking that I could carve through any power. And I felt the energy that she had used split away.

Her staff came apart.

She hesitated, spinning away, and drove one end of the staff down toward Waleith, and then she danced back toward me, bringing the staff back together.

"Interesting," she said, regarding me.

I didn't give her a chance.

Waleith started to get up, but she slipped closer to him and spun her now-intact staff back down, catching him on the shoulder. He grunted, his arm going limp as he was getting up, and dropped his blade. He backed away, and she lunged in, readying another strike, but I was there, already swinging my blade, and I caught her on the staff.

It was far more effective fighting with the sword against her staff than it had been with the short blade. So as it swung forward, I caught the staff and managed to cleave it into separate pieces again.

All around me, I could still hear the sound of fighting. Asi was battling.

The woman turned toward me. She was quiet. Then she moved.

She looked like something out of the night, moving so quickly, so fluidly, that I could scarcely keep up. She was in one place, and then she was in another. Then she was right in front of me. I barely had a chance to bring my sword up. The staff swung once, twice, catching me on either side, leaving pain just rocketing through me.

Not only pain but some uncomfortable—and impossibly harmful—power. I could feel the way it rippled inside me. I felt some part of me rebelling, the part of me that was the Blade. I recognized what she had done and immediately felt some part of my own energy beginning to expand outward, as if it was trying to combat the effect of her attack.

I staggered, falling back.

She turned away from me, away from Waleith, seemingly unconcerned by both of us. And she headed toward the three sacrifices.

There was a small fabrication resting on the ground.

She lifted it, and then she turned to the others.

I couldn't even move. I stayed frozen, everything within me cold, terror filling me as I worried about what she was going to do, and I was not at all sure that I could do anything to stop it. I had never been around this kind of power before.

No. That wasn't true. I had been around this kind of power before. Garridan had this kind of power, though it was different. He had held Asi with this kind of power, and he had done so in a way that I had not been able to fathom. And what this woman was doing now was so overwhelming that it struck me as too much for me to bear.

How could I hope to counter anything like that?

I might be a Blade, but I was neither trained nor equipped to handle this kind of power. How could I?

I struggled. I needed to get moving. I needed to get

up. Yet I could not. Something inside me was not reacting the way that it needed to. I tried.

The woman turned the fabrication, twisting it in her hand, and then she brought it up to her face.

The darkness in it began to swirl.

And something about it changed, rippling, flowing.

It flowed out, running along her hand, running up her neck, and the strange, inky darkness began to slide and slither, as if alive.

Some part of her seemed to swell, changing, almost. I had not seen that before. This ink, or this fabrication, or whatever this was, was changing her.

She brought the fabrication over, and I waited for her to attack the others.

But then everything froze.

I couldn't move. My mind worked, but my body did not. All around me, everything felt still, quiet. The woman with the staff turned, moving slowly. I didn't even know how she could do so.

And I understood what was happening.

Garridan was here.

"That's enough." Garridan's voice rang out.

It sounded musical. Everything about him sounded musical, I realized. I hadn't pieced it together, but the man was a minstrel, after all. He came into the clearing. His every movement seemed to add to that musical quality, as if his footsteps were a march, his voice notes that were joining in that march, and even the way that the fabric of his clothing rustled added to it.

"You have what you came for. You can leave."

"A price must be paid," the woman said.

"The price *has* been paid."

"The price must be paid."

She held her hand out, and there was a strange, suppressed cry.

And then I saw something that I doubted I would ever forget, assuming that I survived this. The blood that erupted from one of the sacrifices—and I couldn't even see who it was—simply hovered in the air, drawn toward the strange fabrication. It swirled, and then it moved downward. Toward the pillar. I didn't need to look over to see that the person had a perfectly made incision, and there was probably no splatter of blood. This was the sacrifice?

For what purpose?

"Enough," Garridan said.

He strode forward casually. For whatever reason, he still had his instrument strapped to his back, and he didn't look like any sort of deadly assassin, but the sheer power that he wielded around us made him seem like one.

"The sacrifice must be made. The debt must be paid. Blood for blood."

"The sacrifice has been paid," Garridan said again. "The others were not involved. They were just meant to feed."

I didn't know if the comment was for her, for me, or for clarification. The others? So one of them was meant for something, but the others... Strange. I didn't know what was going on here.

"The sacrifice—"

Garridan move forward.

I had thought the woman moved quickly. But Garridan simply seemed to go from one place to the next, as if I had blinked and he had simply moved during that time.

He had a blade in either hand that I hadn't even seen him wielding. He had them pressed up to the woman, who had her own staff that she'd somehow managed to reform but did not move.

"I give you this last warning," Garridan said.

"Your warnings mean nothing."

"You do not want me for an enemy."

She regarded him.

I ignored their strange confrontation. This woman had been killing people around the city. But now she was here, and I had my chance.

I was a Blade, wasn't I?

She had attacked me. My body had reacted, and I had survived.

That was the key here, wasn't it?

I had found her. I had uncovered what she was doing.

I could stop this.

I focused, drawing upon my power, feeling it blooming, and let that energy explode inside me.

Then I could move.

I turned, looking around the clearing.

All around me, some of the power seemed to have faded. Was that because of what I had done? It didn't matter. Other Anvil guards were starting to move.

I took that moment, charged past Garridan, and reached a pair of guards that were in front of Asi, and I drove my blade into them before they could react. Asi stirred and lunged, driving her blade into the neck of another.

There were only three remaining. How had we gotten through all of them?

We probably hadn't. Garridan must have taken out some of the others. He was a Guild assassin, after all.

"Let's finish this off," I said.

"I'm not even sure that we can," Asi muttered. She shook herself. "I've never felt anything like that. I was aware, but I couldn't do anything."

"Well, you can do something now."

We hurriedly dispatched the other Anvil guards, and then we moved forward. Waleith lay unmoving, though I wasn't sure how injured he might be. He was going to need help. Jamie was not going to be pleased.

The woman and Garridan simply stood across from each other.

"She's coming with us," I said. "She's going to the prison."

"Your prison couldn't hold her," Garridan said. "Much like your prison couldn't hold Talina."

"It held her."

"It held her because she chose to be there. I don't know what you did to capture her in the first place," he went on, without looking over at me, "though I suspect it was tied to your innate abilities. But you would not have been able to hold her indefinitely. And she became a target. The item that our friend here now holds carries with it the ability to trap Daughter of Inkasa power."

"So you knew that she was there."

"I knew something was amiss. It was what drew me here. First the aelith powder, then reports of the Daughter of Inkasa. Activity like that should not have been possible, but for a very distinct way."

"So Talina was helping."

"She would not have helped. Not like that. She would not dare make an enemy of the Daughters of Inkasa. She is powerful, but not that powerful."

"So are you saying she was used?"

"I do not know." He took a deep breath. "You have what you came for. Leave this place."

"Or what?"

Garridan squeezed his eyes shut for a moment. "Or I will place it under my protection."

The woman seemed to consider that more than anything else.

"You do not want to do this."

"I have already done it."

The strange pressure continued to build around me, and I looked over to see that Asi was once again frozen in place. Garridan had reasserted his power somehow. I could still move, though I wasn't sure if that was because of my strength or because he had excluded me.

I stepped toward the Daughter of Inkasa. She regarded me, and then she backed away, spinning her staff. She melted into the shadows before disappearing.

Garridan stared for a moment, letting out a long, frustrated sigh.

"What is this all about?" I asked.

"It's about a play for power. There was an attempt to claim the power of the Daughters of Inkasa, by those who do not fully understand all that it entails."

"So the Anvil were not working with them?"

"From what I can tell, they were trying to take some dangerous power they couldn't completely control, and it caught up to them."

"What do you mean, it caught up to them?"

Garridan shook his head. "It takes considerable effort for a Daughter of Inkasa to even come here. It takes considerable effort for her to stay here. And the fact that she did suggests that this was designed." He let out a breath. "She has grown stronger. I suppose you saw that."

"I saw..." I shrugged, looking around. It was odd the way that Asi was just standing fixated. Was she even aware? Waleith was still lying motionless. The others were dead, I suspected. "I don't know what I saw. But the first time that I came across her, I was able to deflect her attack."

"Deflect it. Yes. But not stop it. And I don't know if you would be able to now. She will only have grown stronger. That is the mistake that the Anvil made. They did not understand the power they were using. They did not understand the consequences of it. And they did not truly know how to hold it." He shook his head. "And thankfully, you have dealt with it."

I wasn't entirely sure that I had dealt with anything.

At this point, I felt like there were still more questions than answers.

"So the Anvil threat is gone?"

"Gone, yes. Perhaps it will return, as it is clear that they are making an attempt at power they should not have, but this particular threat should be no longer."

"And what of you?"

"I will no longer be needed here." Garridan glanced at me. "The city has its Blade. Well, Blades." He glanced at Asi. "Continue with your preparations, and I will be in touch if another exchange is necessary. And the same should be said for you."

He started away, and I tried to go after him, but the moment that I did, I found myself locked in place. By the time I managed to get free, Garridan was gone.

Asi shook, letting out a frustrated cry.

"Now what?" she asked.

"Well, now we see if there are any survivors, and we question them."

She looked around. "Do you think there are any survivors?"

"Well, maybe not. And we need to get Waleith some help."

Chapter Twenty-Eight

Jamie was most displeased when I brought Waleith to him.

"Why does it seem like my work has doubled since you came into the city?"

"I'd like to say that I'm not responsible for this, but I was a part of this fight."

The constables were pleased that it seemed the threat was over, though Harent had made it clear that he would believe it when he saw it, and the Investigators were happy to know that they had not needed to get involved in something quite so deadly. Jos had been taken a bit aback by the sheer number of dead Anvil operatives, and he had looked at me with a new expression. I hoped it wasn't fear, as we did still have to work together.

"Would you care to tell me what this was about?"

"I'm not sure."

"You got into a fight, but you don't know what it was about?"

I looked at Waleith. "We stopped the attack. I think the Anvil are dealt with. The other aspect of the attack is done. Asi has returned to her side of the city…"

"You seem disappointed."

"I can't deny that it's nice to have somebody to work with. A partner."

"I can't, either," Jamie muttered, shaking his head. "You have made it a little bit more entertaining here, I have to admit. Anyway, I will see what I can do for Waleith."

I thanked him and then headed out to stand on the palace grounds for a moment, looking all around. Something felt off. I couldn't quite place what it was, but maybe it was just the energy of the palace itself that I had started to feel.

I thought about what Garridan had said.

The power of the fabrications.

I hurried back to my home, grabbed the fabrication that I had found outside the city, and then hurried back to the palace grounds, getting a strange look from the guards that had seen me running away and then returning. This was something that I should have done before now. A loose end that I should have dealt with, but I'd been distracted by everything else.

By the time I got to Matherin's workshop, I was slightly breathless. I pounded on the door, and he pulled it open quickly this time.

He looked up at me, frowning. "What is it now? Are you dissatisfied with what I made?"

"No. The blade actually works great, but that's not

why I'm here. I wanted to ask your opinion about this fabrication. I should've brought it to you sooner, but I have been a little distracted."

I held the orb fabrication out for him. Matherin stared at it for a moment before waving for me to come in. I joined him in the workshop. He had a pair of long, slender blades resting on his workbench, with strangely curved cross guards and delicate hilts.

"Are those for Asi?"

"I thought that she would benefit from them. A different type of weapon, for a different type of Blade. They aren't quite ready, though they will be soon enough. Is that why you came?"

"I can let her deal with her own affairs. Although she's going to be quite pleased. She has been waiting for them."

"Blades take time to fabricate, Zaren. I realize that you do not know this, as you *are* relatively new to your position. Anyway, where did you get my fabrication?"

"This is yours?" I asked, pausing.

"Yes. It has distinct features to it. I made about a dozen of them, maybe more than that, several years ago. Though this one has some modifications." He held it up to the light, turning it in place, before setting it back down on his workbench. He picked up a long chisel and then a hammer.

Before I had a chance to say anything, he tapped the fabrication, and it split open. It looked like nothing more than a broken rock. There were some silvery lines that had flecks of green and gold inside, but altogether it looked fairly innocuous.

"That's it?" I asked.

"You cannot imagine the level of work that goes into making such a device as this."

I couldn't imagine, but I couldn't help but feel I needed to. But not yet. First I wanted to better understand what this fabrication was, and why it was here.

"So you made it, but somebody changed it."

I thought about the modifications he had mentioned, and then about how it must have been altered with whatever had been used to hold the Daughter of Inkasa power.

"Fabrications are like that, of course. Your own fabrication is going to look quite different now compared to when I gave it to you only a few days ago. And in a year, it's going to look different still. Time and purpose and use change such things."

"Can fabrications be used for more than one purpose?"

"Can your blade?"

"Yes."

"Then the answer is yes." Matherin seemed pleased with that, and then he picked up the fragments, held them up, and frowned at them. "There was an attack on the city a few years ago," he went on. "Nothing of much significance, but the Blade at the time came to me wanting a way to hold the power. Claimed that it needed to be contained, else it might expand into a more dangerous battle." He breathed out. "His death was unfortunate."

"So not Waleith," I said.

"No. Though they were friends, of course. Ihaned was the one to identify Waleith. Apparently, he came from some small town."

I hadn't known any of that. "Which town was that?"

"You'll have to ask Waleith, though he doesn't like to talk about his background all that much. He claims that his life—and his service—began when he came to the kingdom." Matherin snorted. "Most Blades have felt that way, though perhaps not you."

"Because I'm different."

"Yes. Not in a bad way. I've enjoyed your tenure. I have been a little busier, though I cannot complain about that. I enjoy the work I do."

Something still didn't sit right with me. "So you made these fabrications?"

"I did. And like I said, about a dozen similar ones."

"And you can't tell what has changed within them?"

"I think I could if I had enough time, but this sort of thing is a little difficult to do, as over time, the fabrication evolves. As you have seen, and as I have shared. What is the issue?"

"No—"

I felt something. It was subtle.

I turned, frowning. There was the distinct sense of Daughter of Inkasa power. That was what I had detected before, and now I was still attuned to it.

"Zaren?"

"I need to check on something. Look into that, would you?"

"Of course. I doubt that I'm going to be able to uncover anything. As you know, these change."

I didn't know, but I didn't know that it mattered. At this point, the only thing that mattered was finding the reason that this sense was building. Uncovering why and where.

There was something odd about it.

Familiar.

I hurried around the palace grounds, my blade unsheathed as I tested for the source. It just didn't make sense. Why would there still be something here? Unless the Daughter of Inkasa woman had returned.

She had given off a different sensation.

I kept moving.

I checked in the palace and didn't see or feel anything.

Where was it?

Panic began to set in. I could not fail at this.

Then I detected the location.

Jamie's workshop.

I darted toward it, reached for the door, found it locked, and hurriedly jammed my much shorter blade into it. It came open. I was glad that I had tested the lock before, so I knew that my blade would work. Once I stepped inside, I swept my gaze around and saw Jamie slumped over, though there was no sign of obvious injury.

I hurried over to him. "What happened?"

"I don't know. I was turned away from Waleith, and somebody hit me."

"Could it have been Waleith?"

"Why would he have hit me?"

I shook my head, not certain how to answer that. Not yet.

Though I was starting to make a connection.

"I don't know."

The strange sense of that Daughter of Inkasa energy continued to move.

And it was moving beneath me.

"You have some sort of tunnel network here, don't you?"

"How do you know about that?"

"Answer the question, please. This is important. You do, don't you?"

"I do. There are only a few who know about it. It gives me easier access to the Queen." Jamie flicked his gaze around, rubbing his knuckles into his eyes. "I try not to use it, as we don't need the secret getting out, but from time to time, it is more convenient."

Most of these buildings were probably connected. "Show me."

"Zaren—"

"Show me," I snapped.

Jamie regarded me, saw the blade that I had still in hand, and then nodded.

He guided me to one of his cabinets, where he tapped on a section that I hadn't ever paid much attention to. The entire cabinet slid to the side, revealing a closed door.

He started fishing out a key, but I stepped forward. "Don't bother."

The smaller blade pressed up against the lock caused it to swing open.

"Do you need me to guide you?"

"I don't know. Does this lead straight to the Queen?"

"Not straight to her, but it *can* lead to her."

"Then you're going to have to show me. I need to move quickly. She's in danger."

That seemed to change things for Jamie, and he made me follow, pausing to close the cabinet and the door behind us. I was about to tell him that we didn't have time, but I sensed that would probably not go over well. He hurried to the tunnel and then picked up an arcane lantern, which he used to guide us forward.

We turned a few different corners, headed down a set of stairs, back up another set of stairs. All the while I was continuing to focus on the Daughter of Inkasa power lingering here, too potent. It should not be here.

"Care to tell me what this is about?"

"Well, either Waleith went after the one responsible, or he *is* the one responsible," I said. I hated even saying that out loud.

"Waleith?"

"It's complicated, but things are starting to come together."

"What sort of things?"

"Later," I said.

Jamie watched me for a moment and then nodded. "I'm going to hold you to that."

We passed a few more side halls, but Jamie kept going. And the sense of power began to intensify.

Finally he pointed at a set of stairs. "That way takes you to the Queen's chambers, though I don't know if that is where we need to go. You seem to be tracking something."

"Something. I can feel it. I don't know what it is. But be careful."

"Oh, I'm not going anywhere. I'm going to go back to my workshop, and if you need me, you can come and get me. I told you I was going to guide you, and now you need to save her."

"I will do what I can."

I raced up the stairs. Once I got to the top, I saw a darkened figure at the end of the hall, leaning toward a slightly cracked doorway.

"Waleith," I called.

The figure froze. He turned toward me. It was definitely Waleith.

"There's something here, Zaren," he said. "I'm going to stop—"

I darted forward, switching from the smaller blade to the longer sword. "No. You're the something that's here. I've been trying to figure this out. Trying to piece it all together. The Anvil. The Daughters of Inkasa. The power. And then there were these fabrications." I shook my head. "Talina and her sister. You had an agreement with them. You used them to augment your fabrications." I let out a sigh. "And you tried to make it seem like someone else was responsible, but that wasn't it at all. It was you all along."

"What are you talking about? There is something here that we need to—"

"I can feel it on you. Did you know that? I couldn't with my other blade, but Matherin gave me a raw blade. I tuned it. I tamed it." I walked as I spoke. "I don't know if you were hopeful that I wouldn't do so in time, but now that I have, I can detect the Daughter of Inkasa power. It's there. It's subtle. And it's on you. You were trying to collect what the Anvil had gathered, but you weren't fast enough. You hadn't anticipated that the Daughter of Inkasa woman was going to come."

He turned, and the door started to close. He had something in hand, and for a moment, I hesitated, until he drew the blade along his forearms. He worked quickly. And then he sucked in a sharp breath.

"You could've been useful," he said. "You were supposed to be. All you had to do was let Talina pass. But you stopped her. I hadn't thought that you were strong enough. That's why I let you go after her."

I thought about his injuries. Of course. He had let me go.

"And the aelith powder?"

"Another necessary component. I wasn't able to gather enough. The Guild took that opportunity away from me. But I found a few other options."

"All to attack the Queen?"

"You cannot understand."

"I've been getting that quite a bit," I said. "First from Talina, even Jasar, and Garridan, and now from you. But I think that I understand this aspect. You have some grudge against the Crown. You were dragged away from your home, forced to train at the compound, and forced into becoming a Blade." I watched him, saw no change in his expression. "And you found a way to use Matherin's fabrications to destroy the compound. To destroy the Blades themselves. That was what this was about?"

He took a step toward me. Something about his movement had changed.

"And now you are going after the Queen."

"Like I said, you do not understand. You don't know what it's like to lose everything and everyone you've ever loved. To be dragged to the very place responsible for it, and to be told you must serve it because you have some *talent*. So I did."

"You've been the one bringing these threats to the city. I keep hearing about how everything came because of me, but it wasn't me at all. It was you. You brought me here, maybe to serve as some sort of scapegoat, or maybe to give you the freedom to finish whatever it was that you had started." I hated that I had been used, but I also felt I was close to some answer. "And now you're going after the Queen, but I'm not going to let you."

"You aren't strong enough to stop this," Waleith said.

He moved.

I had seen the Daughter of Inkasa woman, faced her, even deflected some of her attack. She was fast.

Waleith was not that woman.

So when he came at me, I stepped slightly to the side, though the hidden passageway was narrow enough that it

The Anvil's Mark

made it difficult. And in that instant, I thought about all the lessons that I had tried to obtain about fighting. Waleith had wanted me to learn with the smaller, shorter blade. I had tried that, but it hadn't suited me. I had tried to learn to fight like Lijanna, but that hadn't suited me, either. It was when I embraced my size that I truly became what I needed to be.

And so I just swung the flat of my blade.

When I did, I felt some part of me reacting. It was as if some power exploded, maybe the natural part of me, the Blade part of me.

Waleith stumbled. He staggered before my blade even struck.

And then I punched, catching him in the jaw. His eyes widened, and he collapsed.

I was on him in an instant. I drew my shorter blade, jammed it into his shoulder, his other shoulder, and then for good measure, I jammed it into both his legs. I didn't know if it would neutralize whatever power he had consumed, but I wanted to be careful.

"You will never know the truth," Waleith said.

I brought my blade up. His eyes widened, and then I dropped it to punch him once more, knocking him unconscious.

I sat there for a moment, resting on top of him, breathing heavily.

The door that Waleith had been trying to go through opened.

I stiffened. Prince Dorian poked his head in, and I froze. This didn't look good. And I knew Waleith and

Dorian had worked together, especially from what Asi had said about his time visiting the compound.

"Waleith betrayed the Queen," I said hurriedly. "I believe he is responsible for what happened to the compound. He came up here, intending to attack—"

"I heard what he said." Prince Dorian stepped aside. A pair of guards stood behind him. "You have done well. The Queen will be pleased when she recovers." He made a motion. "Bind him and bring him to the prison. I have questions for him."

The pair of guards slipped into the passageway, grabbed Waleith off the floor, and regarded me for a moment before dragging him away.

I straightened, and then realized I was still holding my sword, so I slipped it into its sheath.

"The city is safe?" Prince Dorian asked.

"It is," I said. *Now*, I didn't add.

"And the rumors you brought of some terrifying magic..."

"It has been dealt with."

He glanced back toward the door, and then at me. "It is a good thing that we have a true Blade in the city." With that, he headed out of the door, closing it, and left me in the hidden passageway.

I stood there, debating what I wanted to do, but I knew the answer.

I had to get back to work.

And though I knew that Dorian intended to interrogate Waleith, I had my own questions for the man. And I was determined to get answers.

***

Want more of Garridan? Read on to learn how!

And don't miss the next book in The Queen's Blade: The Traitor's Trap.

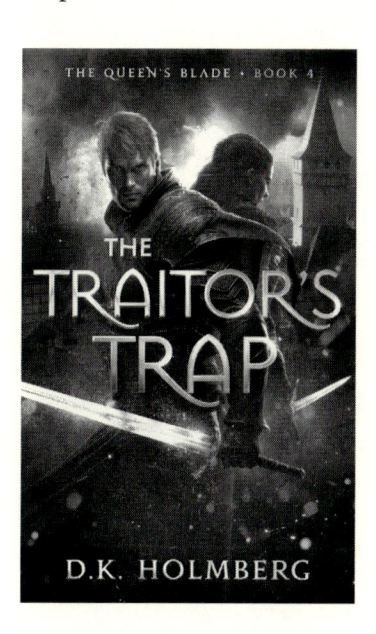

When only the traitor has answers, the Blade must first avoid his trap. The Queen's Blade saga continues.

As Zaren seeks to learn what his former mentor planned, a series of strikes in the city force Zaren to take action.

Worse, he learns the truth of the queen's illness and the steps taken to save her. No longer is magic a danger; now it might be a salvation.

Time is not on his side. Pushed to his limits, what he

discovers may change the course of his service in the city —and to the queen. As the attacks in the city escalate, Zaren and his team search for answers, but it might already be too late to save the queen.

Zaren must rely upon everything he's become to protect the city, but can he remain the Queen's Blade?

* * *

Don't miss another series set in the same world featuring Garridan and the Guild: Chords of Fate.

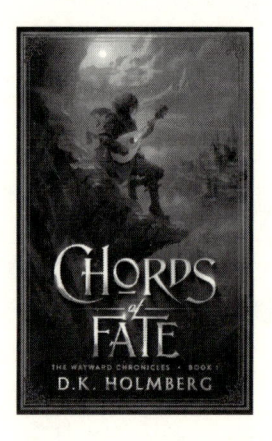

We were called the Wayward. It was a derogatory term for some, but it was one we embraced. Most of us truly *were* Wayward.

Leo Surinar is a wanderer, traveling with his mother in the Wayward caravan in the only life he's ever known, finding their own peace while parts of the world descend into war. When a traveling minstrel joins the caravan, everything begins to change.

As Leo learns the power of song, and begins to dream of a world beyond the caravan—one only the Academy can show him—he starts to think there might be more to the world than what he sees from the top of a wagon.

Until his mother's illness forces him to make a difficult choice.

Leo soon learns about the world beyond the caravan, the power that can be imbued in song, and power even greater than the song. As he's hunted by deadly guild assassins and runs from the fae, he must decide between returning to what he's always known and the knowledge and magic of the Academy.

The Wayward Chronicles begins an epic journey as Leo searches for his place in the world, as he's destined to become more than Wayward. He's destined to become a part of the song itself.

Series by D.K. Holmberg

The Wayward Chronicles Series
The Queen's Blade

The Wayward Chronicles

The Executioner's Song Series
The Executioner's Song

Blade and Bone

The Chain Breaker Series
The Chain Breaker

The Dark Sorcerer

First of the Blade

The Dragon Rogues

The Storyweaver Saga
The Storyweaver Saga

The Dragonwalkers Series
The Dragonwalker

The Dragon Misfits

Elemental Warrior Series:
Elemental Academy

The Elemental Warrior

The Cloud Warrior Saga

The Endless War

The Dark Ability Series

The Shadow Accords

The Collector Chronicles

The Dark Ability

The Sighted Assassin

The Elder Stones Saga

The Lost Prophecy Series

The Teralin Sword

The Lost Prophecy

The Volatar Saga Series

The Volatar Saga

The Book of Maladies Series

The Book of Maladies

The Lost Garden Series

The Lost Garden